A SPECIAL RAMSEY CAMPBELL EDITION

Ramsey Campbell is the greatest inheritor of a tradition that reaches back through H.P. Lovecraft and M.R. James to Mary Shelley's *Frankenstein* and the early Gothic writers. These special, collectable hardcover editions celebrate Campbell's over 60 years in publication. They feature the dark, masterful work of the painter Henry Fuseli, a friend of Mary Wollstonecraft, to invoke early literary investigations into the supernatural.

AN ECHO OF CHILDREN

RAMSEY CAMPBELL
THE NEW NOVEL

FLAME TREE PUBLISHING
6 Melbray Mews, Fulham,
London SW6 3NS, United Kingdom
www.flametreepublishing.com

First published and copyright © 2025
Flame Tree Publishing Ltd
Text copyright © 2025 Ramsey Campbell

All rights reserved. No part of this publication may be reproduced, stored in a retrieval system, or transmitted in any form or by any means, electronic, mechanical, photocopying, recording or otherwise, without the prior written permission of the publisher.

Publisher's Note:
This is a work of fiction. Names, characters, places, and incidents are a product of the author's imagination. Locales and public names are sometimes used for atmospheric purposes. Any resemblance to actual people, living or dead, or to businesses, companies, events, institutions, or locales is completely coincidental.

The cover is created by Flame Tree Studio, featuring a detail of:
Henry Fuseli, *Silence*, 1799–1801, oil on canvas, © Peter Barritt/SuperStock.

HB ISBN: 978-1-78758-978-0
ebook ISBN: 978-1-78758-979-7

A copy of the CIP data for this book is available from
the British Library and the Library of Congress.

Printed in China

AN ECHO OF CHILDREN

RAMSEY CAMPBELL
THE NEW NOVEL

A SPECIAL
RAMSEY
CAMPBELL
EDITION

FLAME TREE
PUBLISHING

for Cat and Colin –
banquet it, folk, it's Chinatown

CONTENTS

AN ECHO OF CHILDREN

One 1

Two 8

Three 20

Four 31

Five 42

Six 46

Seven 57

Eight 71

Nine 75

Ten 83

Eleven 91

Twelve 97

Thirteen 102

Fourteen 110

Fifteen 118

CONTENTS

Sixteen 127

Seventeen 132

Eighteen 138

Nineteen 143

Twenty 151

Twenty-One 164

Twenty-Two 173

Twenty-Three 185

Twenty-Four 194

Twenty-Five 202

Twenty-Six 211

Twenty-Seven 218

Twenty-Eight 228

ACKNOWLEDGEMENTS 244

ABOUT THE AUTHOR 245

AN ECHO OF CHILDREN

ONE

The shrieks of children greeted Thom as he drove into Barnwall. At first he wasn't certain he was hearing them beyond the cries of gulls above the harbour, where boats waved their masts to conjure the clamorous flock down from the August sky. A further burst of screams let him locate the rollercoaster inverting carriagefuls of youngsters inside a loop of the track. "Dean would love that," Jude said. "Maybe we can take him."

"It looks a bit fierce for me. I don't think you should risk it either."

"No need to act our age so much just yet," Jude said and squeezed his hand while he braked for a family as plump as the quartet of rubber doughnuts they were bearing to the beach.

A breeze through her open window tried to tousle her clipped silver hair on his behalf. Though wrinkles had netted her long oval face all the way to the tapering chin, they couldn't tame the quirky snubness of her nose or dim the vigour of her eyes, which were busy relating the promenade to the map on her phone. "Are we turning pretty soon?" Thom said.

"Don't distract me and I'll tell you in a minute."

"I'm silenced." In case this too was a distraction he refrained from adding "Not another word."

The breeze that was rearing ragged crescents of foam from the sea enlivened displays outside shops, where the clappers of plastic spades tolled the dull bells of buckets while mobiles composed of shells kept up a shrill clatter, and inflatables for bathers roused themselves to accost shoppers only to slump back. Presumably Jude ignored all this, instead observing "There's a sign for the park."

A pigeon functioned as a beaky extra indicator on the sign that pointed inland towards Childer Field. A mass of seafood cafes climbed the hill: Nowt Without Trout, Bass With Sass, There's A Plaice For You, Hake No Mistake.... Perhaps an initial jokey name had infected its neighbours. On the corner of a lane a woman in an amber kaftan rampant with the breeze was puffing on a metal cigar outside a shop called Crystal Distillations. At the top of the slope, beyond a disused fire station whose dusty windows looked stopped up with cracked slate, was the park.

Railed gates stood wide beneath a wrought-iron arch displaying a Victorian year. On the path beyond the gates a toddler's protests were substituting for a siren. A phalanx of barely teenage cyclists veered past the howler and his trudging mother to lob bottles not especially towards a concrete bin. A man who appeared to have cast a line to fish over a grassy mound reeled in the lead to reveal he'd caught a sprawling pink-tongued Labrador. "We need the far end," Jude said.

For a moment Thom wondered if she'd sent him wrong, but if anybody was confused it wasn't her. They'd just passed Childer Close, a name that twinged his memory, though Willow Grove was the street he should be looking for. Childer Close in Barnwall – the memory vanished before he could grasp it. The perimeter road extended side streets that seemed to reach for its nature or its past: Pine Lane, Green Row, Woodland Way.... It curved around the park for at least half a mile before Jude announced "There" and more urgently "There."

Though it appeared to lead to the park, Willow Grove was almost a dead end. Beyond a stub of road it expanded into a square composed of broad neat pairs of fifties houses helmeted with shallow red-tiled roofs. The frontages – not just the walls but doors and window frames – gleamed so white they seemed designed to dazzle with their innocence. Number fourteen stood at the top of the square, beside an alley leading to the park. Its hedge enclosed a lawn bordered by flowers and grew several feet higher alongside the alley until it gave way to a solid wooden fence. The street was so quiet Thom could have thought any sounds had been tidied away, so that the muted trundling of his and Jude's small suitcases felt like an impolite intrusion. As they wheeled the cases up the garden path pieced together out of jagged slabs reminiscent of an infant's jigsaw, he noticed there were no toys in the garden.

He was about to ring the doorbell when he heard someone struggling to open the front door, an effort that sounded close to frantic. "What's wrong?" Jude said just as the albino plastic slab swung inwards to reveal their grandson dropping from his tiptoes. Dean dashed to hug her legs and then his grandfather's. "They're here," he shouted. "Gran and grandad Clarendon."

Jude ruffled his turfy reddish hair as much as it would stir. "Have you been watching out for us?"

"Mum and dad said you'd be here by now. They kept saying before."

"You know how far we have to drive. You wouldn't want us going too fast, would you?"

"You mustn't." Concern skewed the six-year-old's lips. "You mustn't get hurt," he begged.

"Don't worry, we aren't planning to," Thom said as Dean's parents and a forceful aroma of coffee emerged from the kitchen at the far end of the hall, which might have been designed to demonstrate cleanliness by remaining unadorned. "Come here now, Dean," Coral said.

"Give my mum and dad a chance to breathe at least," Allan told him.

As the boy retreated they stepped forward to hold his shoulders and make space for the Clarendons in the hall. They could almost have been posing for a portrait that depicted their closeness as a family. Dean had inherited his father's lanky limbs and looked set to be as gangling a teenager, but owed his expansively roundish face and deceptively sleepy eyes to his mother. Having planted him at the foot of the stairs, his parents hastened to embrace the visitors. "You mustn't feel you have to visit if it's giving you any trouble," Coral said. "We'll still have our video calls."

"You're all worth the trouble," Thom assured her.

"So long as driving doesn't start to be a problem," Allan said.

"I don't see it being one just yet or for a while either."

"We've a few years on the road left yet. More than you can count, Dean," Jude said in case he needed reassurance.

"I can count to a hundred. Do you want to hear me, gran and grandad?"

"We'll believe you," Thom said. "Maybe you'll see us live that long."

"Heady says some people only live as long as me."

"Don't start your silliness again," Allan said. "Coffee, is it, mum and dad? Or something stronger if you feel the need."

"Coffee's fine." Once Jude confirmed it Thom said "Shall we take our cases out of everybody's way? There's something for somebody in mine."

"We've given you Dean's room," Coral said to Jude and Thom. "You won't mind, will you? My parents asked for the guest room."

"It's very kind of you to let us use yours, Dean," Thom said.

As Allan hefted Jude's suitcase Dean ran to grab his grandfather's, which he bumped from stair to stair until Allan seized the handle. "We mustn't spoil the carpet, must we? We need to treat our new house with respect."

"You were just trying to be helpful, Dean," Jude said. "You can show us our room instead."

The boy scampered upstairs to stand in a bedroom doorway, gripping the frame as if he was pinned to an invisible cross. He stepped back as his father carried the cases into the room while Jude halted on the threshold. "What a tidy boy you've grown into," she said.

The room was as pale as the hall and not much less plain. A tall stack of plastic baskets full of toys stood next to a wardrobe beside an equally straightforward dressing-table just as white. "Did you clear up your room for us?" Jude said.

"Mummy and daddy say I have to all the time."

"It goes with the house, remember." Allan stood a case at the foot of each bed, a single and its unfolded temporary companion. "Will this do for a couple of nights?" he asked his parents.

"I can stand it if your father can. We'll just have to abstain from each other."

Allan grunted as if he'd been punched in the stomach. "Do remember someone's listening."

Thom saw Jude refrain from telling their son he shouldn't be so untypically embarrassed, either for himself or on Dean's behalf. Instead she crossed to the window, where Thom joined her. The view included swings and slides and climbing frames beyond trees in the park. As he observed none of the trees were willows she said "Is that where you play with your friends, Dean?"

"You'll make some soon at your new school. We'll leave grandma and grandad alone now to unpack."

"Let's just see what there is for a tidy boy," Jude said.

This prompted Thom to fetch the present from his case. She'd wrapped the item in a sheet of glossy paper printed with rings of dancing children and secured it with an elaborate bow. "What do you say to grandma and grandad?" Allan said.

"Thank you very much, grandma and grandad."

"You're entirely welcome." Not just to him Jude added "I'm sure you were about to say."

Dean set the parcel on top of a jovial moon that gave the quilt on his bed a face, and perched on a corner while he tugged at the bow with eagerness Thom thought unusually measured for his age. He stretched the ribbon as long as his arms were wide and straightened it on the bed before unfolding the wrapper, which he flattened small along its folds and placed precisely alongside the ribbon. "No need to make a performance of it, Dean," his father said.

"You and mummy said I'd got to be like granny says I am."

"We aren't that severe, are we?" This was meant for Allan's parents, who responded with a wry smile each. "There's just no need for any mess."

"Do you remember what your room was like," Jude said, "when you were his age?"

"I gave you too much cleaning up you should have made me do myself. Coral and I have enough to do working from home."

Dean had yet to open the Lego box. "Do you like it, Dean?" Thom said.

"It's great. Are there a lot of pieces?"

"There should be, but we can bring more next time if you like."

"How many can I play with, daddy?"

"Now you're just being silly again. Do you want my mum and dad to think we don't let you have any fun? You'd better leave it till you have your room back."

"Can't he take it somewhere else?" Jude rather more than suggested.

"All the other rooms are spoken for. We'll let people finish their unpacking now, Dean. We've bothered them enough."

"You're no bother to us, either of you."

"I can help," Dean said. "I'll take their things to the bathroom."

"Perhaps they won't want to be helped."

"We appreciate it, don't we, Thom? You shouldn't feel embarrassed that you've brought such a helpful boy up, Allan."

"If that's your choice, fair enough." He lingered in the doorway to add "If he's any kind of trouble, just send him down to us."

Jude unloaded toiletries from her case as Allan padded downstairs. When she heard him murmuring to Coral in the kitchen she said "Was there anything you wanted to say to us, Dean?"

"Thank you very much, grandma and grandad."

"We know what a polite boy you are. You're a credit to your parents and yourself." As he mimed awkwardness, skipping from foot to foot in slow motion, she handed him her bag of lotions. "If that's all," she said, "forget I asked."

Once Dean made for the bathroom Thom said lower than she'd spoken "What was that about?"

"Nothing if you think there's nothing. Here's that good boy again."

Thom rummaged in his case for the bathroom bag he passed to Dean. As the boy trotted across the landing Jude said "It felt as if Allan didn't want him staying with us."

"In case he was in our way, which he isn't," Thom barely finished declaring before Jude put a finger to her lips. "What's he saying?" she mouthed.

"My gran and grandad are sleeping in my room," the boy was murmuring. "You have to look after them."

Perhaps Dean realised his grandparents might hear, since he reappeared at speed. "Were you talking to your friend?" Jude said.

His discovered look did its best to hide as if he wished he could. "Yes, gran."

"I think we know why she can't talk back."

"He's a him." Dean looked more guarded than ever. "Why, gran?"

"Were you speaking to him in the mirror?"

"Some of him's in it sometimes."

Jude tried to signify discomposure just with a laugh. "Sometimes he can talk," Dean said.

"How do you make him do that?"

"He does it when he's got a head."

Jude started and clutched at her chest as if to pump out the laugh she manufactured, but Thom couldn't tell whether she was reacting to Dean's fanciful notion or the doorbell. She was making to speak when Allan's shout cut her off. "Here's nan and grandpa, Dean," he called. "Come and let them in."

TWO

The front door was still shut when Thom heard Kendrick Benton. "It looks as if the youngsters beat us to it. Isn't that their car?"

Leigh's answer stayed outside the house, but opening the door turned her husband's volume up. "There's a sight to make our day," he greeted some if not all of the family. "Come and squeeze the air out, Dean."

Thom didn't have to see to know Kendrick had swung the boy into the air before signifying the hug with an extravagant breath that could be heard throughout the house. Jude completed a grin with a comical wince. "It sounds as if Kendrick's on form."

As a conversation that included everybody's voice but Dean's receded into the kitchen Jude said "We can leave the rest of our things in the cases. Let's go down."

She seemed anxious to hear what was being said downstairs, and hurried past a pair of dwarfish cases in the hall. As Thom followed her into the clinically pristine kitchen, where every surface other than the polished metal ones was white, Kendrick jogged his chair away from the table and stood up. "Always a treat to see you both."

"We feel the same," Thom said, though not as loud.

Beneath a shock of permanently untamed ruddy hair Kendrick's extensive flattish face looked loosened in anticipation of a joke his heavy-lidded eyes were dreaming of. He clasped Thom's hand while his other arm embraced Jude. "What do you think of the new home?"

"It feels even newer than it looks," Jude said.

Leigh's small face framed by hooks of greying hair might have been compacted around patience. Her unobtrusively watchful eyes appeared to

AN ECHO OF CHILDREN

keep a constant lookout for a punchline to deliver. "The road's where the park lodge was," she said.

"Not too much of a trek for you young folk, we hope," Kendrick said and released them to take their seats at the lengthily expanded table. "Half as far for us, and that's ideal."

Coral set two scrubbed plastic coasters in front of Thom and Jude before posing a pair of mugs ringed by lines from Shakespeare. "So what was all the chat about upstairs?"

"Just how good Dean is," Jude said, "and how you should both feel proud of him."

"Then I think our little man deserves a present," Kendrick said.

"You two get so many books to read in your job," Leigh said, "we didn't think another one could do anybody any harm."

"That rather depends what it is." Almost without a pause Allan said "We're sure we can trust your judgment."

Leigh made fast if lopsidedly for the hall, where Thom heard the rasp of a zip, a sound that felt close to impolite in the house. She reappeared with a Texts carrier and showed Dean the contents. "Do you love it?" she scarcely asked as she handed Coral the bookshop bag. "Can you tell us what it's called?"

"*Let's Sail to Fairyland*," Dean said not quite at once.

The cover depicted a mass of children on a galleon beneath sails stretched concave by a wind. "Would you like to be on there, Dean?" Jude said.

"Mummy and daddy want me to stay here."

"I mean in your imagination."

"He's got plenty of that," Allan said. "Maybe a little too much."

As Leigh looked rebuffed on behalf of the book Jude said "Show us how well you can read, Dean."

Leigh opened the book at the first story before laying it in front of him. "Once upon a time," she read aloud like a prompter.

"Once upon a time." Dean might have been echoing her until he went on. "There was a little girl who hadn't many shoes, so in the summer she went barefoot and in the winter she wore clods that hurt her feet...."

"Is that a typo?" Coral said as if she were at her copy-editing job, and leaned over to peer at the page. "That isn't what she wore. Take your time and be more careful."

"It's only a tiny mistake," Jude protested. "We wouldn't have pulled anyone his age up for that when we were teaching."

"They would have at the schools we went to," Kendrick said. "Perhaps they'd lowered their requirements by the time you youngsters got involved."

"You've just a couple of years on us, you know," Thom felt driven to object. "And we've always believed in encouraging our pupils, not dismissing their efforts."

"People never got our praise unless they earned it. We thought that made them try to do better. Still," Leigh said, "what do we know? We only ever saw to one child."

"And you did a great job," Allan said, "just like I hope you'd say my parents did."

"Who couldn't?" Kendrick clasped their hands across the table. "Please forgive a pair of old solicitors," he said, "for forgetting how we were brought up to behave."

"So long as we haven't set a bad example," Leigh said.

Thom thought Dean was too intent on reading to have overheard, but everyone fell silent until he used a finger for a bookmark. "I've finished that story."

"Don't say you have just to impress us."

"I have, mummy. The girl gets some red shoes and they make her do things she doesn't want to do because she went to church with them on."

"That's what happens to people who do wrong."

"And she goes to a man who chops her feet off and the shoes run away with her feet in them. That's like Heady."

"Heady's a friend Dean made up," Jude seemed to find it urgent to explain. "I expect you won't need him once you make some real ones, Dean."

"And we're sure they'll be nicer than the children where you used to live," Leigh said.

As Dean reopened the book Allan said "What haven't you said to nan and grandpa for your present?"

"Thank you very much, nan and grandpa." With a six-year-old's pique Dean said "I was going to say but nan said to tell you what my book was called and grandma wanted me to read it to you."

"Don't speak to us like that," Coral said, "or it won't be your book any longer."

When the boy clung to it with both hands Leigh said "Shall we vote on where we're buying everybody dinner?"

"What's the best in town, Dean?" Kendrick said.

"I like the one they bring us here."

"He means a takeaway," Allan said. "It might be a good idea when you've all been driving."

"Give us the name, then," Kendrick said.

Dean kept his eyes on the book but risked a grin. "Cod Is Everywhere."

"True enough round here," Kendrick said and added a guffaw. "Witty into the bargain."

Allan gazed at him. "I'm afraid I don't see the joke."

"Now you're joking," Jude said. "What don't you see?"

"Perhaps we don't want someone else seeing it," Coral said.

The silence this achieved appeared to settle on Dean, who lowered his head as if the book might hide him. His mother took a menu from a drawer next to the one in which she'd laid the bookshop carrier flat on top of a stack of bags. COD IS EVERYWHERE BUT HERE'S THE BEST, the menu proclaimed. Perhaps the pun was inadvertent, then. Haddock and chips and peas proved popular, with Dean doggedly selecting cod despite Leigh's urging to choose whatever he liked. "Half an hour," Kendrick said as he ended his phone call. "We'll unpack and then we'll be down."

"Shall I help you, nan and grandpa?"

"You stay here with your book now," Coral said. "You've been quite enough help for one day."

As Allan headed for the suitcases, Jude identified the tale Dean had just read. "Did you like the emperor's new clothes?"

"I liked how the boy couldn't see them."

"The point is people can convince themselves they're seeing things that aren't there, Dean," his mother said. "They have to be shown where they're wrong or else it's dangerous. Remember how the girl with the red shoes saw she'd done wrong. If she hadn't seen her error she wouldn't have been able to go to heaven."

"Some people can't even if they haven't been very bad."

"That's right, they go to purgatory."

"And some people have to stay here."

"I'm sure that isn't in your nan and grandpa's book."

Dean planted his hands on the open pages as though he feared losing it, unless he meant to hide any questionable content. "I just thought it, mummy."

"Then don't let such ideas into your head."

Thom felt impelled to change the subject. "We haven't congratulated you yet on your bargain."

Coral glanced at Dean as if this might refer to him. "Which are you saying we've made?"

"Why, this house."

"Prices are dropping, and the owners wanted a quick sale. We thought the house was too big for them."

"What were they like?" Jude said.

"We never met them. The agent showed us round."

"What was their name again that made us laugh?" Leigh said from the hall. "The Lettices, that's right. They were involved in education too."

"Wine from your family, Coral." Allan produced bottles from a carrier as Leigh and Kendrick followed him into the kitchen. "I'll put one in the freezer," he said, "so we can have it with dinner."

"Better put a friend in with it," Kendrick said, "and the rest in the fridge."

"That should do for tonight," Leigh said, "unless anyone thinks there'll be more of a need."

"We haven't been driven to drink that much yet," Coral said.

A wry grin or at any rate a twist of the left side of her mouth defined this as a joke. Allan returned from the utilities room to produce a misted bottle from the refrigerator. "Here's one to start the celebrations," he said, "and you'll have orange, won't you."

"Yes please and thank you," Dean said.

"That's an old way to put it," Jude said. "Did you find it in one of your books?"

"It's the way we've started teaching him," Allan said.

"I wasn't saying anything was wrong with it. It just doesn't sound like you."

"So long as it sounds like Dean," Coral said.

She collected the mugs to wash them in the sonorous gleaming metal sink and stood them on their mouths while Allan dealt out the chardonnay and Dean's glass of juice. "Here's to your new home," Kendrick said.

Dean's glass joined in the communal clink, if a little timidly. "And your new life in it," Leigh proposed.

"Your better one," Jude told Dean.

As Thom pondered a wish he could add Dean said "Can I say one?"

"So long as it isn't silly," Allan said.

Dean raised his glass solemnly enough to be honouring a vintage wine. "Everyone who lived in our house ever."

"That's a kind thought," Leigh said. "What do you think they were like?"

The boy glanced at his parents and visibly revised his answer. "Like my friend."

"All right," Coral said, "we've done your toast now."

"Grandpa said we were having fish and chips."

"We don't need that kind of cleverness," Allan said. "Just read your book."

When the boy ducked to it as though his head had been forced down Jude said "I don't know if he was meaning to be clever."

"Then he needs to be clever in the right way. I'd have known what she meant at his age."

Thom wasn't sure this would have been the case. As the elderly quartet began to reminisce about Allan and Coral as children, Dean kept his head close to the book. He looked up eagerly when a bell tolled along the hall – the doorbell sounding the first phrase of a nursery rhyme. "Oranges and lemons," Thom said to Dean, only to recall the candle lighting you to bed and, with an unexpected chill, the threat of the chopper. "That must be the feast," Kendrick said and produced a wallet stratified with plastic cards to hand the boy a fiver. "I've paid, but there's a tip for you to give."

Dean dashed along the hall and succeeded in opening the front door as Kendrick strolled after him. Thom wondered what the pause was until Dean said "There isn't anybody, grandpa."

"Have they rung the bell and run away? That won't earn anyone a tip." Louder Kendrick said "Yes, this is number fourteen. You were right first time."

The answer came across the square. "Just looking for it, sir."

"You didn't ring just now. You didn't see who did." When the man said no to both Kendrick told him "I can't say I care for the example you're setting. You keep what I gave you, Dean."

The front door shut with heavy emphasis, and Dean ran into the kitchen, flourishing his prize. As Kendrick reappeared hugging a carrier stacked with polystyrene oblongs Coral said "Just let me set the table, daddy. That didn't sound like our regular man."

"Can't we have it out of the boxes?" Dean said, closing the book like a lid on Rumpelstiltskin.

"Do you want to save us washing up?" Jude said.

"I thought it'd feel like going by the sea."

"I expect you must do that quite a lot."

Allan broke if not dismissed Dean's silence. "When we can find the time."

"All of us grandfolk have lots of that, Dean. We'll be giving your mummy and daddy a break. I don't mind having a carton, Coral."

"We can sit in the garden like on the prom," Dean said.

"There isn't room for everyone," Coral told whoever ought to be informed.

"Is there room for two old things and Dean?" Jude said. "We always like a picnic."

Sprawling inscriptions with a marker pen identified the contents of the cartons, and Dean's was on top of the stack. He carried it together with a wooden knife and fork to the table on the back lawn as gravely as a priest bearing a sacred object to an altar. "Have some proper knives and forks if you like," Allan told his parents. "We know we can trust you with them."

Surely this wasn't a comment on their age. "We'll use the ones they sent," Thom said. "They're part of the experience."

He followed Jude to the bench across the table from Dean's perch. Apart from the picnic facilities, the long lawn beside a concrete path was bare. A wall about ten feet high separated the path from the alley that led to Childer Field. A multicoloured trinity of bins next to a garden shed stood guard by the back gate, which was secured by a large padlock. "What's happened to the bike you were so fond of?" Jude asked Dean.

"It's locked up safely in the shed. It's brought out when it's called for." Allan nudged Dean's carton aside with his own. "Budge up, Dean," he said. "I'm sure grandma and grandad want some adult company."

"We'd have been happy with Dean's," Thom said.

"Well, I hope you're still happy with mine."

"I'm sure you'll never give us reason not to be."

"You'd hope that about everyone."

Thom could only agree, though he didn't feel entirely certain what he might have endorsed. His carton loosed a polystyrene squeal as he held the lid wide with his glass. Dean was already digging out chunks of cod to munch. "Is that your favourite?" Jude said.

"Mummy and daddy say it's my treat."

"Then you'll have to be good to deserve it." As Allan turned his eyes towards her, the sunlight narrowed them. "We know you are," she appeared to feel prompted to add.

A screech accompanied by echoes did duty as an answer. Seagulls were veering like scraps of ash beneath the implacably blue sky. "Watch out, Dean," Thom said, "or the birds will be stealing your dinner."

A gull swooped down to land on the shed but swerved away with a cry that sounded outraged. "You're safe after all," Thom told the boy. "It must have been something I said."

In a while Dean's performance – thrusting the wooden fork into the fish so hard the tines scraped the carton, opening his mouth in preparation for the next load, brandishing the tiny trident until the mouthful went down with a visible spasm of his throat, spearing a fat chip stained green by peas and biting it in half before following it with the remainder, collecting a forkful of peas to add to his internal mix – grew sluggish, and then he stuck the fork upright like a miniature memorial in half the fish. "I hope you're just having a breather," Allan said. "Remember grandpa can see."

"I liked it, daddy, but I don't want any more. It was big like yours."

"If it's too much you should have asked for a small portion. Nobody's going to want it now."

"It was filling even for me," Thom said and laid his splintered fork and knife down in the carton. The batter was growing bedraggled, while the watery puree studded with peas had softened the remaining chips and turned them alarmingly greenish. "I'm retiring from the competition too," he said.

"Don't anybody feel compelled to finish," Kendrick called from the kitchen. "So long as you've enjoyed what you had."

"You don't need us to tell you," Jude said and consigned her utensils to the carton.

"I remember you both having more of an appetite." The sunlight slitted Allan's eyes again as he gazed at Dean. "If you've really had sufficient," he said, "make sure that's shut tight before you put it in the bin. We don't want to attract any unwelcome visitors."

By now his gaze had settled on his parents, though of course he couldn't mean them. Thom collected the tight-lipped containers and took them to a bin as garishly green as the peas had been rendered. As he dropped the ungainly pile in the bin he heard his nails scratch a carton. Nobody's could have, since he'd felt no sensation. A restless fork must have clawed at the polystyrene as though scrabbling to lift a lid.

Politeness seemed to require him and Jude to stay while Allan finished, and Dean seemed to feel his presence was expected too. Thom could have taken Allan's resolute behaviour as a rebuke to them all. By the time Allan scraped the carton clean his son was swinging his legs under the table, and Allan stared at them until they wavered to a standstill. "I think we've had enough excitement for one day," he said. "Time for your bath."

Jude hurried after them into the house, and Thom felt driven to keep up. "Can the grandparents supervise the ablutions?" she said.

"If you think you'll have the patience," Coral said.

"I can't imagine he takes much." To the Bentons Jude said "Shall we alternate?"

"You and Thom do the honours tonight," Leigh said. "We can hear you're eager."

"We'll be outside with our drinks," Coral said, "if you need any of us."

Dean was already heading for the bathroom. As Thom followed Jude upstairs the boy emerged from the parental bedroom, naked apart from a wad of pyjamas he was using as a fig-leaf. "Can I have bubbles?" he was anxious to establish.

"They're his treat," Coral called. "I suppose you can indulge him, since we're celebrating."

"Don't forget to open the bathroom window," Allan added. "It needs the ventilation."

As Thom propped the frosted transom wide a convivial murmur rose from the garden. A yellow plastic duck, earnestly jovial despite its solitariness, sat on the edge of the stainless white bath like a waterfowl waiting on a snowbank for a dammed river to return. Jude wedged the plump plug into its socket and squirted liquid into the bath before setting an onslaught of water on the pinkish puddle, which swelled into a haphazard mound of soapy globes. Dean hurdled the side of the bath and handed her the protective nightwear, then plunged under the bubbles. "Watch out you don't get lost in there," Jude said. "We wouldn't know where to look."

"I'd still be here, gran. People can be even if you can't see them."

As the conversations down below subsided, Thom heard a bottle encounter a glass and another. "Don't forget your friend," Jude said. "I mean your duck."

"Duck doesn't like bubbles. They hurt his eyes."

"Can't you wipe them for him?"

"You can't fix eyes when something bad's happened to them."

Thom saw this disconcert her. "Haven't you given your poor duck a name?" she said.

"He didn't tell me any."

"I think the idea is for you to make up one."

If Dean disagreed, he kept it to himself. For a while he played with the contents of the bath, raising arms bejewelled with bubbles out of the pallid bulbous mass to watch the fragile swellings disintegrate on his skin, leaving it scaly with their remains. Eventually he said "Please may I have a drink of orange, please and thank you?"

"I'm sure you can," Thom said and made for the kitchen, where Dean's glass was intent on its own vague reflection in the polished metal drainingboard. He was taking the chilly bottle of juice out of the refrigerator when Jude called "Sorry, what did you say?"

Her footsteps padded out of the bathroom. "Was somebody wanting me?"

"Not that I could hear," Thom called.

As he shut the refrigerator it seemed to echo overhead. Filling Dean's glass covered up Jude's voice, whatever she was saying. A throaty gurgle had begun somewhere in the house. Thom was carrying the glass to the stairs, having taken a surreptitious sip to render the contents more manageable, when he saw Jude on the landing. "Come up quickly," she little more than whispered. "The door's shut and I can't get in."

Thom took the stairs as fast as the glassful allowed and limped to twist the doorknob. Though it obeyed readily enough, a soft but stubborn object – surely not Dean – was blocking the door. "Dean," he urged. "Let us in."

"Not so loud, Thom. I don't want anybody thinking I was neglectful."

"I know you weren't." He handed her the glass, in which the juice began to jitter. Gripping the doorknob with both hands, he thrust his shoulder against the door. "Dean," he said with his mouth against the wood, which smelled and tasted faintly of polish. "Dean, answer me."

Perhaps the creaks of the door obscured his murmur. He'd heard no response by the time the door yielded a few inches, only for the obstruction to consolidate its resistance. He sank to his knees as speedily as age permitted and groped through the meagre gap. His fingers found a small limp arm that seemed to deflate as he stretched to grasp it. Before he succeeded in taking hold he realised it lacked a hand. He had to drag it into view to be sure it was a sleeve of the pyjamas Jude had hung on the door. He fished the nightwear through the widening gap and clutched at the doorknob to haul himself to his feet. Dean was seated in the bath, where the last of the foam was gurgling down the plughole. "Why didn't you answer me?" Thom demanded.

"I thought gran didn't want mummy and daddy to hear."

Thom lowered his voice to match the boy's. "Then why didn't you open the door at least?"

"It's slippery. I couldn't get out. I want to now. It's cold."

Jude pushed past Thom to shut the window, although he didn't think the summer evening could have caused a problem. She grabbed one of the fat white towels from the rail to enfold Dean as she helped him out of the bath. "Good heavens, you are cold," she said, having touched his cheek with the back of a hand, and stooped to peer into the bath as she set about towelling him. "What am I seeing, Thom? It can't be ice."

He glanced into the bath in time to see a whitish substance vanish down the plughole. "It looks like snow, but you have to know it's foam."

"It is ice, gran. It's how Heady made the bubbles go," Dean said, and Thom felt glad the window was shut. "He makes it go cold sometimes when he comes," the boy insisted, "and it was him that wouldn't let you in."

"We'll pretend you didn't say any of that," Thom said, "so long as you don't tell anyone we left you alone," and hoped his deviousness was justified on Jude's behalf.

THREE

A touch on his forehead wakened Thom. Was the hand cold, or was that the room? As he struggled towards consciousness the chill receded, and by the time he opened his hesitant eyes it had gone. The room was emphatically warm despite the open window, but the hand could only have been Jude's, reaching out from the unfamiliar bed to establish his presence — either her hand or a trace of a dream. If she hadn't sought the reassurance without waking, perhaps it had let her resume her sleep.

Her right hand lay on the thin quilt, while the left was upturned beside the puffy pillow as though to indicate some item in the dark or to invite a caress, and Thom might have responded if he hadn't been wary of wakening her. Her face was turned towards him, simplified and rejuvenated by dimness. He could almost fancy they were young again, except that he was too aware how the last few years had revised him. His equipment had shrunk faster than the rest of him, and showed even less ability to regain its stature; it required a manful effort to produce the infrequent faltering increase, and he felt as though it had reverted to a second childhood. "It doesn't matter, Thom, I've still got you," he heard Jude say, although this time only in his head, and nearly reached to clasp her hand.

A stab of cramp in his calf made him twist onto his back, striving to keep the movement surreptitious. He'd pushed the beds together for company, but whenever he shifted, the frame beneath him creaked, and he took all the time he could bear to straighten his agonising leg under the burden of the clammy quilt. Only the faint sight of Jude's sleeping face let him wait for the pain to subside while he trapped his voice by pinching his upper lip between his teeth. When at last the pangs dulled to an ache he closed his eyes in the hope of retreating into sleep. If he let thoughts start to swarm he feared he'd be awake well past dawn, but then a final twinge of cramp lost its hold on his consciousness.

Light through his eyelids roused him. When he widened his eyes to restore their reluctant focus the sunlight showed him he was lying by an empty bed. He might have expected Dean to waken him; Allan was always insistently audible at that age. Thom turned on his back in a tangle of quilt and saw Jude at the open window. She put a finger to her lips before beckoning him. "Come and look," she mouthed.

She slipped an arm around his waist as he leaned over the windowsill, bruising his unmanageably advanced stomach. Dean was seated at the picnic table with his book. An illustration showed he was intent on the tale of the ice queen. Rainbow jewels of dew glittered on the lawn around him, though the closest globes were pale and opaque. "He'd have been a model pupil," Thom murmured, "if we'd had him at school."

"I didn't hear him get up even though I must have been awake."

"Sorry if you were. I did my best to let you have a good night's sleep for a change."

Jude's frown underlined by a blink suggested he'd missed a point if not a pair of them. "Let's make ourselves presentable and go down," she said.

She was already showered and dressed. Once Thom left the shower a befogged shape kept him company, eventually revealed as his reflection by a ventilation fan he hadn't previously noticed. Jude turned from the bedroom window as he started hopping perilously from foot to foot in a bid to don his shoes. She supported him with both hands around an elbow until he succeeded in mastering the feat. As a promise of caffeine met them in the hall Coral called "Come and have your breakfast, Dean."

She shook a measured heap of cereal into a bowl and sugared it with a precisely flattened spoonful before moistening it with milk. The adults went for those ingredients too, and for a while the morning ceremony made all the noises – the flimsy rush of cereal into bowls, the faint hiss of sugar, the trickling of milk out of a small beaky jug and the helpless gulps of a bottle of orange juice emptying its contents, followed by a contest to restrict the sounds of breakfasting to the politest level. When Dean crunched a mouthful Allan sent him a critical look, which appeared to prompt Jude to provide a distraction. "Dean?"

He swallowed and dabbed at a spluttering cough with his napkin. "What, gran?"

"Don't try to speak when you're eating. Now you see what happens to you."

"It was my fault, Allan." Jude waited until Dean doused a final explosion with a glug of juice. "I was only going to ask," she said, "were you in our room?"

"When, gran?"

"Last night when grandad and I were asleep."

"He couldn't have been," Coral said. "He couldn't have got past us without our noticing."

"What gave you the idea he did?" Allan said.

"I woke up for a moment and thought he was there."

"I wasn't though, gran."

"I should have known really. You couldn't have fitted between our beds."

"Grandma's saying she was dreaming," Coral said.

As the boy looked unconvinced Thom said "Shall we elders give you both a break today? Dean can show us round the town and what he likes to do."

"Are we included in the merry band?" Kendrick said.

"It wouldn't be as merry without you," Thom felt required to assure him.

"Dean likes the playground in the park," Coral said. "That could be a plan if you don't feel up to walking far."

"We need to give our legs a good stretch," Jude said, "after all that driving."

"There'll be my parents as well to consider."

"We can take him," Thom told them, "if you'd rather have a restful day."

"I hope he won't be giving anybody any other kind," Allan said. "If he does, please let us know."

"Neither of us needs a rest," Leigh said. "We're up to whatever everyone wants."

"Can we go down to the sea?" As both his parents opened their mouths Dean added "Please and thank you."

"Is that all right with everyone?" Jude audibly hoped.

"I think we've made our view clear," Allan said.

Thom wasn't sure Dean's parents had, but Jude took the answer for agreement. "We'll make a day of it," she said.

"You'll have your phones, won't you," Coral told all four grandparents. "Ring us if there's any kind of reason."

"Does Dean have one? A phone, I mean."

"No need." Coral might have been referring to the question too. "Could we drop the subject?" she barely asked. "We don't want anybody being tempted."

Dean swallowed a last resolutely discreet mouthful and planted his spoon in the bowl with a subdued clink. "It looks as if someone's ready to be off," Thom said.

"Bathroom first," Coral said, presumably not to him, "and don't rush."

As Dean scrambled down from his chair Allan said "What have you forgotten?"

The boy looked unsure where to direct his answer. "Please and thank you?"

"Never forget that, but I'm asking if you're leaving your book out for the birds."

"They don't come, daddy. You and mummy said they were the only thing you missed."

"Just bring it in and hope nan and grandpa aren't thinking you don't value what they give you."

"We'd never assume that, Allan," Leigh said.

Dean ran to the picnic table and returned hugging the book as if he feared it would be confiscated. "Sorry, nan and grandpa. I really like my present."

"Put it away safely now," Coral said. "Leave it on your bed in our room and then do what I told you in the first place."

As the boy ran upstairs Jude said "We did buy him a present too. Can't he play with it outside?"

"You wouldn't want pieces falling through the table," Coral said, "and having to be thrown away."

"There'd be no need for that, surely."

"There's every reason if they got soiled, and I shouldn't think you'd want to risk it."

While the grandparents fetched thin jackets from their rooms Thom heard Dean dash downstairs to be told to stay calm. Coral and Allan accompanied the party to the garden gate. As Dean swung it open – playing the doorman, Thom thought, rather than anxious for release – Allan said "Could you all keep an eye on what he eats? No additives, if you don't mind."

"Don't let him go on anything that may make him ill," Coral said. "And Dean, don't you go running off."

By now Thom had begun to feel impatient to be on his way. "We'll see he doesn't," he said and strode out of the gate.

Past the corner of the garden he turned along the path to Childer Field. Twin hedges boxed him in, and then a pair of gapless fences more than a head taller than him. As he heard Jude say "Hold my hand" to Dean, the shadow of Allan and Coral's house closed around him. The sudden darkness cut off all the sunlight from this stretch of the path. It seemed to muffle his senses, so that the noise of children in the park sounded muted by distance if not walled off from him. Presumably a neighbour had been gardening, since the elongated shadow smelled of upturned earth. Thom felt unnecessarily glad to emerge into the brightness of the park.

A picket fence that might have belonged to an idyllic cottage surrounded a play area. Fewer children than he'd thought he heard were clambering across rope bridges or dangling by various limbs from tubular frames or sailing down slides only to sprint back to the ladders and repeat the experience as if they were caught on loops of film. A mother was propelling a toddler on a swing no higher than her breasts despite his pleas to fly. Thom turned to find Dean waving at the house. "Are you saying goodbye to mummy and daddy?" Jude said.

"I can't imagine who else," Kendrick told her.

Thom glimpsed Dean's parents at their son's window before they stepped back out of sight. Had he and Jude ever been so concerned for Allan? Perhaps in their fashion they had, but less oppressively, he hoped. He waited by the play area in case Dean wanted to detour, but the boy urged Jude past the picket gate. "Do the children keep you awake at night?" she said.

"They'd gone home by the time we read his bedtime story, Judith," Leigh said.

"I meant the ones who woke me when we were in bed."

"We didn't hear them, did we, Kendrick?"

"It was as quiet as the—" He edited his comment, having glanced at Dean. "As quiet as I don't know," he said with the force of frustration. "The quietest thing you can think of."

"Heady when he's like this," Dean said and wagged his fingers at his neck to express some notion Thom failed to grasp.

Leigh ignored this, which felt like an unspoken response. "Did you hear these children, Thomas?"

"I'm afraid I didn't, Jude. I slept nearly all night for a change."

"Maybe they were teenagers. I couldn't really tell with the kind of noise they were making. You'd have thought it was some kind of screaming competition. That's how some teenagers behave."

"I hear them sometimes." Dean let go of her hand to stretch his fingers towards a woman on the path the family was following. "There's Mrs Doughty," he said.

"Inspector Doughty, Dean, remember," the woman said gently enough.

"Sorry, Mrs, Inspector."

"Mrs Inspector will do for now." She drew a finger back and forth across her eyebrows as though to focus the scrutiny she trained on his companions. "You'll be the family I haven't met," she told Jude and Thom, thrusting a large hand at them. "Call me Elsie. I live across the road."

She was tall and broad and muscular, with an expansive face squared off by cropped black hair. "Thom," he said as his hand began to twinge from her handshake.

"Jude," Jude said, and he saw her manage not to wince at Elsie's grip.

"Do you go in for lost causes, then?"

"I shouldn't think so." Jude sounded bemused if not resentful. "Why do you ask?"

"Like the saint, I was thinking."

"It isn't short for Judas."

"I'd hope not." As Thom considered pointing out the saint's name had been a biblical truncation, Elsie said "Folk generally know how to behave round here. I can tell you my young neighbour Dean does."

"Do you see much in the way of drugs?" Jude said.

Elsie's gaze was her first response. "I wouldn't have thought you'd be interested."

"I haven't been for many years."

"I'd rather have heard you say never. May I ask why you are now?"

"I just wonder if some children were taking any in the park last night."

"Did you see them doing it?"

"Only heard. They sounded a bit out of their minds."

"If there's any repetition I'd appreciate you reporting it at once."

"Are you saying we should call you?"

"You may as well when I'm so close," Elsie said and scribbled a number on the card she handed Jude. "Keep me in mind while you're in Barnwall."

"We take it you heard nothing last night, Elsie," Kendrick said.

"I must have been sleeping the sleep of the just," Elsie said and turned to Dean. "I don't know how much you understood, but we were saying some children get mixed up with drugs. Don't you ever, Dean. It's a wicked thing to do, and bad things happen to wicked children."

"I know they do, Mrs Inspector."

Presumably he thought she'd authorised the usage. "Excuse me now if I make the most of my day off," she said and strode past the playground.

Dean was visibly battling to contain his eagerness. "Please may we go to the sea now, please and thank you?"

"You've been very patient," Jude said. "Nobody could say you weren't good."

He took this as a liberation, and dashed along the path before apparently remembering to slow down and wait for her beside the first of the high grassy hillocks between which the path rambled. Thom heard children beyond each of them, and occasionally someone would poke up a head to spy out the land or whoever was near. Past the hillocks the path led alongside a lake and bisected it with a bridge, beneath which Dean trotted nonchalantly upside down beside Jude in the water. Beyond the lake a splintered wave of starlings surged up from the furthest trees to veer away from the park. "Look, Dean," Jude said. "There are birds after all."

"Nan's turn now," Leigh said as he reached the gate between the trees, and captured his hand. Tempting noises rose to meet him on the road down to the seafront: the circular tune of a roundabout, the amiable collisions of dodgems, the hearty hoots and miniature tintinnabulation of a fairground train. Beyond the crowded promenade at the foot of the hill the North Sea jittered with glittering as if the fidgety masts in the harbour had electrified the waves. Dean and less urgently Leigh were first onto the promenade, where the boy eagerly obeyed a shop's name, Don't Pass The Glace. "Please may I have an ice cream, please and thank you?"

"Is it rather early in the day, do we think?" Leigh said.

"Not for us," Jude said, whoever this included.

"Why, look who's back at last," the woman behind the glassed-in counter greeted Dean. "I was starting to think you didn't like my ice cream."

She was almost too plump for her multicoloured apron, and looked made up to represent items on the menu – lips painted the red of raspberry syrup, twin symmetrical patches of her cheeks the same pink as the strawberry ice in a trough behind the glass, eyes the brown of the chocolate variety and outlined for emphasis. "And here's the rest of the family," she said, though just to Jude and Thom.

"Does everyone in Barnwall know who we are?" Jude wondered.

"Just us folk who live in the grove," the woman said, reaching across the counter. "Eva Briggs."

"I'm Jude Clarendon, and this is Thom."

Eva's enthusiastic handshake was cooler than the summer day. "So what's my youngest neighbour having?" she said.

"We didn't realise he was," Jude said before he could speak.

"He's the only youngster we've got in Willow."

While Jude gave Dean a sympathetic blink Thom said "Ice cream for everyone?"

"I've said I'll have one," Jude reminded him, "now I've warmed up."

At once, as all too frequently these days, he felt anxious for her. "Aren't you feeling too well?"

"I'm fine. I was exaggerating," she said, confirming it with a laugh. "I meant I was cold in the night. It woke me up."

"It can get cold round here at night," Leigh said as if the issue needed explanation. "It did sometimes when we used to come on holiday with Coral, but she loved the place."

Eva rubbed her lips as if considering her next remark, tinting her fingertip crimson. "It's good to know her memories made her move here."

Thom had a sense too transient to grasp of something left unspoken, but could only say "So what am I treating everybody to?"

"Can we just ask if you use any additives?" Leigh said.

"Never," Eva assured anyone who was concerned. "I believe in keeping everything pure."

She scooped the five flavours she was asked for into tubs and stood a wooden spoon in each. Dean selected vanilla as if he'd been prompted to take care, and resisted Jude's urging to be more adventurous. As Thom paid, Eva said "Watch out for the seagulls."

"Are they much of a problem?" Thom wondered. "They left us alone when we were dining in the garden."

"You're on their territory now. I've seen a few battles on the prom."

"Can we go on the beach?" Dean said almost eagerly enough to omit his display of politeness.

"Perhaps when you've had your ice cream," Leigh said.

She held his free hand at the kerb while a roofless bus fluttery with windblown sightseers passed along the promenade. She let a road train like an escapee from a fairground trundle by as well, then led him to a bench above the narrow elongated beach that stretched away from the harbour. The railings bordering the promenade were staging a seagull exhibition. Whenever any of the birds swooped towards the bench the grandparents competed at driving them off with shouts of "Shoo" and "Fly away" and "Nothing here for you" and from Jude "Leave us alone," a quartet of uninhibited performances Thom found oddly convivial. Beyond the beach the sea was strewn with glittering splinters of sunlight, lined up in parallel towards a horizon carbuncled with tankers. As Jude dug a spoonful of tawny ice cream together with a buried raisin out of her tub she said "Just think if those were Viking ships out there, Dean."

"The Vikings named the town, you know," Kendrick said. "That's why it has such a strange name."

"Where's the barn, grandpa? I can't see any."

"I don't think it means that in Viking lingo, old fellow."

"So you shouldn't keep looking for things that aren't there," Leigh said.

Before the tubs were empty the scrapes of spoons began to sound like a harsh but wordless conversation. Dean collected the containers and utensils and stuffed them in the nearest bin, whose concrete crown bristled with cigarette butts. "That's the sort of thoughtful boy we like to see," Leigh said.

"I believe you've earned yourself a prize," Kendrick said. "What would you say to a bucket and spade?"

"Please and thank you, grandpa." This resembled uncomplicated gratitude until Dean said "But I've got one."

"I'm sure there'll be room for another, or would you rather have a different little item?"

"I don't know any I'm supposed to have, grandpa."

"Then do give the poor man a sale now I've raised his hopes."

A doleful man was attending a flimsy metal stand at the top of the nearest ramp to the beach. His carillon of inverted plastic buckets and their spades intermittently emitted a staggered series of clanks as though searching for tunefulness. Kendrick handed Dean a pristine five-pound note, which he bore like a trophy to the abruptly jovial vendor. He bought a bucket and its matching bright red spade, then hesitated beside the ramp. "You can go on the beach," Jude called. "Just stay where we can see you."

As Dean made his way between tenures marked by blankets on the sand Leigh said "Shouldn't someone stay with him?"

"We can go down if we're needed, but I'd like to have a chat while he can't hear."

"Stay there now, Dean. We'll be watching," Kendrick called as the boy reached an unoccupied patch of sand opposite the bench. A good deal lower he said "What were you wanting to talk about, Judith?"

Jude waited until Dean turned his back and squatted to dig in the sand near the gently restless hem of the ocean. "Is anyone else worried," she murmured, "or is it just me?"

FOUR

It seemed to be up to Thom to speak, though he couldn't tell which of Jude's questions the others were reluctant to answer. "Worried about what?" he said.

"What else could it possibly be?"

The Bentons blinked at this and then at Thom. "We don't know either," Leigh said.

"The family, of course. The children."

"I think they're more than that by now," Kendrick said, "except for our youngest member."

"I appreciate what Judith means, though. Once you're a mother you're always one."

"Then I hope you're as concerned as I am," Jude said.

"I'm certain all of us will be," Leigh assured her, "if we see the need."

"We have."

Thom felt as if this was trying to tug words out of him. "What are you thinking of?"

"Where do I start?" Before he could find a response she turned to Leigh and Kendrick. "Have you had a look at Dean's room?"

"We have indeed," Kendrick said. "We were suitably impressed."

"I think we may have been meant to be," Thom said.

"By whom?" Jude demanded.

"I wouldn't be surprised if it was Dean."

"They shouldn't have made him feel it was necessary. We'd have said if anyone had asked."

"Coral was always a tidy child," Leigh said. "I really don't think there's anything wrong with that."

"You haven't heard the worst. We bought him a set of Lego, but he's not allowed to take it all out of the box at once."

"That's only what he wondered, Jude," Thom said. "You heard Allan tell him off for giving us the idea he wasn't."

"I feel as if I haven't heard much else apart from his parents telling him off."

"Do you think that could be rather an exaggeration?" Leigh said.

"I said it's how I've been made to feel. You saw just now he doesn't even know what he's forbidden to have."

"I shouldn't think it will be much. I expect there must have been toys you preferred Allan not to play with."

"I'll tell you something else I felt, Thom. As if Allan didn't want to leave us alone with him."

"Why," Kendrick said and paused over his words, "what did he think you might do?"

"What could he have? I'm talking about Dean. It felt as if there was something Allan didn't want him telling us."

"Was that how it seemed to you, Thomas?"

As Thom shook his head, a constrained gesture he found marginally less disloyal than speech, Leigh said "I believe we may know what Allan didn't want you hearing."

"If you know something we don't," Jude urged, "please tell us."

"Him and Coral, I get the impression they're embarrassed by this Eddie character he's invented. I shouldn't think you two are any more than us, but perhaps you've noticed they are."

"Heady," Jude insisted more forcefully than Thom understood. "I really think Allan had something else on his mind."

"Well, you should know your own son best." Before Jude could respond Leigh said "Both of you."

"I'm not sure how much we do just now, and you don't seem to be about Coral."

"I think we are, you know," Kendrick said. "What makes you think otherwise?"

"The business with the fish and chip shop. You thought the name was funny, and we saw her reaction took you aback."

"I'll grant you it was unexpected, but she told us what the issue was."

"Since when have they been religious? I won't pretend we are, and Allan never has been. Is it just Coral? Their wedding wasn't, after all."

"We aren't particularly, but we're not proud of it," Leigh said. "Perhaps they've decided to give Dean the option. There's nothing wrong with a bit of belief."

"It didn't strike me as optional."

"I'm sure you'll agree some things aren't at his age."

Jude took a breath she let out louder. "I'm starting to believe nobody wants to hear anything I say."

"Of course we do if it helps to put your mind at rest," Leigh said. "Say anything you'd like us to hear."

"All right, there's this," Jude said not far from a kind of triumph. "Why did they want us to open the window when Dean was having his bath?"

"For ventilation," Kendrick said as gently as he gazed at her, "I should imagine."

"They have a fan in the wall for that."

"Then I expect they were saving on electricity while it's hot enough to keep the window open. What other reason could there be?"

"Maybe they wanted to listen in the garden."

"You'll excuse my slowness, but listen to what?"

"Whatever Dean said while we had him on his own. Did they want you to be quiet while you were sitting outside?"

"I think they may have," Leigh said.

"Don't you think that suggests anything?"

"It doesn't need to, Judith." Leigh might have been bidding to outdo Kendrick for gentleness. "We were all enjoying hearing Dean play in the bath," she said.

Jude slumped into silence as though only her words had been supporting her. In a moment she lurched upright, having heard Dean say "Can't you help me?"

Thom made for the railings so fast a spasm seized the back of his right knee, snagging him with a lopsided limp. The boy was kneeling by a rank of half a dozen sandcastles precisely aligned with the promenade. Progressive stages of disintegration showed which he'd built first. Kneeling must have left the blurred virtually shapeless marks suggestive of incomplete footprints on the sand around him, since none of the other children on the beach were close enough for him to have addressed. "Were you wanting us?" Thom called.

The boy twisted on his knees and almost lost his balance. Thom could have imagined he hadn't expected any of his grandparents to respond. "My castles won't stay up," Dean complained.

"I used to be good at them," Jude said as she joined Thom. "Shall I show you how to make the best ones?"

"Yes please and thank you, grandma."

"You go and have a sit down, Thom. We don't want that old leg giving you grief again."

He hobbled several infantile paces to sink onto the bench and extend his leg, each separate halting inch a new twinge if not an ache. As Jude crossed the beach almost at Dean's speed Leigh said "Age does bring its problems."

"It's just annoying. Just an inconvenience."

Kendrick watched Jude fall to her knees in slow motion beside Dean, who handed her the bucket and spade. "Is Judith having many?"

"Cramps, the kind your legs get. And we're not as steady as we'd like to be sometimes, and there are places we could shin up we can't now. I expect some of that sounds all too familiar."

"We can sympathise from experience," Kendrick said, "but we were thinking more of, let me find the right word."

"Lapses," Leigh suggested.

"Lapses, yes, precisely."

The repetition lay between Thom and the Bentons like an uninvited intruder on the bench until he couldn't avoid acknowledging it was his turn to speak. "I don't think I know what you mean."

"We've started having them," Kendrick said. "Names of films I used to be able to tell you without even stopping to think, a lot of those have gone."

"People's names as well," Leigh said. "That's getting to be my trouble."

"So you can see there's no reason to feel ashamed. You're talking to folk who are going through it too."

"I'm sorry you are. It hasn't come to us yet, but who can say when."

He saw Leigh and Kendrick stop just short of glancing at each other. "I think it has to Judith," Kendrick said.

They'd turned their eyes to her as she loaded the bucket with spadefuls of sand moistened by the receding tide. "It's best when it's a bit wet," she told Dean as if reverting to monosyllables, and dealt the contents of the bucket several triumphant thumps before inverting it alongside his attempts. Of course she was simply enjoying the transfer of knowledge, just as she and Thom had in the classroom, however reminiscent of a second childhood her behaviour might be. "I'm afraid I'm not with you," he said.

"We know it must be difficult for you," Leigh said. "If we can help in any way, please tell us."

"I don't believe that will be necessary. I don't even know with what."

"The ideas Judith seems to have got into her mind," Kendrick said. "We could see you weren't comfortable with them. You did your best to put her right, just as we did."

"I'd rather she was how she is than not. She's always been concerned for children. It's one reason she was such a good teacher."

"Please don't take this the wrong way, but perhaps she isn't quite concerned enough. Perhaps her notions are distracting her. I'm afraid we all heard what she must have hoped we wouldn't hear."

"I'm sure she wanted you to hear everything she had to say."

"We mean what happened last night," Leigh said, "when you left her on her own."

"When she let Dean get trapped in the bathroom."

"I'd hardly say trapped," Thom protested. "His pyjamas fell off the hook on the door and they only needed somebody to move them."

"She left him alone in the bath," Kendrick said, "because she thought somebody had called her when nobody could have."

Thom felt defensive to the point of doggedness on Jude's behalf. "I could."

The Bentons rested sympathetic looks on him. "But did you?" Leigh said.

"I'm just saying she'd have no reason not to think so. Or maybe with the window open it could have been somebody in the park."

"There's a lot to be said for loyalty. We don't see enough of it these days." Kendrick sighed as a preamble to his main theme if not a wordless summation. "Please pardon this," he said, "but could you possibly arrange it so that Judith won't be caring for our grandson by herself in future?"

"Coral and Allan were so unhappy about asking," Leigh said, "we told them we would when the right moment came."

Thom fended off the implications, which he found monstrously unfair, by saying "We stay together all we can. We don't know how much longer we will be."

He'd caught their sympathy again or reminded them how they felt about each other, and they shared a wistful glance politeness made him look away from. His gaze strayed to Jude – at least, it searched for her, because Dean was alone on the beach. He was struggling not to think she'd confirmed the Bentons' view of her, and clutching at the bench to lever himself to his feet, when her head appeared above the edge of the promenade as she climbed the ramp. "What have I been missing?" she said.

"Just three old folk rambling on," Thom said at once.

"That's all it was, Judith," Leigh was eager to confirm.

"Nothing you'd have been anxious to hear," Kendrick said.

She took the hand Thom offered as she sank onto the bench, but her touch refrained from conveying her thoughts. He felt hemmed in by a mass of words nobody wanted to utter. As she brushed at her crumbling knees – at sand the colour of her linen trousers – he risked saying "You've still got it. You haven't lost the knack."

"Thomas was telling us how splendidly you used to teach," Kendrick said.

"And we've been seeing how you do," Leigh wanted her to hear.

Everybody turned to watch the result, Dean planting strong castles to replace insecure towers he'd knocked down. Thom thought one or more of the children playing by themselves might have joined him, but they seemed to think he was sufficiently companioned. Whenever he raised another castle he cocked his head as if to listen, no doubt contemplating his latest achievement. Was he murmuring to himself, or were the responsive whispers just the ocean? The lengthy row of castles resembled defences against an invasion by the time he shuffled around on his bare knees to ask "Did I do enough?"

Until the boy looked towards his grandparents Thom might have assumed he was addressing someone hidden by the wall beneath the promenade. "You've done wonderfully," Jude called. "Give yourself a rest now if you like."

Thom heard footsteps acquire substance while they climbed the ramp, Dean stamping sand off his shoes. As he dislodged a final sprinkle on the promenade a man shouted across the road "Is that the best boy in the grove?"

He was standing in the doorway of the Ample Amusements arcade. Enough light and clangour for an entire fleet of fire engines flashed and clamoured at his back. His costume – white shirt and bow tie as black as his suit – let nobody doubt he was the manager. Jowls tugged at his face, which illustrated the adjective above his head, but left his wide plump lips straight. "It's Mr Bowler," Dean enthused. "Please may I go and see him, please and thank you?"

"We all will," Kendrick said.

Leigh took Dean's hand to usher him across the road. Thom might have thought it was Jude's turn, but she'd fallen behind Dean and the Bentons for a private word. "Why are they such a twitchy lot round here?"

"Who do you mean?"

"Dean's friend over there. Look at him."

The arcade manager had folded his arms to drum his fingers on his biceps as if the rapid rhythm could speed Dean across the road.

"And don't you remember the ice cream lady," Jude said, "rubbing her lipstick off?"

"Eva. Eva Briggs."

"I heard her name. I don't need reminding any more than you do. And don't forget how the policewoman couldn't leave her eyebrows alone."

"Just a mannerism. We all have them."

"Not like those, I hope. You'd wonder if there's something in the air round here."

As Thom resisted wondering, Kendrick glanced back. "Aren't you two with us?"

They caught up as a gap in the sluggish traffic let everyone cross. As they passed Swanky Swimwear next to the arcade Thom seemed to glimpse a decapitated child-sized mannequin sprouting or otherwise donning a head – his own reflection in the window, he guessed without needing to look. The arcade manager uncrossed his arms to deal out greetings. "You'll be the last of the family," he informed Jude and Thom. "Eric Bowler at everyone's service."

His moist handshake was emphatic and capacious. "Does someone deserve a free ride?" he said.

Jude seemed to think this needed translating. "Mr Bowler's asking if you'd like a ride, Dean."

"Yes please and thank you, Mr Bowler. Please may I go on the racing car, please and thank you?"

"Now you know I'm Eric to my friends." As the boy looked uncertain Eric said "But you've said more than you need to earn yourself a race. Go and strap yourself in and I'll start you off."

As Dean ran to clamber onto a seat that faced a screen depicting a racetrack, Jude murmured "Do you think his parents might be a bit less strict with him, Eric?"

"Not my place to say. Why do you ask?"

"I thought you seemed to feel he was overdoing the politeness."

"I'd rather have too much of that than not enough," Eric said and swung around, having scowled at an overhead mirror. "You lot carry on straight past," he called. "You're not coming in here any more."

The trio of teenagers sent him a selection of gestures before strutting onwards. "I'll take one of your grandson against three of their sort any time," Eric said. "They act like they're possessed, some of them. They nearly wrecked a pinball last time they were in. On drugs, the lot of them, I shouldn't wonder."

"I heard some in the park last night," Jude said, "even if nobody else did."

As Thom avoided looking at the Bentons, Eric activated the race. Dean trod on a pedal, rousing the roar of an engine while the track beyond a simulated windscreen rushed at him. When a car overtook him he tramped the pedal flat, drawing level with the rival vehicle just as they reached an unrealistically sharp bend. "Slow down," Jude cried as if she were a passenger.

Dean floored the brake so fiercely his car spun off the track. The rudiments of a landscape turned over several times before the car crashed upside down into a wall and shattered into cartoon flames with a lingering thunderous explosion. "I'm sorry, Dean," Jude said and gripped his shoulder as if to lead him and herself back to reality. "I was caught up in your game. I'll buy you another ride."

"Grandma doesn't have to, does she, Mr Bowler? It gives you three more goes."

"If it doesn't I will. Just keep it in your head it's nothing but a game. We don't want you growing up like those villains I had to chase."

"I don't see how that would follow," Jude said.

"It's been kids like them who've been turning our prom into a racetrack and doing wheelies in the middle of the traffic. They'll be getting themselves knocked down or worse, and then it'll all be the driver's fault. We aren't supposed to blame kids any more whatever they do. Maybe it's time a few more of us did."

He'd begun to drum his fingers on his upper arms again. Above the uproar of the renewed game Jude said "You don't need to be told it's not real, do you, Dean? You couldn't put everything back together like that if you were really in an accident."

"Mr Bowler was just saying children who aren't careful could be badly hurt," Leigh said.

Though Dean's speeding car was flanked by an equally headlong pair of vehicles, this didn't prevent him from answering. "You could still come back."

"Not if you were killed, old fellow," Kendrick said. "Killed like you just were or any way at all."

"You might. Bits of you could."

"Now you're being imaginative again." Jude plainly meant to defend him against potential criticism. "It was one of the things we liked most about teaching," she told Leigh and Kendrick.

"I've begun to think Allan may be right, though," Leigh said. "You can have too much imagination."

She turned to watch Dean win his race, a victory celebrated with a series of explosions, though only of fireworks. "Thank you very much, Mr Eric," he said.

"Any time, Dean. We try to mind our friends in the grove."

Once he was out of earshot Jude halted outside a shop displaying nostalgic jars of sweets – headless snakes of liquorice, elongated honeycombs of rock, humbugs resembling zebras rendered to their essence – but seemed unaware of how they might tempt her grandson. "Just let me ask you a question, Dean," she said.

"You can, grandma."

"When you were in the bath last night, did you hear anybody calling?"

As Thom deduced Leigh's last remark had provoked the question Dean said "Which bit of when, grandma?"

Jude gave the Bentons a belated wary look. "Don't mind us, Judith," Leigh said. "We heard you were shut out by accident. It's been discussed."

"Has it now." Her gaze trailed across them and Thom on the way to fastening on Dean. "In that case, just before I went out."

"He called you, grandma."

"Your grandad Clarendon, do you mean? He says he didn't, so he couldn't have. I was only wondering if you remember hearing any kind of voice at all."

"Yes, grandma, his kind," Dean said and pointed at his cranium. "Sometimes you hear him in there and you don't know where he's talking from."

"Now who would that be?" Leigh said.

Her tone seemed to make him feel safe to say "Heady."

"So that's why you made up that name, because he lives inside your head."

"He doesn't, nan, only sometimes his voice gets in."

"It sounds as if he can throw it as well," Thom said in an attempt to recapture rationality. "If you remember you told us he'd shut us out of the bathroom."

"He did, grandad."

"If mummy and daddy heard you saying that," Leigh said, "they'd tell you you were being silly."

"I'm not. I'm telling the truth like they say I've got to."

The complaint was on the way to growing petulant, and Thom heard Jude try to calm him before anyone rebuked him. "Then tell us how he could be in two places at once."

"Because," the boy said with all the seriousness his six years conferred, "most of him was in the bathroom with me. Just his head was somewhere else."

The silence this prompted was multiplied by four, and Thom felt as if a shadow too misshapen to be looked at had brought a chill, even though the sun that stood high overhead was unobstructed. "I believe that's all we need of that conversation," Kendrick said to end the hush, "and I think it's time we found some lunch."

FIVE

Thom was hardly in the bedroom when Jude said "Shut the door."

She was sitting naked on the end of Dean's bed, where a dog's ear of the quilt exposed the mattress. He might have fancied she had some intimate pleasure in mind, though he feared the proximity of so many other people would render him even less adequate than he'd lately proved to be. The prospect dwindled as she drew her legs up to slip beneath the quilt and cover herself like a gift she'd exhibited only to withdraw the offer. "Get into bed," she told him.

It was obvious she didn't mean the same one, since there was scarcely even room for her. Its rudimentary companion creaked as he lowered himself onto the mattress, and he imagined the occupants of the other bedrooms wondering whether the sound betrayed some marital activity. When he propped himself on a shaky aching elbow and leaned down to Jude she suffered a kiss on her forehead. He was reaching for the cord that hung above the junction of the beds when she said "Don't you want me to see you?"

"Why would I ever not want that? If you can stand how I look these days I can."

"It's me who's turned into a rotten old caricature of myself."

"You've done nothing of the sort, and you never will."

"So long as I don't for you." She pushed away his hand as it reached to stroke her face. "I don't need that just now," she said. "I want to hear what all of you have been saying about me."

At least she hadn't confronted Leigh and Kendrick, instead waiting until she was alone with Thom. Tonight the Bentons had looked after Dean's bathtime, which Kendrick had graced with a medley of ditties, rowing a boat gently down a stream and seeing three ships sail by and another on instead of in an alley, commandeering Leigh and eventually Dean to join in. The Bentons had introduced a bedtime story too, reading him to sleep as a girl found her magical way through a wardrobe. Now the house was quiet except for Jude's demand. "All of whom?" Thom said.

"Keep your voice down. All right, not all. You know exactly who I mean, so don't try to make it sound as if I'm imagining that too."

Matching her murmur made him feel as though someone unseen might be eavesdropping. "I'm not. I'm just not sure who."

She didn't whisper so much as mouth it. "Coral's parents."

"You heard what they thought. They don't believe you need to worry about any of the things that were bothering you. They gave us explanations for them all."

"That's what they tried, and you sided with them."

"You shouldn't look at it like that, Jude. I only wanted to reassure you if I could. No point in getting yourself in a state when there's no need for it."

"And then you carried on talking about me when I went on the beach. You told them I trapped Dean in the bathroom."

"I didn't have to tell them. They said everybody heard."

"Then why didn't they say so?"

"Jude, they did. Really they did. You must have misunderstood."

"I've started doing that, have I? That's what you think." Just as bitterly she said "So that's what you were discussing while I was looking after Dean."

"The business with the bathroom did come up."

"And what else were you saying about me?"

"They mentioned they've been having some elderly interludes, and they wondered if we had."

"Elderly interludes."

She sounded as if she was holding the phrase at a distance to fend off infection. "Lapses, they called them," Thom said.

"Like an incompetent old crock who's started hearing voices and oughtn't to be left in charge of children any more."

"Jude, you're none of that and never will be." The resemblance to the undertaking the Bentons had extracted from him made Thom all the more anxious to persuade her. "They're just concerned for you," he tried saying, "the way you are for Dean."

"You think that's necessary, do you?"

"I don't think they need to worry about you any more than you need to worry about Dean."

He was afraid she could take this for the opposite of what he'd meant until she said "So why didn't they tell me what they've been thinking about me?"

"I couldn't say, but does it matter now? I'm sure I showed them they were wrong."

"You didn't bother telling them they ought to wait till I came back so I could hear."

"I just felt it was important to find out what they thought so I could put them right." With belated inspiration he said "And I didn't know if you'd be bringing Dean back with you. Surely you wouldn't have wanted him to hear."

Weariness overtook her as if she'd been striving to ward it off, unless his answer was the cause. "I want to go to sleep now," she said and tugged the dangling cord. "I just hope I can."

Her hand retreated beneath the quilt before Thom could reach to squeeze it if not to keep hold. Her dim face sagged against the pillow as though exhaustion had rendered all its muscles slack. Her initial breaths sounded more like sighs – like bids to leave distress behind. The emotion drained away as they grew longer and shallower, and Thom willed her to have found sleep. Perhaps he would too, although the inch that separated the beds felt like a chasm that had cut him off from her. He could only lie with his face towards her and leave his left hand on top of the quilt in case she might want to find it in the dark.

At last his cluttered thoughts let him sleep until a bony creaking wakened him. He'd disturbed the skeletal frame of the bed with a shiver. He hoped this wouldn't waken Jude, who had taken hold of his hand while he was asleep. Hers felt unexpectedly thin, unreasonably so. It felt somehow incomplete, and at least as cold as the chill that had roused him. He thought he might prefer not to look while he hoped the sensations went away, but another shudder twitched his eyes open.

As his vision strove to focus he grasped how empty his hand had grown. Both of Jude's arms were under her quilt, along with practically all the rest of her, but a silhouette was standing between the beds. How could it fit into such a meagre gap? Perhaps because it appeared to have no more bulk than a shadow. It was similarly bereft of detail, and Thom couldn't judge which way it was facing, not least since its head was ducked so low it was invisible to him. He blinked in search of clarity, an action that seemed to send the intruder leaping over Jude's bed to flatten itself on the wall beside her. He twisted onto his back in order to sit up, jerking a creak out of the bed, and stared around him. He and Jude were alone in the room, and the wall was blank.

He began to turn over an inch at a time to hush the bed, only to find Jude watching him. "Don't say you didn't see," she said.

SIX

As soon as Thom returned from showering Jude said "I think I know what's going on."
She was at the bedroom window with her back to him. "What's that, Jude?" he said.

When she turned he saw she was holding her phone. "I've been looking this place up," she told him.

"Which place? Not their house."

"That for a start, yes, of course."

Was he nervous of learning what she'd discovered or how her mind had begun to work? He could think of no alternative to asking "So what have you found out?"

"About their house, not a thing. No history at all that I could see. I wouldn't mind talking to the people who sold it to them, but otherwise it might as well not exist for all the information there is."

"That's a relief, I suppose." When she didn't respond Thom tried saying "Isn't it?"

"It just means we have to look elsewhere for the explanation."

"Of what, Jude?"

"What we both saw last night."

He had one: that it had just been a shadow, which prompted him to say "Did you hear anything?"

"The children in the park again, but now I'm not so sure they're what I thought they were."

No doubt they were the kind of youngsters Eric Bowler had decried, and they would only have needed a powerful flashlight to project the shadow into the room as a prank. The way Thom's eyes took time these days to focus once he wakened, it was no wonder he'd misperceived the sight, while the sensation of a hand in his had been the last trace of a dream brought on by missing Jude in bed. "I'll tell you what I've found out while you get dressed," she said, "if you like."

He couldn't very well retort he wasn't sure he would. As he dressed a hanger in the shoulders of his bathrobe he said "I'm listening."

"Do you know what Barnwall means?"

"I haven't really thought about it, but no."

"It's Old Norse, so it's nothing like it sounds to us. Barn is the same as bairn, and wall means field."

"So it's like Childer Field."

"Exactly right," Jude said, but her gaze expected more of him. "Doesn't that strike you as odd?"

It didn't, and she mustn't either. "In what way, Jude?"

"That so many places round here should be named after somewhere that has to do with children."

"I wouldn't have said two was so many."

"It is when the whole town's one of them."

Thom refrained from searching this for logic while he leaned a shoulder against the wall to help him wobble on one foot and then the other to don underwear. "Is that all you found?" he rather hoped.

"No, I found out where the name comes from."

Thom sank on the end of Dean's bed and lugged his right foot as close as it would advance – barely close enough for him to haul a sock on. "Where did they?" his gasps of effort left him just sufficient breath to ask.

"From all the children who were slaughtered here."

Thom might have liked his struggles to distract him. Once he'd dragged the left foot within reach he tugged on the sock, only to have to clutch at his ankle to heave the foot closer while he strained to adjust the heel. "Where?" he protested. "You don't mean right here."

"More like the park as far as I could see. That's where a village was the Vikings raided. Their leader, I won't try to pronounce his name, he was the cruellest Viking of them all. He had everybody in the village killed, starting with the children so their parents had to watch. He was supposed to have thought they'd sent the children to swim out and damage his boats, but nobody's sure if they tried or even if they were told to."

"Are you saying he named the place after the massacre? That doesn't seem to make much sense."

"He didn't name it, the Vikings who came later did. They settled here and built a new village after they made a treaty with the English. It sounds as if they named it as a memorial, maybe even an apology for what he did."

Thom stood or rather staggered up to hop by clumsy stages into the right leg of his trousers, tottering more than once against the wall, before he shoved his left foot in a series of unbalanced jerks into the remaining leg. "So," he said as patiently as his antics would permit, "what do you think you've actually established?"

Jude waited for him to finish desperately pirouetting. "You know how the Vikings executed people, yes?"

He punched his way through the truncated sleeve of a shirt and twisted in search of its opposite number. "Remind me," he still had to say.

"They beheaded them. They chopped their heads off, Thom."

"I do know what beheading means."

"And you see what it has to mean where we are. Dean's friend, the one Allan and Coral don't like him mentioning. They don't believe in him, but now we've both seen him."

"What do you think you saw?"

"A child. A boy. I don't know exactly what age, but I know he didn't have a head."

Thom's question felt like a grotesque joke. "Then how could you tell it was a boy?"

"Because Dean says so, and I believe him." As Thom wondered where to start with this she said "And I've realised it was a boy I heard calling me out of the bathroom."

This silenced Thom as he made to speak. "I'm not afraid of him, are you?" Jude said.

At least this let Thom feign straightforwardness. "I can't see any reason."

"I don't believe he means any harm. That business with the bathroom, it was just the kind of prank boys play. Or maybe he's trying to let us know he's here. He only wants to be acknowledged, like I should think a lot of ghosts do." When Thom found no answer to any of this she said "There's one thing I don't understand."

"Only one?" He managed to stifle the retort by saying "What's that?"

"If all those children were killed, why is it just him who's stayed?"

Until that moment Thom hadn't grasped how much he might secretly hope she'd pieced the truth together. It would mean nothing was amiss with her mind, after all. "I've no idea," he said and wished it weren't the case.

"Perhaps he's some kind of I don't know, a representative. Perhaps he's standing for the rest of them to remind us. Let's see what everyone else thinks."

"Hadn't we better keep all this to ourselves?" Thom said and found a desperate reason. "We don't want to risk Dean overhearing."

"I suppose not, but I wonder how much he understands."

"For heaven's sake don't ask him."

"I wouldn't. I hope you don't think I'd be so thoughtless." She turned her back on Thom to look out of the window. "There's somewhere we can take him," she said. "Let's try and get his bike out for him."

Beside the playground, where two boys competed at inversion on a climbing frame while a girl on a swing aspired to kick the sky, a cycle track imitated the route of the adjacent footpath. "Come on before anyone has another idea," Jude urged and was first out of the room.

An aroma of coffee merged with a blur of conversation to meet them on the stairs. Everyone was at the kitchen table, where Dean turned a page of the Lewis book and paused the story with a finger and thumb. "We've all had our breakfasts. You can have yours, though."

"Don't be so rude, Dean," Coral said.

"I didn't think he was," Jude protested. "You were meaning to be helpful, weren't you, Dean?"

As if she felt it wise to intervene Leigh said "You looked as if you had something to say to us, Judith."

Unhappy anticipation snagged Thom's nerves until he heard Jude say "We were thinking it was time somebody went for a ride."

In a bid to maintain the same style Allan said "You mean the contents of the shed."

"That's it, the healthy item."

"I expect he can give it an outing so long as you'll all be with him. Grandma was asking if you'd like to go out on your bicycle."

Dean looked up from reading or pretending not to listen. "Yes please and thank you, grandma."

"Let me just give it a check," Allan said. "Make sure it's still fit to ride."

"Why," Jude said, "how long has it been since he's had it out?"

Allan gazed a reprimand at her before unlocking the back door. "A while."

As Thom and Jude set about their bowls of cereal he let himself into the shed, rousing a clatter of tools that sounded sharp and eager for release. He wheeled Dean's bicycle out to examine the chain and the brakes before pumping the tyres firm. At last he called "Just try it now and see if it needs adjusting."

Dean ran to hurdle the crossbar and perch on the seat, then wobbled along the path so precariously Thom might have fancied he was recalling how to ride. Once he regained his balance he said "It doesn't really, daddy."

"Leave it now till everyone's ready for you."

As he followed his father into the kitchen Jude said "And then maybe you can ride all the way across the park."

"Don't listen, Dean," Coral said. "You know you won't be doing that."

"I'm sorry," Jude said less than apologetically. "What will he be doing, then?"

"He knows how far he can go," Allan said. "No further than the first little hill in the park."

"We like to be sure where he is," Coral said.

"But you didn't feel that way yesterday," Jude protested.

"Don't be so certain you know how we feel, and anyway, that was before."

"Before what, can somebody tell us?"

"Before Allan and I had a talk. Shall we leave it now? Some little ears pick up far too much."

Thom sensed Jude's question this had headed off. She plunged her spoon into her cereal with a fierceness reminiscent of a frustrated child. Hoping she was only eager to be off, he matched her pace if not her vigour. As he carried their bowls to the sink Allan said "Let me deal with those. We don't need anyone to feel we want to hold you up."

"Use the back gate," Coral said, "and leave it open. Then we can see the park from our workroom."

There was indeed a view between the railings on the far side of the alley that crossed the path from Willow Grove to Childer Field. Dean pedalled sedately through the entrance to the park and looked over his shoulder once he reached the cycle path as if seeking permission to put on speed. "Go ahead," Thom called. "Just be careful."

"Remember you aren't on your ride in the arcade now, old fellow," Kendrick said.

For the moment Dean was alone on the cycle track, and the grandparents sat on benches by the playground to watch. He glanced at the footpath beside the track so often that Thom wondered whether he was playing at racing a companion. Leigh waited until the boy had almost reached the nearest turfy mound, several hundred yards away, before she spoke. "Well, I must say I've been made to feel as if I can't be trusted any more."

"I know exactly how you feel," Jude said.

As Thom hoped the Bentons would assume she meant their present situation Kendrick said "I expect Dean's parents just like to know he's safe."

"I thought that was what we were for," Leigh said.

"We used to get pretty anxious when Coral was his age, didn't we? I should think you two were the same with Allan. I'd rather they cared a bit too much than not enough."

They all watched Dean coast up and down the track, dismounting to turn the bicycle whenever he reached either end of his permitted route. Thom glanced back to see Allan and Coral at computers in the room beyond the open gate, but couldn't tell whether they were intent on their screens or on their son. As Dean measured the stretch of track yet again, a cyclist appeared around the miniature hill.

He wore a summer suit clipped at the ankles, but the tight pallid plastic ring that encircled his neck made his calling plain. His ruddy round resolutely humorous face looked determined to escape the restrictions of the collar. While he cycled after Dean, Thom heard him striving to dictate to a phone fastened to the middle of the handlebars. "And a little child shall lead them…. No, not liquor…. Delete liquor…. Delete no not liquor…. Finish taking dictation," he tried saying, only to have to jab the screen with a defeated finger. "Why, there's one now, except he's not so little any more. Bigger and better every day is young Dean."

He halted opposite the family as Dean did. "They're my grandmas and grandads," Dean said.

"Father Nicholas." The priest sent them a wave that stopped short of sketching a cross. "Call me Nick," he said. "Just not Old Nick."

Dean giggled before glancing towards the house as if he feared being overheard. "It's all right, Dean," Jude said. "It must be if Father Nick is saying it. Do you live in the grove as well, Father?"

"Nick without the trimmings is absolutely fine. No, I live up by my church."

"How do you come to know Dean?" More doubtfully than Thom thought polite she said "Do they all go to your church?"

"Not yet if ever." He seemed untroubled by her tone or by their absence. "I was passing by when they were moving in," he said. "I just stopped to say how do and welcome to Barnwall, not to drag them off to worship. Forgive me for inflicting my thoughts for a sermon on you, if you could even call them thoughts."

"You shouldn't say that," Leigh protested. "Those words mean a lot to some people."

"I'm glad to hear it's still the case. Do look in at the church any time it's open if you care to," the priest told all of them. "I promise no harassment. I don't believe in imposing faith on anyone. I'd much rather they found their way to the spirit by their own personal road at their own pace."

Into the silence this appeared to warrant Dean said "Please may I cycle now, please and thank you?"

"Race away with my blessing," Father Nicholas said. "Don't waste a splendid day like this listening to me drone on."

"But only as far as your daddy said," Kendrick reminded Dean.

As the boy set off for the mound Jude beckoned the priest over to the bench. "You believe in spirits, then."

Although Thom found her approach contrived if not worse, the priest seemed to welcome it. "I was thinking of the spiritual in general, but I wouldn't say that necessarily excludes them."

"You're saying you believe in ghosts."

"If that's the term you favour," he said, keeping hold of a handlebar now he'd dismounted. "I think a case can be made for them, yes."

"What kind of a case would that be?" Kendrick said.

"As long as we accept there has to be an afterlife I don't see why it should be too unlikely that people sometimes linger."

"What would you say might make them do that?" Jude said.

"Perhaps they find it hard to let go of the world. They cling to somewhere that's familiar. Or perhaps the way they left this world was so traumatic it traps them where it took place."

"That's the kind of thing I thought. I'm glad you think so too, you and your church."

"Do you mind if I ask if you've any special reason for asking?"

"I believe there's something of the sort in our grandson's house."

"Would you know the history?"

"I've just been looking into it. It's the first I'd heard of it or Thom had."

"It might well explain the situation."

Thom was disconcerted less by the agreement than by who had voiced it: not the priest but Kendrick. "It could," Leigh said.

Jude stared at each of them before she spoke. "You've known about it all along."

"For a while," Kendrick said. "I'm sure you can see why we haven't brought it up."

"Remember the ears," Leigh murmured and touched hers while she nodded towards Dean.

"We didn't want to disturb anyone, Dean in particular."

"So what do we think should be done?" Jude said.

Though she was addressing the priest, it was Leigh who said "What are you saying ought to be?"

"Father Nick, excuse me if I don't feel comfortable calling you just Nick, you said people can be trapped after they died. I'm sure that's happened here, so mustn't he need somebody to set him free?"

"That does sound like a solution."

"Would you be able to, or if not someone in your church you could bring in?"

"What did you have in mind for them to do?"

"I was thinking along the lines of an exorcism."

A memory glimmered in Thom's mind – an exorcism in Barnwall – before shrinking out of reach. Was the priest reminded too? He looked less than happy with the notion. "Do you think that's a shade excessive?" Kendrick said.

"We don't mind if it makes the house a better place."

Thom swung around to see Coral and Allan on the path a few feet from the benches. "If that's what it takes," Allan added to his wife's remark, "go ahead."

"I should have asked you both before saying," Jude said. "It just came to me."

"It's good to know we think alike. Dean, stay on the track while the grownups are talking." As the boy pedalled to the mound so fast he might have been miming escape Allan said "We wanted to catch you while you were here, Father. Would you have room for Dean at Sunday school?"

"I'm afraid we no longer run one. These days it's regarded as rather an old-fashioned notion."

"There's nothing wrong with some of those," Coral retorted. "I hope you don't think exorcisms are."

As a memory evaded Thom again Jude said "Sorry, this has just caught up with me. You both think there's something in the house as well."

"Something we can do without," Allan said.

"But you keep telling Dean he's being silly."

"Would you rather we encouraged him?"

"Encouraged him how?"

"To believe he's got some kind of friend in the house," Coral said.

"Surely he has," Leigh protested. "The two of you."

"And the rest of us just now," Jude said.

"I think everyone knows perfectly well what I mean."

Jude nodded and then gave her head a shake as if to enliven an insight. "Won't having an exorcism just confirm what you don't want Dean to think?"

"Not if all of you keep him out of the way while it's being done. How long do these occasions generally take, Father?"

"I'm afraid I don't believe an exorcism would be appropriate."

"How can you say that when you've no idea how much it's been troubling us?"

"I give you my word it would help to put our minds at rest," Allan said.

"It has to be about a good deal more than that. It's a very serious business."

Allan stared at him so hard his eyes twitched. "We couldn't be more serious."

"You must appreciate you can't simply book an exorcism. They have to be argued for, and I wouldn't know how in this instance. Would you say there's any actual threat? Has anyone been injured?"

"You're telling us you have to wait till someone's hurt?" Coral demanded.

"Maybe the worst hurt isn't physical. I should think you might say that," Allan said and with heavy emphasis, "Father Nicholas."

"I'd say neither ought to be involved."

"Then I'd have thought you'd want to do your best to protect our son from them."

"I can't recommend a course I don't feel is called for." As Coral opened her mouth to argue or to mime disbelief the priest said "Perhaps there's someone who can help instead. You may have seen her Crystal Distillations shop down by the promenade."

"And what's she supposed to be able to do?"

"They call it cleansing. A gentler form of exorcism, you might say. Chloe Sissons is the name. Tell her I sent you if you like." Father Nicholas stood on a pedal to hoist a leg over the crossbar. "Now if you'll forgive me, I must get back to that sermon. Delighted to have met the family. Do look after one another."

Leigh waited until the priest had cycled into Willow Grove and Dean was at the mound again. "I don't think any of us realised you were so bothered by developments at home."

"Well, now you know." Coral's rejoinder sounded close to a general accusation. "Let's go and see this Sissons woman now," she said, "if the rest of you can look after Dean. We'll be as quick as we can."

She lingered while Allan told Dean "Just make sure you behave while we're away." As she and Allan strode past the mound, apparently too purposefully to hold hands in the way Jude found so appealing, Kendrick said "I hope this psychic lady or whatever she is will do some good."

"I'm sure she will when a priest recommended her," Thom said and told himself Father Nicholas hadn't done so merely to preclude an exorcism. Perhaps the priest didn't even realise how unwelcome such an activity might be in Barnwall. Just the same, Thom found he needed reassuring that the case he'd remembered at last had been years ago and all the way across the park.

SEVEN

The Days – Joan and Daniel – had lived in Childer Close on the far side of Childer Field from Willow Grove. Their neighbours thought them amiable enough, if a little taciturn, and hardly worthy of remark except for how often they attended church. Soon after moving to Barnwall the couple had adopted a six-year-old boy. He was a quiet child, though some said he hadn't started out that way, and soon the neighbours scarcely noticed him or his eventual absence. In fact they hadn't seen or heard him for months; at least, they testified they hadn't, and some of them grew distressed or enraged if not both when this was questioned in court. The anguish the Days had displayed when they'd reported the boy missing had impressed the police, and the couple had insisted on leading the amateur search that had lasted nearly a week before the portion of a small corpse wrapped in a supermarket bag had been found under the rubbish in a concrete bin just inside the park. The Days had maintained their innocence until a neighbour told the police he'd seen them dump an item in the bin around midnight, and then they'd claimed the child had died by accident while they were attempting to purge him of wickedness. Afraid of being misunderstood – the phrase Joan Day had used in court – they'd prepared the remains for distribution, using tools in the shed. Among the items the police had removed from the property was a heavy child-sized cross. "Those who don't believe in Christ," Daniel Day had told the court, "deserve to suffer as Christ did." In the course of the trial it became clear that the couple had subjected the boy to months of torture in the belief he was possessed. After the verdict and the sentencing – life for both – the officer in charge of the investigation had spoken to the press. "If anybody was possessed," he'd proclaimed in several headlines, "it was them."

Thom had remembered far more than he welcomed. All the talk of exorcisms had brought it back, but the ritual scheduled for tomorrow wouldn't be the kind the Days had tried to perpetrate. If his thoughts were keeping him awake, at least he could stay still so that the flimsy bed wouldn't creak. Was Dean awake too, or muttering in his sleep beyond the wall? Of course the indistinct childish voice was his, which Allan confirmed by saying "Stop that right now, Dean. You've been told." Eventually the silence let Thom's thoughts subside, and he succumbed to a jerky slumber.

A touch on his forehead wakened him. A silhouette was leaning down to him. The sun was in the window, and when the silhouette gained substance as Thom's eyes reclaimed clarity he saw it was Jude. "People are about," she said. "We need to be."

A shape without a face loomed in the fog her shower had spread across the bathroom mirror. It lurched to meet him when he clambered out of the bath. Jude had laid his clothes out on the bed like a flattened figure awaiting assembly. Once he'd struggled into them and his shoes he followed her to the kitchen, where everyone seemed to be waiting for them. "Finish your breakfast, Dean," Allan said.

Not much less than immediately Coral said "Don't rush your food."

Thom thought all the grandparents were avoiding one another's eyes. He attacked his cereal at a defiant speed, though the gesture felt childish. Any solidarity it might have shown Dean was lost on him, and the boy was the last to finish. As he laid his spoon to rest, the doorbell tolled its quartet of ecclesiastical notes. "I'll get it," he declared as though it had released him, and ran along the hall.

"Surely that can't be Chloe Sissons yet," Coral said and hurried after him.

When Jude followed, Thom felt he should. The newcomer's waist-length hair sprawled down the back of her amber kaftan. However delicate her small face was, it announced an inner strength her slight but wiry body rendered physical. "Who are you?" Dean was impatient to learn, along with "What's that smell?"

"It's only sage." She was visibly unsettled by his directness. "And I'm—"

"Your mummy and daddy will tell you that, Dean," Leigh called. "Just let the lady in."

"Yes, come here, Dean." Too close to a contradiction Allan said "And just apologise for being so rude."

"I didn't think he was," Chloe said. "He was only acting his age."

"Then it's time he grew out of it," Coral said. "Say sorry anyway, Dean."

Thom willed him not to make the joke he could almost think she'd challenged Dean to perpetrate. When the boy said only "Sorry" Thom let out a breath, though Coral didn't seem too taken with her son's performance.

"Maybe I'm the rude one," Chloe said, "if I've turned up too early. You did say I should come as soon as I could."

"You're more than welcome," Allan said, having advanced to the foot of the stairs. "Go and do the washing-up, Dean."

"Please may you tell me what nan said you were going to?"

"Ms Sissons will be giving us a cookery lesson."

Thom would have appreciated the inspiration if he hadn't seen how much his son resented being forced to fib. As Dean disappeared into the kitchen Jude stepped forward to whisper and eventually to hiss "Are you sensing anything here, Ms Sissons?"

"Chloe by all means, but that isn't how I operate. I've never had that talent, but I don't need it to know what works."

"I'm sure you must," Coral said and lowered her voice, "or Father Nicholas wouldn't have sent us."

"You can leave that for me to deal with, Dean," Allan called. "I'm sure you're eager to be out and about."

It was Allan who was eager, Thom knew – concerned to send the boy away so that Chloe Sissons could start work. As Dean scampered out of the kitchen Coral said "Can we just ask everyone not to buy him toys while you're staying, especially not ones he already has. The house is cluttered enough as it is."

"We only did because it was a long walk back to fetch the ones he has," Leigh protested. "And we might have interrupted both of you at work."

"Well, I'm sure there won't be any need in future. Dean, don't you be tempted if anybody offers. You know exactly what to say."

"No thank you very much," Allan told him to abort any other notion.

The boy and all his grandparents were on the garden path when Jude called "Here's hoping everything goes well. We'll look forward to finding out what you add to your cuisine."

No doubt she meant to consolidate Allan's explanation, but might she have left Dean expecting some evidence? Thom made for Childer Field, only to be detained by a voice across the road. "There's a sight I like to see."

The speaker underlined his enthusiasm by tracing his lower lip thrice with a forefinger. He might have been determining whether his small mouth had gained more proportion with his straight thick nose and large eyes, all of which his broad face had ample room for, and Thom took care not to glance at Jude in case she was reflecting on the local prevalence of mannerisms. "Oliver Dodd," the man announced. "Your friendly neighbourhood social worker."

He latched his garden gate before crossing the road. Once the introductions were completed and hands shaken – his grip resembled a promise of support – Jude said "What were you saying you liked, Mr Dodd?"

"Oliver. Always Oliver, and I meant seeing families together."

"Unless they shouldn't be. I imagine you see some of those in your job."

"Regretfully, but I don't expect to see it here," he said and outlined his lip again as he glanced past her at the house. "Are you missing someone?"

"We're giving them a break," Leigh said. "Every parent needs a few."

"Mummy and daddy are having a lesson."

"Let me guess what it's not about," Oliver said.

Dean responded with some of a laugh he seemed to hope would be appropriate. "Go on then."

"Being your mummy and daddy. They don't need anyone to teach them that." As Jude parted her lips with a sound reminiscent of a tut he said "Did I guess right, Dean?"

"No, they're learning to make dinners."

"I'm sure they must do that for you. Don't we all think he looks a healthy boy?"

"Of course they do. Of course he is," Leigh said. "They're just trying something they haven't tried."

"Always room for improvement," Kendrick said.

"I don't know anyone who'd want to argue with that. Now I must dash off to see a client," Oliver said but lingered to tell Dean "Have a marvellous whatever you're going to do."

As the social worker sped away in a car resembling the front half of one Jude said "What would you most like to do, Dean?"

"Please may we go to the fairground, please and thank you?"

"Has anybody said you can't?" Kendrick wondered.

"No, grandpa."

"Then here's to the adventure."

Dean sprinted to the entrance to the park out of eagerness, Thom felt certain, not because the boy wanted to leave behind the chilly shadow the house cast in the passage. From the gates Dean said "Can I please may I run, please and thank you?"

"Remember the drill," Kendrick said. "Just as far as we can see."

As Dean set off on a solitary race his grandparents trotted or limped at a clip in pursuit. On their way past the playground Thom glimpsed a child sailing down the slide, having left his head at the top to watch. No, the head belonged to a boy who'd dealt his friend a push and was craning over the edge to observe the result. Dean loitered at the nearest mound and kept pace with his grandparents as far as the next clear stretch of path, then dashed from hillock to hillock. Thom thought the truncated sprints suggested bids to escape, but could hardly blame the boy for wanting to outrun his plodding relatives. "Hand, Dean," Leigh said as they reached the lower gates, and Thom told himself she meant their grandson had to hold hers – could mean nothing else.

A hulking van had perched two of its wheels on the pavement of Childer Close, so near to the corner that its pallid anonymous bulk hid half the name of the road. Thom risked a long look, hoping he wouldn't have to explain his behaviour. Childer Close seemed as innocent as Willow Grove – just another suburban street off the Childer Field perimeter road – and how could he have expected to identify the house the Days and their victim had lived in? When he heard faint childish cries he had to remind himself they were coming from the fairground.

They rose like a celebration of the final week of the summer holidays as the family made their way downhill. An assistant was keeping Crystal Distillations open. Seafront shops rattled windblown toys and souvenirs, challenging the grandparents not to buy Dean any of them, but he urged Leigh past them. "Let's see what they'll let you on, Dean," Thom said, only to feel as though he was trying to restrict the boy on Coral and Allan's behalf.

He meant the column marked in inches at the entrance to the fairground. "No tiptoes, lad," an attendant burly enough for a bouncer warned Dean as the boy ran to the post. "Keep them feet flat down." Thom watched Dean try to hide a bid to stretch an extra inch, and had a sense that the boy was attempting to grow more of a head. The notion almost roused a memory that could only be a dream, and he put it out of his mind.

Dean's stature barred him from the rides the shrieks were coming from, but a roundabout prompted a contented grin. As a horse bared its glossy painted teeth while it elevated Dean and bore him away at a paralysed canter, children's heads bobbed up and down on the far side of the carousel. The spinning mass of steeds must have confused Thom, leading him to expect more children to sail into view around the ride than did.

A siren loud and harsh enough to signify some lethal danger brought dodgems to a halt. Since an adult had to drive Dean's vehicle, Thom volunteered. Several adult drivers were chauffeuring young passengers if not using them as an excuse to revert to youthfulness. When the siren howled again Thom strove to avoid the other cars until Dean pleaded for some thumps. Each impact throbbed up Thom's legs, replenishing a generous selection of aches. Once he thought he glimpsed a small figure leaping from its seat to be flattened in the midst of a collision. It must have been a shadow thrown by the indoor lightning that flared at the tips of poles overhead.

When the siren released him Thom limped to sink onto a bench near the scaled-down rollercoaster Jude and the Bentons took Dean on. Some of the slopes the train laboured to ascend were impressively ominous, and the plunges they portended earned girlish cries from both women. As the train raced down the steepest section of the track a boy behind Dean craned his head backwards so far that he seemed to have none. He must have disembarked on the opposite side of the train from the platform, since Thom couldn't see him when the riders left the rollercoaster.

Dean climbed on the roundabout while his grandparents recuperated on the bench. Thom kept observing a boy crouched so close to the neck of his steed that his head was nowhere to be seen, but he must have straightened up each time the horse came around to the bench, whichever child he was. "Would you like to go in the maze?" Leigh said when Dean ran to rejoin them.

"Yes please and thank you."

Its glass corridors feigned straightforwardness. Dean had to be deterred from running ahead to peer through the walls at his trudging guardians, a lark that lent him the appearance of a specimen trapped in a display case. The maze led to a hall of mirrors, where a boy was prancing in front of his reflection to separate it into restless fragments: a leg whose kicks suggested bids to fend off an assailant, a hand wriggling like an impaled spider, a head jigging above the stump of his neck. When the family managed to reach the mirror room Thom felt oddly glad the boy had gone.

As they left the maze by an exit far less distant from the entrance than Thom had anticipated, Dean said "Please may we go on the ghost train, please and thank you?"

"Do you think mummy and daddy would want you doing that?" Leigh said.

The boy gave her a look so comforting it seemed to age him. "They're pretend ghosts, nan. They aren't really real."

"Well, that's me reassured," Leigh said, still frowning at the ride – the toothy mouth that yawned around the entrance, the frieze of skeletons capering alongside the track, the quartet of two-seater cars grinning demoniacally at an unlit tunnel as if they'd acquired faces that had been at large. "Is anybody giving it a miss?" she said.

"I'll go on with grandma," Dean said at once.

Leigh seemed to take this as a challenge. "I'll ride with you, Kendrick."

"I'll pay for everyone," Thom said, apparently the only contribution left to him.

Dean's gleeful vehicle lurched forward to lead the procession, and then the Bentons blundered into the tunnel. As Thom left the daylight behind, a spider caressed his forehead. No doubt it was the same simulated cobweb that had drawn theatrical squeals from Jude and a few seconds later Leigh, if indeed the strands were artificial. The sensation appeared to enliven the darkness, not to mention its denizens, the first of which – a glowing figure so emaciated it looked desperate to be fed – greeted the newcomers by raising its top hat along with its relentlessly jovial head. "That's funny, isn't it, Dean?" Jude seemed to feel compelled to tell him.

"It's not like a real one, grandma."

If this was meant as more of the reassurance Dean had offered Leigh, Thom wasn't sure it worked, but he doubted anybody needed it. The ghost train's cut-price manifestations were unthreatening enough – a timidly swooping bat with embers for eyes, a cadaver chattering its teeth as if its lack of flesh had left it vulnerable to chills, a tentatively shuffling monster with a square green head that apparently needed a pair of bolts to hold it on. Thom presumed the effect he could have done without was inadvertent: the shadow the intermittent illumination kept producing, a variably incomplete silhouette that dodged across the dim walls to make its rapid although ramshackle way ahead of the helpless procession to wait in the renewed dark. Given its size, he thought it could belong to Dean, even if he couldn't quite see how. Perhaps he might ask the boy to wave next time it showed up, just to confirm it would imitate him, but how could Thom explain? He was urging the shadow to reappear and verify his supposition when a spasm seized his chest. It felt as he thought a pacemaker would feel, a fancy that persisted until it rang and said "Allan."

Everyone but Dean turned to stare as if they were rebuking a noisy member of an audience. The skeleton that sat up in its coffin ahead of them might have been expressing disapproval, though its lack of eyes made it hard to tell. Had a shadow like an uninvited passenger darted away from the foremost car to hide in the dark? Thom was too busy quelling the ringtone to judge. "Allan," he said.

"It's me all right, but why aren't we seeing you?"

"Sorry, why do you think you should?"

"You just said you could see me."

Thom was seeing darkness that could hide any number of shadows if not consist of them. "No, the phone told me it was you."

"We're finished here. Everything's done that was needed, and we're looking for you. Where are you in the park?"

"We aren't. We've gone adventuring. We didn't think you'd mind."

"Where?"

"Just the fair down on the prom."

"Why didn't you tell us where you were proposing to go?"

Thom had begun to feel like a child accused of putting somebody younger at risk. "I can't speak for anyone else, but I had the impression you just wanted us out of the house."

"Why should we have wanted that?"

Didn't Allan realise Dean could hear, or had he abandoned caring? "So we wouldn't be in your way," Thom said, "while you were having your lesson."

"I think we've learned all we need to know. So whose idea was the fairground?"

"Everyone's."

"You must have realised by now we like to keep an eye on our son. Why didn't you stay in the playground at the back?"

"I think I may be speaking for everybody when I say we don't want to do nothing but sit all the time. We'd rather get out and about and see some of your town."

"I wouldn't call what you're doing much of that. Where are you now exactly?"

"On a ride."

Thom was hoping to leave it unidentified, though he saw no reason why Dean's parents should object to any of the goblins he'd encountered, when the foremost car roused another apparition. The lid of an upright casket tottered wide to release an extravagantly toothy vampire who stretched out his elongated claws to Jude and Dean. The boy giggled while his grandmother struggled to truncate an automatic squeal. As if to concentrate his concern into a solitary forceful syllable Allan demanded "Which?"

"Don't mind me being silly," Jude called. "It took me by surprise, that's all. It's only an old ghost train."

As the coffin lid wobbled shut Thom saw the shadow dodge into the dark — just another shadow. In that case, how could it make a noise? Whatever had sounded like scrawny scurrying must have been caused by the mechanism of the ride. Allan's voice distracted him, not least with how cold it had grown. "Please bring Dean home. Please do so at once."

"I think we'll have to finish our ride first," Jude told him.

"Make the most of it, whoever thinks they have to." Coral plainly endorsed everything Allan had said. "There won't be any of that sort of thing in future."

"We'll be waiting," Allan said and terminated the call.

Thom was pocketing the phone when Jude gave a genuine scream. She and Dean had vanished into blackness that looked not much less solid than a wall of coal, and Thom was glad Dean's parents couldn't hear him shout "What's wrong?"

"Nothing really, is there, Dean?"

In a moment the blackness engulfed the next car. Perhaps Leigh was determined not to react, but Kendrick emitted a gasp he swiftly qualified with a laugh, just audible above a rush of rumbling that had already carried off Jude's voice. Thom had time to brace himself for the surprise – a precipitous unlit incline like a displaced section of a rollercoaster track. He went some way towards relaxing until a hand clutched at his shoulder as though to detain him in the dark. It had to be yet another muscular spasm, which he left behind as the car bumped the exit doors open and coasted out of the ride. As he hauled himself and a generous helping of aches onto the platform Jude said "I'm sorry for spoiling your treat, Dean."

"You didn't, grandma. You were having fun like me."

"I'm glad you did, but I meant it's my fault it's over."

"I don't mind really. It was silly," Dean said as if, Thom thought, he was trying to impress his parents despite their absence. "I told nan all those things weren't real. They wouldn't put real ones in there."

"I shouldn't think anyone would." Jude confirmed this with a laugh. "But I'm saying," she said, "I'm sorry your whole treat's finished."

"It was a big one. It was good."

"You're a good boy," Jude said and hugged him so hard he squeaked like a toy with just that for a voice.

Thom hoped she didn't notice the regretful glance Dean sent back to the fairground as she ushered him onto the promenade. Surely his disappointment deserved compensation, and Thom said "Would anyone like an ice cream?"

"I'm certain someone would," Jude said, since Dean seemed wary of assuming the question had referred to him.

Eva Briggs was carrying a two-faced blackboard menu out of Don't Pass The Glace. Thom could have fancied he'd succumbed to double vision, whether caused by drink or age, since the remains of an erased name showed through the latest listing chalked on the board. "This is still your treat, Dean," Jude said.

He appraised the board at length before saying "Please may I have a rum and raisin, please and thank you?"

"That won't get anybody tiddly, will it?" Kendrick said.

"Not even slightly," Eva assured him.

Thom bought tubs for all the family, selecting rum and raisin for himself. "We'd better eat on the trot," Leigh said, "before anybody's missed."

They were tramping uphill past Crystal Distillations when they saw Chloe Sissons heading for the shop. "Was it a success?" Jude seemed eager to learn.

"I think I gave them what they wanted," Chloe said.

As the family toiled towards Childer Field the sun glared over the treetops to blot out their surroundings, not least the street names, but Thom sensed when he came abreast of Childer Close – imagined the plaque on the corner was commandeering the dazzle to deny its own identity, espousing any ally that would help it pretend innocence. Dean was tramping past the junction when he hesitated, and a drip darkened the pavement at his feet as the tub he was holding tilted. "Mummy and daddy," he said.

"Are you missing them?" Leigh was audibly moved. "We're nearly home," she said. "You'll see them very soon."

"I can now. Can't you?"

"Don't start seeing things the rest of us can't again, old fellow," Kendrick said. "I thought we were done with all that business."

Thom sensed Jude suppressing disagreement. The trudge towards the park sank the sun behind the trees, and he saw Dean's parents striding through the lower gates of Childer Field. "You said you were going to wait for us," Jude protested.

"We did," Allan said. "We thought we'd waited more than long enough."

"We only meant to give you time to get on with some work while nobody was in the way," Leigh said.

"Not much chance of that," Coral said, "when we weren't able to concentrate."

"Then I'm sure we're all as sorry as we should be," Kendrick said. "It was a group decision."

Coral stared at the tub in his hand. "Making a detour after we spoke to you, you mean."

"I don't know about anybody else," Thom said, "but I'd have been parched by now if we hadn't stopped off at your neighbour's establishment."

"I see someone's been a lucky boy." Allan peered into Dean's tub, which let another drip fall like a hint of panic. "What have you got there?"

"Ice cream, daddy."

"We've told you it's not clever to be clever. You know quite well I'm asking you what kind."

Perhaps the concern Kendrick had expressed about the ingredients reduced Dean to a mumble, but he certainly couldn't have said "I'm in heaven."

"You can speak better than that when you want to," Coral said. "Answer your father properly."

Dean surely had no cause to mutter "Rhyme and reason."

"He's telling you it's rum and raisin," Kendrick intervened. "We checked with your friend at the ice cream parlour that it's entirely teetotal."

"Then I wonder," Allan said, "why he's behaving as if he's done something wrong."

Thom saw Jude struggle to tone down her retort before letting it fly unrestrained. "Because the two of you keep making him feel he has even when he hasn't. Since we arrived we've hardly seen anything else."

"Walk ahead, Dean. Further than that. Just make sure you stay in sight." As the adults followed the boy at a distance into Childer Field, Allan said "I'm sorry you feel that way, mother."

"I'm sorrier I've been made to."

"We're just doing all we can to bring our son up properly," Coral said.

"Then perhaps you should start doing a bit less of it. I hope we never treated you the way you're treating him, Allan."

"Maybe you should have, though."

"Well, we never realised you wished we'd been harder on you. If you'll excuse me now I'll walk with our grandson, assuming I'm still allowed," Jude told him and did her utmost to stride well ahead.

She left silence in her wake. As she caught up with Dean his father said "I didn't mean to upset anyone."

"I think you'd better leave it now," Thom said as much for himself as for Jude. "I'll talk to your mother when I can."

She held Dean's hand and stayed remote from the rest of the family all the way back to the house, and retreated out of Allan's reach when he made to unlock the front door. "It's smelly," Dean said and advanced along the hall like a mime of exploration. As an overwhelming scent of sage met Thom on the doorstep, the boy scampered upstairs to his room. Thom heard door after door thrown open, and then a dismayed wail. "What is it, Dean?" Jude cried and stumbled along the hall.

He reappeared at the top of the stairs and sent the family a look that seemed to hold them all responsible. "He's gone," he complained. "He mustn't have liked that smell."

"Never mind, Dean," Leigh said. "I'm sure you'll make some real friends at your new school next week."

"They won't be here in our house."

"Your mummy and daddy will. They're all you need in here."

"I want him." Perhaps Dean grasped how disloyal this might sound. "I wanted him as well," the boy amended and turned away as if to hide his distress, so that Thom barely heard his final murmur. "He told me he wouldn't let anyone hurt me," Dean said, "like somebody hurt him."

EIGHT

Jude had been quiet since they'd left Barnwall. While Thom assumed she didn't want to distract him from driving, he sensed her thoughts gathering like a storm. At last she said "What do you think he meant, Thom?"

The view ahead confused Thom. From the brow of a hill, fields rejuvenated by the high sun sloped to a distant sea, but no sea ought to be visible on the way to Manchester. He could have thought he'd turned too far on one of the many roundabouts that interrupted the road and was heading back to Barnwall. "Who?" he blurted before he was able to think.

"Who else am I going to be worried about?" Jude gave a sigh that brought more words. "No, you're right. We should be concerned about Allan as well."

It was mist, not a sea, that lay low on the horizon. They were indeed bound for Manchester. Since Thom's mind hadn't failed him after all, he felt safe both to drive and to talk. As the car sped down a steep hill, requiring frequent applications of the brake despite the tentative stabs of a cramp in his calf, Jude said "Do we even know him any more?"

"He's still our son. He's had to change a bit, that's all. Life does that to us."

"I can't believe you don't see what's happened to him, or are you determined not to? If you carry on like that you'll have me feeling I don't know you either."

"You know you do. If you're wrong about me, why can't you be wrong about him?" Thom protested, only to feel he should already have said "Try not to let what he was saying in the park upset you. He was just defending how they've brought Dean up."

"Not how they've brought, how they've started bringing. Don't you see the difference? Are you saying I shouldn't have spoken up?"

"Perhaps you could have been a little more tactful."

"I think I was about as much as he was to me."

Had her mind reversed the order of events? Thom preferred to think she was being irrationally emotional, not least when she said "So you agree with him."

"About what, Jude?"

"About how we should have treated him when he was Dean's age. About all the rest of the childhood we did our best to give him."

"Of course I don't agree." Thom trod on the brake as the incline grew so extreme the hedges alongside the road appeared to be clutching at the verges with their bared roots, and a cramp made a grab at his leg. "With him, that is," he thought it best to add. "I hope, I mean I know he had a happy childhood, but we used to see that wasn't always how it worked when we were teaching, didn't we?"

"I don't know what you're trying to say."

"Just that it's natural for the next generation to grow away from their parents, however well their parents looked after them."

"You think his behaviour is natural."

"Not natural but maybe understandable. I wonder if the two of them were so anxious to impress us and the Bentons they ended up trying too hard. It's the first time everyone's been there together, after all. You saw how eager Coral was last night for everybody to like her dinner."

"None of that has anything to do with how they're treating Dean."

"It could have." The road had levelled out at last, and Thom risked flexing his leg, which sent the cramp back into hiding. "Maybe they just wanted everything to be perfect for everyone," he said. "Maybe they were trying to show off their new life as well as their new house."

"It's not perfect for Dean. It's anything but, whatever they think. If that's how having a new house affects them I'd say they were better staying where they were."

"You know they moved for Dean's sake. That's how much they care about him."

"There's such a thing as caring too much." As Thom withheld agreement in case she took it to be aimed at her Jude said "They got away from the break-ins and the dealers and all the rest of it, but at least they looked after Dean while they were there."

"They're still looking after him, just in a different way."

"If that's all you saw you're nowhere near as perceptive as you used to be."

"It wasn't just me, though, was it? Leigh and Kendrick didn't seem to think too much was wrong."

"I think they may be more concerned than they let on."

"Then maybe they're having a word before they go home. Maybe that'll do the trick along with what you said."

Though he hardly knew what he was saying any more – his instincts were speaking for him, or thoughtlessness was – he fancied he'd placated her until she broke her silence. "This isn't even what I started talking about till you distracted me. I asked you what you thought Dean meant."

"Meant when?"

"Do you really need to ask that? When we went back to the house."

"I thought he didn't like the smell, and that made him feel his friend wouldn't either."

"He said more than that and you know it. He said someone was going to hurt him."

"I don't think he quite said that, did he? I think he was just missing the idea of a companion. As Leigh said, he'll be making friends next week."

"And you think they'll be able to protect him."

"From what, Jude? You can't honestly feel he's in any danger."

"You don't think being constantly put down will do him any harm."

"Put down or pulled up? All the neighbours think he's a credit to his parents. Maybe we're so close to him and them we can't see what other people see that's positive. And he does seem happy enough."

"That's children for you. We know that from teaching. They think their childhood's normal just because it's theirs and they don't know any better. They don't realise what's being done to them till it's too late."

"We can keep an eye on things, and I'm certain Leigh and Kendrick will." At once Thom regretted being driven to allow for any need. "Only maybe nobody will have to," he said with the rest of a breath. "Maybe once everyone's gone home Allan and Coral won't feel they have to show Dean off any more, and they'll relax with him."

The road dipped between hedges barbed with thorns and wire. At least the slope was gentle, and showed the distant motorway stringing cars towards Manchester. "I hope so," Jude said, and Thom thought he'd helped her achieve that state until she added "I'll be worrying till the next time we see them."

NINE

At thirteen minutes past the hour Jude said "Do you think something's happened?"

"I shouldn't start worrying just yet. I mean, I'm sure we don't need to at all."

"I don't have to start. I already was."

"Really, I'm certain you shouldn't. We don't want you making yourself ill." Thom reached to squeeze her arm, both of which lay on the kitchen table in front of her phone on a stand. "They're never all that punctual," he reminded her. "Round about noon, that's what they always say."

"It's well past that by now. Do you think they've forgotten about us?"

"I'd say that's most unlikely. Make that impossible."

"Perhaps they want to, though. Someone might. Not Dean."

"I don't believe anybody there could feel that way. Don't you remember what Allan said?"

"I don't need reminding. I keep hearing it when I'm trying to get off to sleep."

"Not that nonsense about how we brought him up. He did apologise, after all."

"Only once we'd had a good few drinks. It doesn't mean he didn't mean it when he said it."

"It doesn't mean it's true either. I've come to the conclusion that he said it because he thought he had to defend Coral."

"I don't recall anyone attacking her."

"We were finding fault with both of them, weren't we? With how they've shaped up as a father and mother. We shouldn't be surprised he reacted how he did." In the hope he'd convinced her Thom said "Besides,

I wasn't talking about that. I meant what he said when we were leaving. They were looking forward to seeing us again, and Coral backed him up."

"Seeing, maybe. Not having us to visit. There's a great deal of difference, and I wish there weren't." Jude jabbed the phone screen to display the time. "Nineteen past," she unnecessarily announced. "I'll give them one more minute and then I'm going to call."

Thom could tell she felt vindicated by finding further reason to be anxious. Nothing in the week since they'd left Barnwall had distracted her enough from her concern. At last month's meeting of the book group they'd voted for *Lord of the Flies* as the next novel to read, but now the theme of children in peril from without and within seemed to have gathered an unwelcome significance. This week's subject at the discussion group was how to deal with criminals, and this too had acquired unwanted resonance: the constant threat of crime that had made Allan and Coral relocate to Barnwall, the unnumbered youngsters in danger, whether of attack or of being enticed into the underworld. Even the days Thom and Jude spent helping in the children's section of the community library failed to work as a diversion, since the readers put Jude in mind of Dean, not least by behaving sedately. At home Thom tried playing discs of comedies and musicals, but even Jude's favourites seemed to fall short of her: Cary Grant had earned scarcely a giggle, and she'd begun to find Gene Kelly relentless, not least since his search for perfection had injured Debbie Reynolds so much she'd had to be carried off the set. Today Jude had lingered over preparing an elaborate dinner, but that couldn't occupy all the hours until noon. Since well before midday she'd been seated next to Thom, gazing at the phone while she clasped her hands together as though considering a prayer. The tiny digits beside a colon on the screen skipped up to twenty, and she snatched her hands apart. She was reaching to poke the phone when it emitted a series of notes like the start of a child's party trick on a keyboard. "You see, we only needed to be patient," Thom said.

In a moment the family in Barnwall crammed onto the screen. The youngest member sat between his parents, who rested hands on his shoulders as if to hold him as still as the icon had rendered them all. When Jude touched the phone to accept the communication, her finger hid Dean until she drew it back. She'd wiped out the family, at least while the screen stayed as blank as the silence, and then their faces filled the screen – Allan's and Coral's did. "Here we are for you," Coral said. "Sorry we're a bit later than usual."

"Coral wanted to finish editing a chapter," Allan told his parents, "while it was all clear in her head."

"You're keeping busy, then," Thom said.

"Every day. Sometimes we wish there were more of them in a week."

"So long as you find time for Dean as well," Jude said.

Coral didn't quite let her smile down. "He's another reason why we're busy all the time."

"I only wish we lived closer. We'd help like I hope we did last week."

"All of you were welcome."

"I expect you'll be seeing your parents more often." This sounded less regretful once Jude added "They'll be able to take some of the pressure off."

"We'll be seeing to it there won't be much of that," Allan said.

Jude gave way to asking the question Thom knew she must have struggled not to raise too soon. "So where's the star of the show?"

"No need to let him hear you call him that. We don't want it going to his head."

"It's only a manner of speaking, Dean. I meant you light up all our lives."

Thom guessed this was designed to prompt at least an offscreen response if not to bring Dean into view. Jude's fingertip marked off several seconds by tapping the table like a counterfeit ghost at a séance before she said "Where is he, then?"

"I'm afraid he couldn't seem to grasp why he had to wait to talk to you," Coral said.

"Nothing wrong with wanting to see his old grandma and grandad, is there? I hope it didn't make any trouble for him."

"We're sure you never intend to."

"I hope we don't, but I meant I hope he didn't make any for himself."

"Just for us," Allan said.

Surely he couldn't be accusing Jude of wishing this on them, but she said "Of course not for you either."

"Coral would have finished sooner if we hadn't had to deal with him, and then you wouldn't have been kept waiting so long."

"We're here now as Coral said, so can he be as well?"

Allan gazed at her – at any rate, in the general direction the computer in Willow Grove would provide – and Thom wondered if their son meant to chide her for cleverness. When Allan turned his back Thom could have thought he was rebuffing her until he shouted "You may come down now, Dean."

"Please may I show grandma and grandad what I made with my present?" The pause might have conveyed a breath the distant voice required to add "Please and thank you."

"I think you should. We don't want them getting the idea you never put it to any use." The second comment could have been for nobody to hear, and then Allan shouted "Just take care carrying it down. The last thing we want is you hurting yourself."

With that he turned back to the screen. His gaze might have been inviting if not challenging his audience to speak. Jude's finger had begun to drum again, as though counting footsteps they couldn't distinguish. How long would Dean take to appear? Longer than the stairs and the hall ought to need, it seemed. Perhaps he'd been making sure to act out the care his father urged. A patch of bright red intruded between Coral and Allan, who moved apart so that Dean could plant the item on the desk. It was a square red Lego building with a steep roof and a tower. "That's lovely, Dean," Jude said at once.

"So it is," Thom said.

"It's supposed to be a church."

"I thought it might be," Jude said, "only oughtn't it to have a cross on top?"

"You didn't give me any, gran."

"We should have realised that was missing." Allan's stare loitered on the church. "Put it on mummy's desk for a minute," he said, "and then you can come and talk to grandma and grandad."

Thom sensed Jude's closeness to hoping aloud the minute wasn't literal. Dean retrieved the crimson church, cradling it between his hands as if it was more fragile than its substance. He backed out of sight and reappeared so swiftly Thom could have thought the boy was making sure his grandparents hadn't vanished. Jude was ready with a question. "Are you happy now you've got your room back?"

"He was happy to lend it to you both, weren't you, Dean?" Coral said. "It was a special occasion, after all."

"Yes, mummy." Less dutifully Dean said "It feels different now."

"I hope that isn't anything we've done," Jude said. "I mean, I hope if it is that's how you want it to be."

"It feels empty when I'm in it."

"Well, it can't be if you are," Allan said, "and we've told you enough times about silliness. We don't want any more of it or you can just go back up."

"He won't really have to, will he?" Jude protested. "Can't he stay and talk to us? He hasn't even had a minute yet."

"I don't know why you'd think we'd want to stop him."

"We don't, of course," Thom said before Jude could speak. "Your mother wasn't saying that. It's just that she's been looking forward to seeing him all week."

"I thought you had too," Jude said.

"Both of us, obviously," Thom said and squeezed her supine arm. "You get us as a team."

"By all means talk to him about anything you think you should."

Thom found the invitation unexpectedly careless, or was Allan ensuring he and Coral monitored whatever was said? In some haste Thom responded "How's your new school?"

"It's good."

"You can say more than that," Coral said.

Was this permission or an order? Thom thought Jude didn't care for the sound of either. "I like my teacher," Dean said. "She's Ms Thorndyke."

"What do you like?" Jude was eager to prompt.

"She likes you to tell her things."

"What things?"

Jude might have asked that, but not as forcefully as Allan did. "Just things about us," Dean said.

"What about us? If you can tell a teacher you can certainly tell us."

"About us in the class, daddy, not us at home."

"I'm glad to hear you aren't discussing us with anyone. You've no reason to, so kindly don't."

How uneasy was Dean's silence? It provoked Coral to say "So what have you been telling her about yourself?"

"I said we'd got a new house."

"Just that it's new."

"And I said it was smelly. It's not now, gran and grandad."

"I don't know why you'd need to tell anybody that," Allan said. "What exactly did you say?"

"The lady from the shop was giving you and mummy lessons."

"Just that," Coral said. "Just lessons."

"She was showing you how to make dinners."

"You didn't say which shop."

"The one with all the crystals in."

"She'll know that's wrong, the teacher," Allan said, but not to Dean. "We'll need to have a word."

"Quite a few of them," Coral said and as they both stared at their son "You said you hadn't been talking about us. Make absolutely sure you don't again."

They appeared to have forgotten they had a distant audience, unless they'd ceased to care, and Thom thought it reasonable to remind them. "What else have you been up to at school, Dean?"

"No more mischief, we hope," Allan said.

"What has your teacher been teaching you?"

"English, grandad."

"I'm sure your parents did a lot of that before you ever went to school."

"Ms Thorndyke says I'm good at it. She says how I talk and write is proper."

Jude gave her head a minute shake suggestive of a nervous repudiation if not a bid to bring a thought up. Had Dean's grammar betrayed him? Perhaps she imagined it had. Thom was close to asking why her gaze had grown blank when their grandson said "And she's been saying about where we live."

"Where's that supposed to be?" Coral demanded more than asked.

"Barnwall, mummy."

"Of course she'd be talking about the town," Coral said as though somebody had been irrational. "What did you learn?"

"The Vikings called it Barnwall when they came to live here."

Jude's gaze remained blank, and Thom gathered she was searching for some notion – prompted by what, he didn't know. "Did she tell you all about them?" she said.

"They kept invading us and we had lots of battles, and then some kings gave them places to live in. Shall I show grandma and grandad what I drew?"

"I expect they'd appreciate seeing it," Allan said. "Take your Lego up with you while you're going."

When Dean backed away and disappeared Jude stayed so preoccupied Thom felt he was speaking for her. "Has he been making new friends?"

"He tells us several," Allan said.

"You haven't met them."

"We'll be looking them over," Coral said. "They're invited to the park tomorrow."

"Not to your house," Jude said.

"We like to know what we're inviting. We'll decide tomorrow after church."

Thom fancied Jude meant to react to this, but a different issue took precedence. "I was wondering," she said, "if we could do this more often."

"Keep an eye on us, you mean," Allan said.

"We'd call it keeping in touch," Thom said, hoping Jude would.

"I think we're doing that as much as we are with Coral's parents."

"I expect they'd like to see more of you as well."

"It depends how work is going. I think we've had enough distractions for a while."

"I hope you don't feel that's all we are," Jude said.

"Of course we wouldn't say you were." Presumably unaware of any contradiction Allan added "And we don't just mean you either."

He might almost have been summoning his son, who reappeared behind his parents. "Don't creep up on us like that," Coral protested. "You'll have us thinking somebody's got in."

Dean ventured forward to display an exercise book open wide at a drawing of a horned man brandishing an axe. "That's very fearsome," Jude enthused. "He looks like a devil."

Coral seized the book to twist it towards herself and Allan. "I hadn't thought of that. He does, too much so."

"I think he's meant to have horns on his helmet," Thom observed, "not on his head."

"You'd better go and fix that," Allan said. "Say goodbye to grandma and grandad."

"Goodbye, grandma and grandad."

"We will as well," Allan said and seemed to find a joke. "Just the first part. We aren't saying you're that old."

"Goodbye till next weekend," Coral said.

"Goodbye for now."

Jude echoed Thom and was saying "Next weekend if not sooner" when the screen erased Allan and Coral. "I want to see them properly," she said.

"Maybe they can fit us in again soon."

"I don't mean that, or at least I don't mean only. Seeing them like that is giving me eyestrain. Let's invest in a computer." As Thom welcomed the solution, which felt like an undefined relief, she said "I just hope something helps me think what I nearly thought of while we were all talking. I know it's important. I think it may be crucial."

TEN

"What do you need a computer for?" It was plain the salesman's head used to surmount a smaller form. His girth left it looking apologetic for its disproportion, while the large square lenses that covered half his face suggested an attempt to compensate. "We're still capable of using one," Thom retorted, "even at our age."

"I beg your pardon, sir. I was wanting to find out if you had a particular purpose in mind."

Thom had felt he was defending Jude, but now he saw he'd interrupted her. "Research," she said.

He tried and failed to postpone an observation. "I thought you just wanted to see everyone."

"That as well."

"Everything we sell can do that for you," the salesman said. "Any special kind of research?"

"Where our son and his family live."

"Here's our best buy of the month." As he led them to a laptop garlanded with tinsel stars the salesman said "Do they live far?"

"All the way across the country on the east coast. I shouldn't think you've ever heard of Barnwall."

"Barnwall." The salesman poised his hand above the keyboard as if he meant to bring up the name. "Isn't that where," he said, "no, forget I spoke."

"We can't now," Jude protested. "What were you starting to say?"

"I was thinking of the couple who are never going to get out."

"Which couple? I've no idea what you mean."

"I don't recall the name just now. Shall I show you what this can do? I've got one myself at home, but it wasn't half the bargain when I bought it."

The interest Jude focused on his performance felt close to an unasked question. At least she seemed eager if not anxious to take the computer home. Certainly it promised to live up to the slogan on the store window: IT'S A LAPTOP, NOT A CRAPTOP. Thom thought she'd forgotten her question by the time they returned to the car, but she said "What do you think he meant?"

She'd used precisely the same words last week, although about Dean. This disconcerted Thom more than he could define, so that he didn't speak until he'd edged the car out of the parking space alongside Zap That Lap into the sluggish suburban traffic. "About what?" he said.

"The couple he was saying can't leave Barnwall."

"Did he say that?" Thom was sure the man had meant the Days and prison, not the town. "I can't think it has anything to do with any of the family," he said. "So what's this research you had in mind?"

"I don't know yet. Maybe once I start it'll show me what I'm looking for. I'm hoping it will help me think what I should have realised when we were talking to the family. Just remind me what we were talking about and then maybe I'll see."

Thom did his best to find a theme that wouldn't turn contentious. "The church Dean built."

"I wonder whose idea that was."

"His, I should think."

"Then I wonder who it was meant to impress."

"I imagine all of us if anyone. Or maybe he just enjoyed building it."

"But why did he build it like that?"

"You've lost me, Jude."

"I hope I never do that." Not much less anxiously she said "There weren't any windows or even a door, unless it was on the side we didn't see. It made me feel as if anyone in there could never get out."

"It didn't make me feel that way at all. I just thought he did a good job."

"I don't want to argue about it. It isn't what I'm trying to pin down. What else was there?"

"Dean's schoolwork."

"Yes, I wouldn't mind meeting his teacher. She sounds like our kind. I just wish I hadn't said his Viking looked like a devil. That didn't seem to go down too well."

"It did rather look like one. I'm sure nobody could think that was intentional."

"Quiet a moment. I'm thinking." A frown contained her deliberation as the car turned along an avenue sectioned by shadows of trees. "I thought I had it but now it's gone," she said. "Go on. What else?"

"How good his teacher says his English is."

"I don't think his parents can object to that." As Thom made to agree Jude said "Be quiet again."

She didn't speak until he'd backed the car into the drive, dislodging a windfall of sparrows from the silver birch in the front garden. "I'm sure you nearly told me just now," she said, which sounded too close to an accusation.

By the time Thom finished lining up the car in the garage Jude had let herself into the broad squarish house and was setting up the laptop on the kitchen table. "Do you know what I ended up thinking when we were visiting?" she said.

Not entirely eagerly Thom said "Tell me."

"I really wouldn't mind a kitchen like theirs."

"Let's think about it if you like."

"I will when I can," she said as if he'd attempted to distract her. "Make us both a coffee while I see what this can show us."

The laptop had its back to the kitchen counter. When Thom glanced around, having filled the percolator, he saw Jude's intent face above the black slab. He was lifting two mugs off the topmost wooden hooks when she took a sharp breath like an imploded gasp, and he turned to find her staring wide-eyed at him. "You did help," she said. "I knew you would."

His wariness was back. "How did I do that?"

"The things you thought were so significant did." As though taking pity on his slowness she said "Vikings and English."

This only left him feeling more obtuse. "They were just what came to mind, and I don't see—"

"We've been assuming Dean's friend they got rid of must have come from the time of the Viking invasion."

"I thought all that was dealt with," Thom said as inexplicitly as he could. "Why should it matter any more?"

"Don't you see even now?" As if she were indulging Thom she said "How could Dean have understood what he was saying?"

Thom didn't know whether he felt triumphant or dismayed to bring some form of rationality to bear. "If he was what you say he was, he wouldn't have been speaking Norse."

"No, Thom, he'd have been speaking Northumbrian."

"We can still understand that, can't we? It's just a dialect."

"Here's what it's like. Can you even guess what it means?" As uncertainly as a child learning to read she pronounced "Fore thaem needfairae I naenig ooioorthit…"

Thom felt betrayed by his appeal to reason. "What on earth is that supposed to mean?"

"It's a poem about being judged for what you've done in your life."

"A poem doesn't mean the ordinary people talked like that. I can't imagine many people ever spoke the way Shakespeare wrote."

"It says here the poet was using everyday language."

"In any case, does it really matter? If there was ever anything at the house it's gone."

"I'd like to know where it came from, wouldn't you? Maybe that'll help us understand why it was there and what it wanted."

As bubbles began twitching in the percolator Thom said if not wished "Perhaps there isn't anything to find."

"Barnwall. Children." She was voicing the words the rapid clatter of the keyboard signified. An ache grabbed Thom's spine as he stooped to take a carton of milk out of the refrigerator, and kept hold of him when he straightened rather less than wholly up. It took the place of thoughts and even left him unaware of Jude while he crouched over making the coffee, and renewed itself as he returned the milk to the refrigerator. It made him wary of turning too fast, and he took a painful time to plant a coaster next to Jude and another in front of the chair that faced the left edge of the laptop. Well before he'd finished placing the mugs on the coasters he was ready to sit down, which he gradually did. "Are you all right?" Jude said.

"I will be. Just a twinge." When her frown didn't fade as the pain had begun to he said "What's the matter?"

"It doesn't look as though it's ever been much of a place for children."

"Which place?"

"Barnwall."

At least he could acknowledge having hoped she didn't mean Allan and Coral's house. "It's good for them now, don't you think? We saw plenty having fun."

"I'd have been happier just seeing one."

"I do think we saw some of that. What were you saying about the town?"

"Where do I start? There was a child his parents named Sufficient-unto-the-Day."

"Is the evil thereof," Thom completed the homily, and felt as if he'd made a tasteless joke. "They must have been Puritans. They had some odd ideas about naming back then."

"I'd call it worse than odd when you consider everything else." She stared at the screen as if she could find nothing there to like. "Before that there was the Black Death," she said.

"A lot of people died of that, not only children."

"Yes, but a family in Barnwall killed their children because they were convinced they'd brought the plague."

"I imagine people had some crazed ideas back then. You'd hope nobody would have them now. It was a long time ago."

"It's just the start, Thom. No, it wasn't even that. There was the Viking massacre, and some people think the Druids were sacrificing children pretty much in the same place centuries before that."

"Except most historians believe the Druids never sacrificed anyone. It was just a tale the Romans used to dehumanise their enemies."

"Then you'd wonder why the Romans never said it about anybody else."

"I suppose the point is it's too far away for us to be sure what really happened."

"Other things aren't." With a kind of dismayed triumph Jude said "When they were hunting witches all over the country they hanged more than a dozen children in Barnwall."

"Didn't they do that to children elsewhere too?"

"You really think that makes it any better?"

"I'm simply saying it wasn't only there. Do we know whereabouts in Barnwall?"

"It looks as if all these things happened around Childer Field."

Thom would have preferred them to be further from Willow Grove, but at least he could hope "You're saying those were all."

"Not even nearly." Triumph was yielding to distress. "Before there were anaesthetics," Jude said, "there was a surgeon who specialised in operating on children."

"Wouldn't they have needed somebody to operate on them?"

"Yes, but people thought he enjoyed causing them all the pain he could."

"I haven't seen a hospital anywhere around the park, have you?"

"Apparently it was only as big as a couple of houses. He owned it and nobody dared to stop him doing what he did."

"At least that was still quite a long time ago."

"Are you going to say the Victorians were? There was a family in Barnwall who sent all their children up chimneys. Sent them when they were three years old, Thom. When they got bigger they starved them so they'd still fit, and when they got too big anyway their parents put them on the streets, except it was in the park they were selling themselves. Prostitutes at ten, apart from the one who suffocated in a chimney when she was four."

In a bid to placate the rage she was audibly gathering Thom said "At any rate, that kind of thing can't happen any more."

"No, but worse can."

"What are you saying is worse? Surely not the way they're bringing Dean up. I don't think it deserves that or they do."

"Not them yet, no. I'm not quite that obsessed, if that's what you think I am."

"I've never said that, have I? I just think you can be too concerned when there's no need to be."

"If any of the neighbours had been more concerned they might have saved a child from, I don't want to think how he must have suffered for months."

"Whose neighbours?"

"A couple who adopted a child and tortured him to death because they'd convinced themselves he was possessed and needed exorcising, and that wasn't even thirty years ago in Barnwall."

"You mean the Days. Joan and Daniel Day, and I can't remember what the boy was called."

"His name was Eddie. They changed it to Peter because they thought that was more Christian. They didn't even leave him that bit of himself." Thom thought dismay had silenced her until she said "So you knew about it. Why didn't you say?"

"I didn't want to trouble you with it when there's no need."

"If you don't see any, I do. They're too fond of exorcisms in Barnwall for my liking."

"The family didn't have one, did they? Our family, I mean. It was only something like. The priest put them off."

"Yes, and now we know why he was so anxious to."

"What the Days did was appalling, but I really think we can forget about it. They weren't anywhere near Willow Grove. They lived in Childer Close, all the way across the park."

"You think that's far enough." As Thom refrained from asking in what sense, she made another search. She narrowed her eyes and leaned closer to the screen, shading her vision as if the side of her hand could balance on her frown. It was evident she didn't know how she ought to sound as she said "There's no Childer Close in Barnwall."

"There is, I promise you. We passed it several times."

"Show me where."

Thom dragged his chair around to her side of the table, rousing a reminiscence of his ache. A street map of Barnwall occupied the screen, and she'd typed Childer Close in the search box. Why was the map resisting the request? He could almost have fancied the town was determined to deny having permitted the atrocity. He pointed at the street opposite the lower end of the park. "There," he said.

"That isn't called Childer Close, Thom."

"Of course it is." He snatched his finger back and shoved his face so close to the screen the street name blurred: the first letters of the second word appeared to sprout extra branches while the penultimate character withered like a dead worm. "Have another look," he said and straightened up.

"That's Childer Grove," Jude said, and at once he saw it was. How could he have misread the street sign so frequently? Had his subconscious set out to delude him? His eyes began to sting with glaring at the obstinately unhelpful name, and he closed them. "Then I don't understand," he said.

"Let's see what we can find out. There has to be an explanation."

Her search was relentlessly audible, perhaps to keep him informed. "Joan and Daniel Day. Childer Close in Barnwall," she said as if to translate the clacking of plastic aloud. Soon she added "Number fourteen Childer Close," which he gathered she was reading from the screen. He would rather not have heard part of that, however coincidental it must be. He didn't care for Jude's ensuing silence either, since the insistent skeletal chatter of keys failed to convey what she was seeing. When she sucked in a loud breath he liked that even less, given its force that might have been designed to hold her words in. He felt as though her muteness had glued his eyes shut until she said "They changed the name."

"From Close to Grove? That's not much of a change."

"No, Thom." Her response was so wearily toneless that he couldn't leave her unseen any longer. She was staring at a street diagram opposite a paragraph concerning Joan and Daniel Day. "The council changed it to Willow Grove," she said as if he couldn't see what he wished he weren't seeing on the screen, "and our family are living in that house."

ELEVEN

Thom felt as if the realisation had paralysed them both until Jude planted her phone on the table like the winning card in a game or else a reckless bid. It roused him to blurt "Are you going to call them? Do you think we'd better talk about it first?"

"We will. We have to. No, not them just now."

She sounded impatient with spending the time the few monosyllables took. "Who, then?"

"The firm that sold them the house. Do you remember which that was?"

"I don't, and even if we did—"

"You're not just saying that, are you? I thought Allan told us."

"I don't recall any more than you seem to."

"So long as I know you're on my side, Thom. I don't think I could bear to feel you aren't right now."

"I don't know when you've ever needed to feel that."

Jude searched his face, surely only to confirm what he'd just said, before turning back to the screen. "Let's see if anything sounds familiar."

Bat, well, eat, age, bay… Eventually she controlled her fingers enough to complete typing *barnwall estate agent*. Swell Dwellings was first on the screen, followed by Properest Properties and Get You Home. "They all sound like jokes," Jude said at some distance from mirth. "Are you remembering any of them?"

"I don't. I think Allan just mentioned whoever he and Coral dealt with."

As she typed digits on her phone Jude said "Maybe the name will come back."

"What are you planning to say?" Thom felt he should learn if not stall.

"I haven't any plan. What I'm feeling will do." As a bell ceased repeating itself she demanded "Hello?"

"Swell Dwellings House Sales and Lettings." Having spoken over her with mechanical impoliteness, a woman's voice proceeded to enumerate reasons for the call. "Any other business will do," Jude declared and jabbed the number.

"Charles Bailey." As Thom shook his head at the name the man said "How may I be of assistance?"

"Are you the firm that sold a house in Willow Grove this year?"

"We aren't, madam."

Jude frowned at his swiftness. "You're sure of that."

"I am, yes."

"Without even looking it up."

"That's correct, madam."

"Can I ask how that's possible?"

"Because my partners and myself took the decision some time ago not to handle such a sale."

"To sell a particular house, you mean."

"Rather more than one. May I enquire the reason for your interest?"

"If you tell me first why you wouldn't sell them."

"It was a professional decision, madam. If other agencies make a different choice, that's theirs to make. I wouldn't want it thought we were condemning them for it."

"Can you tell me which of them would do it?"

"I'm afraid I couldn't say, madam."

Thom thought Jude was going to doubt this aloud. Instead she muttered "Sorry to have troubled you" and ended the call. "He's troubled me," she said. "Why won't they touch anything there?"

"Maybe it's to do with reputation."

"He did sound the type to be concerned with that." Jude typed another number on her phone. "It's not what I'm concerned about," she seemed to feel Thom needed to be told.

She didn't speak until the automatic response finished postponing any human contact while it listed permissible reasons for some. General Enquiries sent her finger to the screen. The young man or at any rate the youthful voice that answered might have been demonstrating mastery of the twister. "Properest Properties," he said much as the machine had.

"I'm sure some are. Have you any up for sale in Willow Grove?"

"We've nothing in that area. Were you looking for somewhere close to the park?"

"I'm only interested in Willow Grove."

"We haven't any houses on the park itself, but if you don't mind just a short walk—"

"That isn't what I'm after. I keep saying, only Willow Grove."

"Then I'm sorry but I can't help you."

"You sell them though, don't you?"

"We sell plenty. More than any other agency in Barnwall."

"I think you know exactly what I'm asking." Jude might have been rebuking a persistently unreceptive pupil. "Did you sell a house in Willow Grove?"

"Please hold on and I'll transfer you to someone who can deal with this."

"Don't you dare admit it? Would you lose your job?" Jude was wasting her challenges on an emaciated fragment of Mozart that had taken the agent's place. Before Thom could grasp the chance to speak, a woman said "Hello, can I help?"

"Who am I talking to now?"

"I'm the manager. Melissa Foster. I understand you're asking after properties in Willow Grove."

"You could put it that way."

"Are you looking to buy?"

"What if we are?"

"Do you mind if I ask why that street in particular?"

"Suppose I say for a good view of the park."

"There are quite a few houses around the perimeter with that view or better. We've none on our books currently, but we could certainly contact you next time we take any on."

"Including ones in Willow Grove."

"Nothing there, no. I can guarantee that."

"Why shouldn't there be?"

"Because too many people have a morbid interest in the area."

"I hope you aren't thinking we have."

"I don't think you've explained why your enquiry was so specific."

"Because—" Thom saw Jude decide to trust the manager or else risk carelessness to reach the truth. "Because someone in your town sold our son the house where, where what happened happened."

"That was most certainly not us. You have my word."

"Can you tell me who it would have been?"

"I can't really be expected to speculate about that, whatever I may think of what they did."

"Will you say what you think of it at least?"

"May I take it your son had no idea of the history of the place?"

"I can't imagine for a moment he or his wife knew."

"In that case at the very least the vendor should have informed them."

"I hadn't thought of that. You would, of course. Thank you for being professional." Apparently in the spirit of a tribute Jude added "Swell Dwellings is another firm that wouldn't sell the house."

She ended the call but kept hold of the phone. "Well, now we know who did."

"I'm not sure what we can achieve by calling them."

"I'll decide that when I hear them," Jude said with a fierceness he thought she might have saved for them.

"Get you home."

Thom couldn't help hearing this as an archaic command. New Enquiries completed the roster of options to press. "You won't have had this one before," Jude said, fingering the digit, and then a thought twisted her lips. "Unless you have."

"Gee why haitch agency. What can we do for you today?"

"I'm calling on behalf of Allan and Coral Clarendon."

"Are they interested in a property we've advertised?"

"No, you sold them one."

She sounded as efficiently official as any lawyer would. Identifying the agency responsible must have lent her the conviction, but suppose a firm from outside Barnwall had handled the sale? "Has there been any issue?" the bright high male voice said.

"Yes, the nature of the house."

"Can you give me details?"

"I'll give you the address, which should be enough. Fourteen Willow Grove."

"Do your clients see a problem with that?"

"Very much so, with what happened there far too recently for comfort. They should have been informed about it before any sale was agreed."

Having striven to stay bright, the agent's voice settled for competence. "That would have been the vendor's responsibility if they had the information."

"Then you'd best remind me of their names. Lettice, I believe the surname is."

This brought a silence Thom could have taken for refusal, but apparently the agent was looking up the information. He reappeared to say "Stanley and Deborah."

"And their present address."

"We can't give out those details over the phone, if we do at all. You'll need to send us an official request on your notepaper." Apparently emboldened by the opportunity to resist Jude's insistence, the agent said "I'm not so sure they had to tell your clients what you're saying they should have."

"Your competitors would disagree with you."

"Maybe not if they realise it isn't the same house."

"Don't—" Jude retorted this much before regaining her adopted personality. "The council tried to disguise it by changing the name of the street," she said. "They didn't manage, and there's no point in your trying to."

"They didn't only change the name, they knocked the house down. They didn't stop there either. They pulverised every brick."

"Then where did the house that's there now come from?"

"A local builder bought the site and put up a new house."

"So that's another kind of pretence."

Would a lawyer say that, especially so vehemently? Perhaps Jude realised her subterfuge had faltered again. "Thank you for your cooperation," she said and seemed to find it prudent to terminate the call at once. "I don't know what difference building a new house was supposed to make," she told Thom, "but I know it hasn't made enough."

Her stare at the phone let him know she was pondering her next move. "Who are you thinking of calling now?" he was anxious to establish in advance.

"Who do you suggest?"

His preferred solution would be nobody at all, but he could only take the chance to say "Shall we have a word with Leigh and Kendrick? They're as involved as we are, after all."

He was hoping they might reassure her in some way he'd failed to achieve. "Yes," she lingered over saying, "we'll do that," and he wondered if he was about to regret proposing the call.

TWELVE

A clamour of children answered Jude's call – laughter and shouts and cries of excitement or of temporary woe. However she'd meant to begin, it distracted her enough to make her ask "Where are you?"

"Where do you think, Judith?" Leigh said.

"You sound as if you're in a park."

"Full marks to the young lady," Kendrick said closer than the children. "We're making the most of the sun while it's here."

"I wish I were."

"I'm sure you must have some of it even in Manchester."

"In a park, I was meaning. The one we were all in with Dean."

"I expect you may be soon enough. You and Thomas if he's there."

"I don't know what kind of if that is."

"I was simply wondering if he's the silent participant today."

"Only because there hasn't been anything for me to say yet," Thom said. "Hello to you both."

"Thomas." He thought Leigh was releasing an audible hint of relief. "What can we do for you?" she said.

"You'll be doing it for me as well." Jude barely bothered adding the last phrase. "Did anything happen after we left," she said, "that we ought to know about?"

"I think we could say that," Kendrick said.

Thom saw Jude grow anxious at once, if only to hear "What did?"

"We had words with Coral," Leigh said. "Allan too, if you'll excuse the interference. We saw how they upset you, and we thought there was no need for it. How they bring their son up has to be their choice to make, but it's certainly no reason to denigrate the way you two brought up Allan. We think he's a credit to you both."

"Well, thank you. Thank you too, Kendrick." Thom sensed she was eager to clear this aside in order to say "I was thinking more of Dean."

"We hope he won't upset you either."

"He never does, but the way he's treated might. Was there much of that after we'd gone?"

"There was some discussion of it," Kendrick said. "We did suggest a little easing might be warranted. He's at least as well behaved as Coral was at his age. I hope you'll agree she's grown up as she should."

Thom saw Jude consider her response and thought it politic to contribute. "As I'm sure you must know, we were happy with Allan's choice."

"We were," Jude said. "Do you think what you told them had any effect?"

"We did our best to be gentle about it," Kendrick said, "so they might be gentler with Dean. Now we think we should wait and see."

Might Jude feel reprimanded for her own approach? She restrained herself to saying only "I was meaning to ask you about the Lettices."

Leigh sounded wary. "Could someone explain?"

"Stanley and Deborah Lettice. They sold the Barnwall house."

"Ah, the education couple," Kendrick said. "I know you and Thom wouldn't call them teachers."

"That's because they aren't. I'd forgotten they were involved in education. I wonder where they're working now."

"I should think they must be academic if they work in an academy." Before Thom could judge how jokey this was meant to be Kendrick said "Didn't they decamp to Cornwall?"

"St Ives," Leigh said. "I remember Coral saying they could hardly have moved further without ending up at Land's End."

"What's the interest, Judith?"

"If they saw what Dean did, it might have scared them off."

"What are you saying he did?"

"Nothing to disturb anybody. I mean, nothing at all. What he saw, that's what I said."

"I don't think we have any reason to believe they'd have seen anything of the kind," Kendrick said.

"Why do you say that? Even if you didn't see it for yourselves, you agreed it was there."

"I don't know where you gained that impression."

"When we were talking to the priest you said the history explained why it was haunted. We thought the same as you were thinking then, it must be the ghost of one of the children the Vikings massacred."

A pause made space for a confusion of childish cries so entangled it was impossible to judge what they expressed. "That wasn't what we were thinking at all," Kendrick said.

Jude stared at the phone as though her fierceness could bring her the sight of his face. "What were you, then?"

"Something more recent. I do apologise if there was any misunderstanding. Shall we leave it behind? It's hardly worth going over again."

"You mean the Days case."

"That's what we had in mind. We didn't realise you were familiar with it as well."

"We only just found out, but you're saying you knew all the time and you'd been keeping it to yourselves."

"Hardly all the time," Leigh protested. "We learned about it after the family moved in, but we couldn't see any point in upsetting anybody over it."

"So when did they realise what they were living in?"

"We assume they don't know the background, and I'm sure we all hope nobody decides they should."

"That can't be right. They believed there was a ghost even if you didn't, and where did they think it came from?"

"They never said they believed in it, Judith," Kendrick told her. "Allan said there was something unwelcome. Not really the same kind of issue."

"What then if they didn't think it was a ghost?"

"Does it matter now? I really think we ought to let it go now that it's been dealt with."

"Exorcised, you mean, or the version they go in for these days. You don't need those unless you're dealing with something supernatural."

"It was just a cleansing of the house," Leigh said. "Some religions have one before you move in. Maybe that should have happened with Coral and Allan's, but at least it has now."

"So everyone ought to be happy," Kendrick said.

"Well, everyone isn't."

Perhaps Jude intended only Thom to hear; he couldn't tell whether the Bentons failed to catch her riposte or pretended to have failed. "I hope we've helped to put your mind at rest," Leigh said.

"Don't hesitate to call us whenever you need it," Kendrick said.

"I will whenever I do." It plainly required more of an effort for Jude to say "Thank you for making things clearer."

How ironically did she mean all of this? "Goodbye both for now," Leigh said. "Look after each other."

"Do that by all means," Kendrick said. "We do."

As a boy's voice rose out of the nearby hubbub, calling a solitary syllable if not just the truncated start of one – "Na" – the phone cut him off. "Who was that?" Jude demanded.

"I've no idea," Thom said and tried to have none. "Who do you think it was likely to be?"

"I thought it sounded like – no, if you didn't, forget it." Before he could decide on a response she said "What weren't they saying?"

"I don't know how we'd know that either."

"I think I've a good idea. For a start, they didn't seem too keen for us to know where they were."

"They didn't need to tell us. They were in a park."

"But they weren't saying which, were they? Why not, do you think?"

"I should say because we wouldn't know it if they said."

"You've a good heart, Thom. It's one of the reasons I married you. Just don't let yourself be taken in."

"I don't intend to be." More warily he had to ask "By what?"

"I think they're back in Barnwall and not wanting us to realise. I think we just heard Dean calling to Leigh before Kendrick could stop us. I'm afraid I'm not sure I trust the Bentons any more," Jude said, and Thom tried to accept her suspicions, because to think her mind was giving way would be far worse. "Shall we give the calls a rest for a while?" he came close to pleading. "Let's take some time to think."

THIRTEEN

Thom would never have expected anyone to enjoy shaking dice so much. He thought Dean might never let go of the shaker. Was the boy relishing the illusion of control or trying to delay the outcome of the throw? His shadow on the game board appeared to enliven the snakes while it sent dark indefinable shapes fleeing down the ladders. As the insistent rattle began to suggest the warning some snakes offered, Allan said "That's enough, now. You're not the only person here."

"Other people want to play as well," Coral said.

Presumably she meant Jude along with Thom, though for the moment Jude was nowhere to be seen. Why had she wandered away from the game? She must be at large in the Barnwall house. He supposed she was searching but had no idea what for – might prefer not to know. The relentless rapid clatter of the dice gathered in his skull, crowding out any further thoughts. "We said enough," Allan declared and grabbed Dean's hand to tip the dice onto the board.

"Don't," Thom cried as he imagined Jude would have. Allan was twisting Dean's hand too far, even if it seemed to cause the boy no pain. He didn't let go when the dice scuttled across the board to gaze blindly upwards with a pair of pinpoint pupils. The hand sprawled after them – the hand that had come loose as if Allan had unscrewed it from the wrist. It flopped on its back, continuing to shake the empty plastic tube as though desperate to revive its voice. Worse still was the sight of Dean gazing in bewilderment at his handless arm. The boy raised his eyes to gaze at his grandfather, parting his unsteady lips, and Thom didn't think he would be able to bear the helpless appeal. "Couldn't," he protested, which sounded shamefully inadequate, if it was even audible. "What could I do?" he begged so loud, however blurred the words were, that he lurched out of the dream.

Or had he? He could still hear the rattle of the dice. Either the hand had managed to scoop them into the shaker or one of Dean's parents was taking a turn, perhaps to distract the boy from his mutilation if not to ignore it in favour of the game. Dismay jerked Thom's eyes wide. He was at home, not in Barnwall, and a high fierce sun showed him he was alone in bed. As he blinked his eyes into sluggish focus he identified the persistent clatter. It was the sound of a computer keyboard.

What might Jude be researching now? Thom eased his legs off the bed and wobbled to his feet, hindered by a minatory twinge of cramp. He fumbled his bathrobe off its hook on the door and groped to shove his fists through the unhelpful sleeves, the second of which played at staying unlocatable and then out of reach. He dug his feet into his slippers and performed an impromptu hopping dance to fit them, all of which felt like a delay in venturing downstairs if not a bid to postpone a discovery. Putting it off would be worse than timid, and he sent himself out of the room.

Jude was at the kitchen table. As the keyboard ceased its plastic chatter she raised her face towards Thom while keeping her attention on the screen. "I've found something," she said.

"What now?"

"No need to ask that way. I'm only trying to save the situation. You'd think I wanted to make it worse."

"Of course I don't think that, but what—"

"I've found some houses near us I fancy everyone might like."

The sight of an estate agent's list on the screen was more bewildering than reassuring. "What are you thinking could happen?" Thom said.

"We have to get them away from that house, don't we? We can say we want them closer at our age. They'll still be pretty close to Coral's parents. Everybody ought to see that's fairest."

"You think they'd be prepared to move again so soon."

"I'd hope they would for us, yes. I certainly hope Allan would, and I can't believe she could influence him that much." With a prolonged look at Thom she said "You must know I'm not really being selfish. We won't be doing it for us, we'll be doing it for them."

"I know it's because you care about them, but how do you imagine it could work?"

"I've found them houses that don't cost as much as the one they're in. We can make that point as well."

"But they'd have to sell their house."

Her gaze might have been indulging an obtuse pupil. "That's the whole idea, Thom."

"How are they going to do that without letting people know about the history? Are you saying they should hide it or sell the house to somebody who'd want it for that reason? We know there are people like that, and I don't think you'd want Allan and Coral mixed up with them."

"They needn't be or hide anything either. They don't know what was there, and I'm sure you wouldn't want to tell them any more than Leigh and Kendrick do."

"But then we'd all be responsible for hiding the truth."

"Would you rather be responsible for keeping the family in that house?"

"If they don't know about it I can't see where the harm is."

"And I don't want to wait till we do see. I think it could be an evil place, and I won't be able to rest till they're free of it. I'd like to call Allan right now."

"You don't want to interrupt him at work."

"I said I'd like to. I didn't say I will. We'll leave it till lunchtime. At least Dean will be at school so we can talk."

The wait entailed glancing at her watch and the slightly more precise time on her phone at least as often as she returned to searching for houses for sale. At last a pair of zeroes opened their blind eyes, imitated by their miniature twins in a corner of the laptop screen. Jude had added an icon to the onscreen throng, Thom saw – an image of a phone contained within a pallid wafer or else marked on a tiny moon. The icon brought up the rudiments of a contact list, in which Allan's was the solitary entry. His name trailed away from a vignette that fixed his and Coral's smiles along with Dean's as the parents towered over their son, resting hands on his shoulders as though poised to guide him elsewhere. Triggering the photograph appeared to turn the screen into a mirror, and when Thom sat beside Jude he showed up on it too. An electronic repetition distantly related to a ringtone gave way to silence, and then Allan said "It's my mother. No, it's both of them."

This earned no answer Thom could hear. "What's up over there?" Allan said. "This isn't your usual day."

"If it isn't convenient," Jude said, "just tell us when."

"It's as convenient as it's going to be. I was only wondering why you've changed the schedule."

"We don't need to be so formal, do we? We're your family, remember."

"We still wouldn't mind some warning when you're going to call."

"As I say, if we've interrupted you or Coral at work—"

"Not at the moment, no. You were right if you thought we'd be taking a break, but you haven't told us why you're calling."

"We'd just like to see more of you than we've been seeing. Why aren't we now?"

"It looks as if you're using a different app."

"You can deal with whatever needs it, can't you? I don't think we can at this end."

"We've had to deal with quite a lot lately. Just give me a minute."

Thom heard a confusion of movements he would have thought had little to do with the computer. All at once his and Jude's faces shrank into the topmost right-hand corner as Allan appeared on the screen. Beyond him Coral swivelled her chair to face the callers, switching on the kind of smile he'd already adopted. "There you both are," Jude said. "How's the house?"

"It's absolutely fine," Coral said. "Why do you ask?"

A pain gripped Thom's chest, hindering his nervous breath until Jude spoke. "I was just saying to Thom I was jealous of your kitchen."

"You could have one like it if you wanted. Richest Kitchens, they're a national firm."

"I'll certainly keep that in mind. Meanwhile do you both think you can bear our house as it is?"

"I always did. I mean," Allan added with barely a pause, "there was nothing to bear."

"I'm glad you can say that. So when will you all come to visit? It's your turn."

Allan turned away without eliciting any visible response from Coral, and resumed his smile as he faced the screen. "I don't think that's going to be possible right now. We're pretty overwhelmed with work."

"You told us you could work anywhere."

"I did say that, didn't I." He sounded as if he regretted the admission. "We'd still be losing work time while we got to you," he said.

"It's just that we want to show you more round here. Show you things you haven't seen we think you'd like, and things Dean should."

"There's plenty for him to like here," Coral said.

"I wasn't saying otherwise, but perhaps he'd like a change and you two would. Couldn't you all come to us for a weekend?"

Thom thought the silence this achieved might mean she'd persuaded or at least defeated them until an offscreen voice said "Please may I go, please and thank you?"

Coral twisted her chair around as though confronting an intruder. "You won't be going by yourself. You won't be going anywhere."

"I meant with you and daddy."

"Just you remember you're not to go off with anyone unless we've said you can."

"I know, mummy. I promised."

"Oh dear," Jude said. "What's wrong with Dean?"

Allan stared at her or close to it. "What do you think is wrong with him?"

Coral swung around to scrutinise Jude too. "What do you think you heard?"

"I was only wondering why he's off school."

"I'm not, gran."

"Can we see him, do you think? It feels strange just hearing him when we're seeing you both."

"Why wouldn't we want you to see him?" When Jude found or at any rate uttered no answer Coral said "Sit with me, Dean. Bring your chair."

Thom heard a succession of muted thumps that made Dean's parents frown. While Allan rubbed his forehead, a gesture suggestive of a bid to drive ridges into hiding on his scalp, Coral said "Pick that up, Dean. Look what you're doing to our carpet."

The boy took some time to plod into view, hugging a rudimentary office chair a few inches above the floor. He planted the chair next to his mother and scrambled to perch on the edge, swinging his legs. "Here I am, gran and grandad."

"Keep still," Coral said. "We don't want you kicking the chair."

"We weren't expecting to see you, Dean," Jude said. "Are they having some kind of special day, then?"

"Mummy and daddy are making it special."

"I'm sure that's good to hear, but I was talking about your school."

"Mummy and daddy say that's here."

"I'm not sure I understand. Maybe one of them will explain."

Coral pinched the corners of her mouth between a finger and thumb as if trapping a response, and Allan glanced at her before he spoke. "We've decided he's better educated at home."

Thom knew Jude would have answered if he hadn't said "What gave you that idea?"

The smile Coral sent in his general direction looked indulgent. "You did, Thom."

"I really don't believe so. Tell me how and when."

"You said we didn't need his teacher when we could teach him English ourselves."

As he sensed Jude's look – reproachful if not accusing – Thom protested "I'm sure I never said he didn't need her."

"Well, we don't," Allan said. "She's a good deal too inquisitive for our liking. We'd call it interference. We know what's best for our own son."

Jude turned her look on him. "But she doesn't just teach English."

"Nor do we."

"And schools aren't just about learning in the classroom. They help children learn to interact with one another."

"We don't want Dean associating with their kind."

"Which kind is that?"

"The kind he brought to meet us in the park. We're just glad that was where he did. We wouldn't have had them in the house."

"What was so bad about them?" Thom felt someone had to ask.

"Squabbling half the time. Impoliteness. Loudness even when they'd been asked to make less noise. Some of their hygiene wasn't too pleasant either." The memory if not some other thought momentarily contorted Coral's lips. "Heaven knows what they'll be like as teenagers," she said. "We're just relieved Dean won't be going anywhere near them."

"Anyway," Allan said, "I think it's time we all got back to work."

"And thank you for helping make our minds up," Coral said, "even if you didn't think you did."

Thom was fending off the gratitude, which he found dismayingly unwelcome, when Jude said "As long as you feel that way you can let us help you more."

Thom felt Coral was expressing his own wariness by saying "How would that work?"

"You've got a pair of teachers here. We can give Dean some lessons and save you some stress."

"We're hoping not to have too much of that," Allan said.

"In that case you'll have even less." Thom didn't know if he was alone in hearing how carefully Jude added "I should think he'll need a computer of his own."

"I've got one, gran," Dean said and pointed offscreen.

As Allan chafed his brows again while Coral pinched her lips Jude said "Then we're ready whenever we're needed. When shall we start? Anything you'd like us to teach?"

"Let's see how you fare with religious knowledge," Allan said.

Coral freed her lips to recapture a smile much like the one he found. "We'll work on that," Jude said with audible determination. "We'll have it ready for tomorrow."

"We keep school hours," Allan said. "Perhaps we'll see you then."

"Say goodbye now, Dean," Coral said.

"Goodbye, gran and grandpa."

His parents echoed his first word but not his wistfulness. The Barnwall family vanished at once, leaving Jude's reflection to outdo Thom's for concern. "At least now we'll be keeping an eye on them," she said.

"I suppose that will come with it." More reluctantly Thom said "What makes you feel we should?"

"Couldn't you tell something isn't right with them? It was obvious right from the start, Thom."

"Not to me."

"They shouldn't be able to do it tomorrow. If they do I hope you'll wonder why." As Thom failed to experience any hope in response she said "I don't think they wanted us to realise Dean was there. I felt as if they didn't want us seeing them at all."

FOURTEEN

"Wake up. Wake up now, Thom. We don't want to be late."

Jude's urgency suggested they were about to be. Would he have to drive to Barnwall? He felt less than equal to the task, but he didn't want to burden her with it when she disliked driving such a convoluted distance. Perhaps they could take the train or rather a haphazard series of them. "Playful mock?" he thought he came close to mumbling, and tried again. "Lay for what?"

"Don't say you've forgotten. Our first lesson for Dean."

He feared he almost had, though they'd carried on discussing topics last night in bed. Perhaps their deliberations had sent him to sleep, since he seemed to recall Jude suggesting themes as he'd dozed off. "Of course I haven't," he tried to reassure them both.

As he blinked his eyes towards a sluggish focus, he saw Jude was wearing a plain dark suit and white blouse, an outfit that helped her resemble a probationer anxious to impress her first employer. "Am I supposed to dress up too?" Thom wondered, if with fewer consonants.

"Dress how you feel you should. I just want to make sure they see how serious we are about the job."

Thom felt gently reprimanded. He eased his legs off the bed, hoping not to rouse a cramp, and stumbled to the bathroom once an eager spasm in his left calf let him walk. A shower assailed his skin and jerked his mind towards alertness. By the time he returned to the bedroom he'd decided Jude was right, and donned a shirt and suit and as an afterthought a tie. He expected Jude to welcome the sight, but she met him in the kitchen with a frown. "How are we going to do this? We haven't got Dean's details."

"Then they'll have to call us this first time."

"I'll be calling them if they don't when they said they wanted us."

She'd made coffee and set out a pair of tubs of yoghurt, which she seemed to think was all the breakfast they should have time for. She finished hers before Thom was half done, and then she set about looking up religions on the laptop. "Just in case Dean asks about any we didn't think of," she said.

She was on the outer fringes of her research when the laptop uttered the approximation of a ringtone, and Thom saw the time was precisely nine o'clock. The cramped image of Dean flanked by his parents appeared on the screen, to be ousted by Allan's face. "Shouldn't Dean be on his computer?" Jude said.

"He will be."

"I mean shouldn't we be connected with his."

"You are."

"I only asked because we didn't see his icon."

"I don't know why that would be."

"We saw yours instead. You and Coral with him."

"That's his as well now. You surely wouldn't expect to see him without us."

"But then how are we going to know who's calling?"

"Because," Coral said as she appeared beside Allan, "you'll know it will always be one of the two of us."

"Before you start, can we just hear what you're planning to teach?"

"We thought we'd talk about a few religions," Jude said. "I expect Dean will have come across some of them."

"You'd only confuse him. It was one of the reasons we took him away from the school."

"What was, Allan?"

"The way they taught the subject. We just want him learning about ours."

Thom felt as bemused as Jude visibly did. "Which is that?" he said.

"We're sorry if you need to ask," Coral said.

"I take it we're talking about Christianity." When she and Allan gave this an ostentatiously patient look Thom said "It comes in quite a few varieties. Do we need to know which?"

"You'll be confusing Dean again," Allan warned him. "There was only ever one saviour. He's what we want to hear you teach about."

"Won't listening distract you from your work?" Jude said.

"It's a distraction everyone should have," Coral said, "if that's how you choose to regard it."

"I wouldn't normally." When Coral accepted this with a wordlessly ambiguous nod Jude said "Is there anything special you'd like us to include?"

"Everything about Jesus is special, Dean."

Coral might have been summoning Dean if not permitting him to show himself. As the boy ventured into sight beside her he said "He did magic, didn't he?"

Allan swung around so fiercely Thom heard his chair squeal. "What on earth do you mean by that?"

"A boy at school told our teacher Jesus did some things that were like magic."

"And what did the teacher say to him?"

"She said it was a funny way to put it but he wasn't wrong."

Allan turned less than swiftly to face the screen. "Those are some more reasons Dean's at home."

"We didn't think the boys at that school were very nice, did we?"

"No, mummy."

As his parents gave the hint of wistfulness a sharp glance, Jude intervened. "Would the teacher have been talking about miracles?"

"That's the proper word, yes," Allan said. "We'll expect you both to use it."

"You'd like us to talk about them."

"Unless you don't feel comfortable with it."

"Of course we do. It was part of our job."

Dean's parents seemed to find the answer less than ideal. "I must say you're both looking very official," Coral said.

"We thought we should dress the part."

"No need to make too much of it. You're just helping, after all."

"And we're grateful, obviously."

As Thom wondered how dutiful Allan's contribution might be, Coral said "Sit at your desk, Dean."

Allan vacated the chair, only to stoop so close to the screen that his eyes collected darkness. "Remember we're here if we're needed," he said and stood back to steer Dean onto the chair, holding him by the shoulders. "Tell grandma and grandad which miracles you know."

"Jesus had to feed a lot of people with just some bread and fish, but there was lots left when they'd finished."

"Five loaves and two fishes," Jude said. "Just imagine how miraculous that must have been."

As Allan moved out of sight, leaving her a tentatively satisfied look, Dean informed her "Our teacher said they didn't really know how many, so they made some numbers up."

"It was a big crowd and a tiny bit of food. As many people as you'd see on the prom and the beach put together."

"I remember, gran."

"Perhaps your teacher got mixed up by the numbers," Thom said. "There was another time when Jesus fed four thousand people with seven loaves and it doesn't say how many fishes. Just a few."

He had a sense of trying to placate Dean's parents, of seeking to convince them he and Jude would be more to their taste than the school. "What else are you going to tell us about, Dean?" Jude said.

"Jesus went to a party where they drank up all the wine, so he made them some more out of water."

"It was a wedding like the one your mummy and daddy had. We were there and it was lovely."

"I wish I'd gone."

"That would have been quite a bit of a miracle, don't you think?"

"One of the boys in my class went to his mum and dad's."

Dean's gaze flickered aside as though he'd been caught committing mischief, a reaction that reminded Thom they had an unseen audience. "What else did Jesus do besides catering for people?" he said.

"He wanted some figs off a tree to eat but there weren't any left, so he cursed it and it died while everyone was watching."

"I don't think we'd want to say he cursed. Perhaps he was meaning to show them whatever you've got, you should use it to help other people."

"I try and help mummy and daddy."

"I'm sure you don't just try," Jude said. "How else did he help people?"

"He put them back together."

"I don't think I remember that." More warily than Thom wanted to believe was called for Jude said "Tell us about it."

"Someone chopped a man's ear off and Jesus stuck it back on. And there was another man who couldn't see till Jesus fixed his eyes for him."

"We know what you meant now. It was just a funny way of putting it. I don't think we'd usually say a gentleman who was blind had his eyes put back."

"If someone dug them out we would."

"That didn't happen, Dean. There's no need for you to think such things."

"It did another time. It wasn't Jesus's fault. I don't think he'd have wanted it. It was supposed to be about him, though." The boy sent the screen a concerned look well in advance of his age. "Don't worry, gran," he said. "He got his eyes back so he could see."

Thom found the silence beyond Dean oppressively ominous. "Shall we return to our lessons?"

"That's a sort of miracle though, isn't it, grandad?"

"Let's stay with Jesus," Thom said not far from desperation. "Do you know any other things he did?"

"He showed people there were really ghosts."

"I shouldn't say he did that. If you're thinking of the Holy Ghost—"

"He did, grandad. There was one called Lazarus."

"I see what you're trying to say. Jesus could raise people from the dead is how we always put it."

"That's still like a ghost. They're someone people want to be dead but they won't go away."

"Nobody wanted Lazarus dead, Dean. I shouldn't think anyone wanted it for any of the people Jesus brought back." To forestall any further uncomfortable argument Thom said "Have we run out of miracles now?"

"I liked another one our teacher told us, the one with all the pigs."

Perhaps Jude welcomed the subject as appearing to be safe. "Which pigs were those?"

"When Jesus made them all run off the cliff into the sea."

"That's because he'd sent demons into them. He'd cast the demons out from some men who were possessed."

"The demons asked to be pigs instead, but it doesn't say what they got to be after they all drowned."

"It just shows you can't always trust that kind of thing to work."

Thom couldn't judge whether he and Jude were meant to hear Allan's muttered comment or Coral's response: "He said himself casting out a devil may simply bring worse back."

Thom thought it best to give Dean no time to ponder this. "Can you remember anything Jesus said?"

"If your eye does something bad it has to be dug out. And if your hand does it has to be chopped off."

"That's part of what we call the Sermon on the Mount," Jude said. "It's the only nasty part. You shouldn't concentrate on that kind of thing so much. I know your mummy and daddy wouldn't want you to."

Thom sensed she hoped to prompt some confirmation, but their silence withheld any meaning. "Some people do it, gran," Dean insisted.

"Then I'm sure none of us want to hear about them. What else did Jesus teach?"

"We have to love everybody, even people who do bad things to us."

"I hope there's nobody like that in your life."

"There aren't many people in it, gran."

"You know there's always me and grandad."

Thom thought it politic to contribute "And your nan and grandpa too."

Jude sent the image on the screen to occupy the upper right-hand corner so as to bring up the text of the sermon. "See if you can finish any of these," she said. "Blessed are the poor in spirit..."

Dean knew the meek would inherit the earth and the pure in heart would see God, though he needed an explanation of each beatitude. "What do you think God looks like?" he said.

"If you're good perhaps you'll see when it's time."

This left Thom aware how readily Jude feigned belief, unless she was reaching for it as a consequence of age. He might have liked to have more faith himself, given the inevitable increasingly imminent end. "What do you think was the best thing," she said, "Jesus told everyone to do?"

"I think we've learned enough now," Allan said. "We thank you both."

Before Dean could answer Jude's question, his parents moved to flank the boy, and Coral intervened by saying "We'd like to hear what you think it was."

"I had love one another in mind."

"May we suggest one?" This was clearly not a request. "Honour thy father and thy mother," Coral said.

"Jesus did everything his father wanted," Allan said. "That's why he died on the cross."

"He came back, though," Dean said. "You can."

Allan began to rub his embossed brows while Coral clamped her lips, not so much denoting pensiveness as trapping an exclamation. "Then I hope you'll both honour yours," Jude said.

"If you can show us anywhere we haven't," Allan said, "we'll listen."

"Just remember our advice. It's for everybody's benefit. Remember we've been parents like you, but we can look back on it and see what was best and what wasn't." Thom sensed she yearned to be more explicit but was restraining herself. "When do you want us again?" she said. "Every day if you like."

"We'll discuss it and be in touch. What do you say, Dean?"

"I'd like it every day there's school."

"We mean," Coral said, having freed her lips with a fierce twist of finger and thumb, "what do you say to your granny and grandad for everything they've tried to do for you."

"Thank you very much for my lesson, granny and grandad."

"And once again thank you from us," Coral said, "for showing us what you can do."

She and Allan closed their hands around Dean's shoulders, Thom couldn't judge how vigorously. They might have been manipulating the boy to imitate the farewell waves they sent his grandparents. Allan's knuckles swelled towards them, and the family in Barnwall disappeared from the screen. "That wasn't a lesson," Jude said. "It was a test."

"I think he passed it, don't you?"

"Not of Dean." Jude dismissed the image of herself and Thom, leaving the monitor as blank as an uninscribed slab. "Of us," she said.

"Let's hope we passed as well."

"I hope so too. I want to see them all again as soon as we possibly can. We need to be keeping more of an eye on Dean."

"Why are you thinking that now?"

"Couldn't you see how nervous he was? I just don't know of what yet. I'm not sure I want to know."

"I didn't think he seemed too nervous." When Jude gave him a look close to an accusation, Thom said "Perhaps he hasn't got used yet to being taught remotely."

"I think you're more right than you realise. He was wishing we were there with him, not hundreds of miles away." A thought appeared to freeze her, and then she shook herself or shivered. "There are people we need to speak to," she said.

FIFTEEN

Although the closest school to Willow Grove was about ten minutes' walk away – perhaps five at a concerted run – it was called Childerfield Primary. Viewed from above on the computer map, the building with its stubby transverse wings resembled a cross designed to point its apex towards the park, and Thom imagined alerting Allan and Coral to the similarity, though he doubted this would achieve much. The map simplified Willow Grove as well, so that it looked like a snake stretched out straight, bloating the stylised cobra head that was the square alongside the park. As Jude set about phoning the number listed onscreen Thom switched the map to its photographic mode, which displayed a frozen moment from the past. An undefined notion made him zoom in on Willow Grove. Who was that outside the family's house? The boy must have been dashing somewhere if not striving to flee, since his speed had split his image into fragments. Thom reverted the map to its overhead view in the hope Jude hadn't noticed the incomplete figure, just as a brisk female voice said "Childerfield Primary."

"Could I speak to Ms Thorndyke," Jude said, "if she's on her break?"

A pause suggested she'd called the wrong school. Perhaps the receptionist was consulting a roster, since she said "She will be. May I ask what it's concerning?"

"One of her pupils."

"Are you a parent?"

"I've been one for quite some time. Mrs Clarendon."

"Good morning, Mrs Clarendon. Excuse me a moment." The request was evidently prompted by a nearby murmur that led to a muted discussion. None too soon the receptionist returned to say "We understand you've taken your son out of the school."

"That's what I'm calling to talk about."

"Let me see if I can find Jane for you. I'm just putting you on hold."

This roused a recording of children – presumably pupils at the school – singing the colours of ink and a page. As the chorus declared that a child should understand the law, Thom said "Do you really think you should—"

"I'm only letting them assume. I haven't lied, have I? I'll do anything that's needed if it's going to help Dean."

The song had turned the world from day into darkness when the receptionist left it there. "Putting you through, Mrs Clarendon."

"Mrs Clarendon." Thom imagined the newcomer might be repeating the name to test its authenticity. "Jane Thorndyke," the teacher said.

"Thank you for taking my call."

"I'm more than happy to if it involves Dean. May we hope you're thinking of bringing him back to us?"

"I only wish I could. That's all I seem able to do just now, think."

"You'll pardon my asking, but aren't you very well? You don't sound yourself, if you don't mind my saying."

Thom had time to rest his gaze on Jude's face before she spoke. "I'm not that Mrs Clarendon."

"Then please accept my apologies for the mistake, and can I ask you to forget what I said to start with?"

"You won't want me doing that. I'm Dean's grandmother."

"I see." Jane Thorndyke's tone kept her reaction to itself. "How is he getting on?" she said.

"You're concerned about him, then."

"I'm concerned with all my pupils. I don't stop when they leave us."

"We know exactly how you feel, Dean's grandfather and I. We were teachers too. No, we still are."

"I should think that never stops either."

"We've been trying to help to teach Dean at home, but it isn't the same as a real school for all sorts of reasons. From everything we've heard about you we wish you were still his teacher."

"So do I."

"And we're certain his parents shouldn't have used you as a reason to take him away from the school. Do you have any idea why they did?"

"They seemed to feel it wasn't religious enough."

"But our son was never like that," Thom protested, "and we don't believe his wife was either. They weren't even married in a church."

"Mr Clarendon? Welcome to the conversation. Perhaps having a child changed them. I've seen that happen in my job. Maybe you both have."

"Never to anything like that extent, and it's only been since they moved to Barnwall."

"They told me where they moved from was pretty rough. Do you think they might have felt they ought to give some sort of thanks for where they've ended up?"

"Where are you saying that is?" Jude demanded.

"Your husband just said. Barnwall."

"Willow Grove is what they call it, and what do you know about that?"

"It's a quiet little road that takes you straight into the park."

"Hardly enough for anyone to get religious over," Thom said.

"I wonder if they decided Dean needed some kind of moral foundation. I know they thought the kids where they'd moved from didn't have much of one. I'm afraid they started thinking some of ours at the school didn't either." More hesitantly Jane Thorndyke said "Between ourselves, and please don't say I said so, I did find them a little bit fanatical."

"When was that?" Jude was impatient to learn.

"The day they told us they wouldn't be bringing Dean back."

"What else do you remember about that? Anything at all."

"They said they'd taken the decision and there was nothing we could do about it. You'll know that's true, of course. They said the school was having a bad effect on Dean, some of his classmates were. They didn't say which ones, but I had the feeling they meant all of them, and maybe blaming me as well."

"We're sure your influence was positive, aren't we, Thom? They gave us the impression they didn't like you asking Dean about his home life."

"I didn't mean to pry. It's just my way of finding out about the children."

"We aren't saying you shouldn't. It used to be ours. Did he tell you anything they could have objected to?"

"As far as I could make out he had a friend who stopped going to visit because he was allergic to some ingredient they used in cooking. Would they have minded I heard about that?"

Thom thought Jude might give her version of the incident, but she only said "Anything else?"

"That I remember? Nothing really." With a pause too terse to let Jude speak the teacher said "Except I don't want to make too much of it, but I did hear them when they took Dean away."

"Why, what did they say?"

"It was how they led him off as well. They both had hold of him, and I heard his father tell him now he was going to be home with them for good."

"That doesn't sound too terrible," Thom felt compelled to tell Jude in particular.

"I think you'd have had to see it and hear it to make your minds up," Jane Thorndyke said. "You'll be doing some of that, will you? I take it you live locally."

"We've begun to wish we did," Jude said. "We're on the far side of Manchester."

"I didn't realise. That's really quite a distance."

"Do you ever go through Willow Grove?"

"I often do. I like to walk here through the park when the weather's in my favour."

"Do you think you could keep an eye on the house and call me if there's anything we ought to know about? Let me give you my number." Jude enunciated the digits at a pace she might have used to dictate a mathematics problem. "Have you noticed anything when you've been passing?" she realised she should ask.

"It's been as quiet as I don't know, a church. Good to talk to you, but will you forgive me if I shoot off now? I've got a class."

"Goodbye," Jude said, possibly in time to be heard, and turned from the mute phone to scrutinise Thom's face. "At least now you can't say it's only me."

"What isn't, Jude?"

"Thinking Allan and Coral have changed more than they should. More than we'd call healthy too."

"But you heard why she thinks that may have happened. It needn't have anything to do with their house."

"I wish you'd stop looking for explanations when the truth is there in front of us."

"Haven't you been looking for them as well?"

Her gaze lingered on his face as though not liking what she found had snagged it. Before she looked away her fingers darted to the keyboard of the laptop, and he wondered how long she proposed to punish him with silence. In one way he felt relieved when she spoke while typing in the search box on the map. "Perhaps hearing someone else will show you I'm right. I don't want to keep having to deal with this all by myself, but I will if I have to." As the map raced to St Ives she turned her gaze on him again. "Do you remember what Kendrick said?"

"Nothing comes to mind."

"It's a good job my memory's still working. He thought he was making a joke." She typed in the box, and then her triumph faltered. "There's more than one academy," she said.

"He didn't say which."

"Obviously he didn't. How could he have known that? Don't make out I'm more irrational than you already think I am." Before Thom could protest, however dutifully, she copied on her phone the topmost number in the list beside the map. "Let's see if this is where they're hiding," she said.

"Ouseside Academy. For student absences press one..." Jude's gathering impatience found release at "For any other business," and she jabbed the fifth digit at once. "Ouseside Academy," the phone began again.

"I know that. You already said." The receptionist did indeed sound like an understudy for the automatic message. "Can I have a word with Stanley Lettice?" Jude said.

"I'm sorry, you've made a mistake."

"I've hardly even spoken yet. What mistake?"

"Mr Lettice isn't on our staff."

"I don't suppose you'd know which school he's at."

"I wouldn't, sorry. I can see how you might make the mistake."

"How might that be?"

"His wife works here. I can ask her where he works if you like."

"I'd prefer to speak to Deborah myself."

"Let me see if I can find her." A folk song or at least a ditty in that style, concerning fish and sewage in the River Ouse, took her place while she conducted the unheard search. The song was halfway through a repetition when she reappeared to say "Sorry to have kept you."

"So long as you've tracked her down."

"She took a bit of finding." As Jude gave Thom a sidelong glance expressive of suspicion the receptionist said "She had a free period but she's been looking after a girl who was sick in class."

This visibly took Jude aback. "Does she go in much for that sort of thing?"

"Whenever she's needed. She's our most caring carer, always in demand."

"So does that mean I can't speak to her?"

"No, she's taken the girl back to class now. She still has a few minutes before her next class, but if you just want to know where her husband works—"

"I'd like to ask her something else as well."

"Can I tell her who you are and what it's about?"

"Judith. I'm a teacher."

Thom watched her squeeze her eyes so tightly shut the lids wrinkled as she willed the information to suffice. "Please hold on," the receptionist said.

The song about the river recommenced by groping for notes on a species of keyboard, but the voice that followed the bid for a melody refrained from singing. "Judy? Debbie. I'm pretty fully booked at Ouseside, but it looks as if Stan may be available next term."

Thom saw Jude take a grim pleasure in saying "I'm not that Judith."

"Oh dear." Debbie Lettice thought this worth an embarrassed laugh. "I'm afraid you've been put through to the wrong person somehow," she said.

"It depends what you mean by wrong. I'm calling about your house in Childer Close."

The brusque noise this prompted bore no relation to mirth. "That isn't where we live," Debbie Lettice said.

"It was till you got rid of it."

"Forgive me," Debbie Lettice said without desiring any kind of absolution, "who am I speaking to?"

"We're part of the family you sold the house, the family you couldn't even face."

"The agent dealt with the sale for us. We didn't see any need to meet."

"So you stayed well clear even though you were living in the house."

"We were away for the summer. We love working with children, but it takes quite a lot out of you."

"We're entirely aware how much it takes. That's never an excuse to mistreat them."

"I hope you aren't suggesting we ever would."

"We don't know anything about that, but we do know you kept quiet about the house and what it used to be. Never mind trying to blame the agent for that. It was your responsibility to say."

"We didn't know what used to be there when we bought it either."

"Then how are you telling us you found out?"

"A neighbour told us, a social worker. He was still upset he hadn't realised what was going on with the couple and the boy."

"Oliver Dodd," Jude said as if naming an accomplice. "So what exactly did he say?"

"The council made the house into a compulsory purchase and knocked it down. People had been coming to look at it because of, well, you must know why. Some of them were even trying to get in. And while it was being demolished they started stealing bits of it, so the council had all the bricks smashed."

Thom saw Jude losing patience with the information. "And then the council changed the street name. We know all about that," she said.

"But then a builder bought the land for not much and put the new house up, and you'd never know what happened there by looking."

"Some people might. What did you see that made you so anxious to get out?"

"Nothing at all."

"Don't try and tell us there was nothing. We've seen some of it for ourselves."

"I've no idea what you're talking about. The place worked on our nerves, that was all."

Thom thought it was past time he was heard from. "Worked how?"

"You're the backup, are you? We didn't like the way we started feeling about children. We never acted on it, and you can look into that all you want, you won't find we ever did. What happened where we lived must have been affecting our minds somehow. Knowing about it must have."

"Affecting you how?" Jude was determined to learn.

"Making us intolerant of every little thing they got wrong and even some they didn't. You mustn't have that kind of attitude if you're going to work with children."

"We're very well aware of that, and we wouldn't want a child living in that house either."

"Are there any?"

"Yes." The syllable condensed all Jude's fierceness, and so did "Our grandson who's six."

"We didn't know there was a child. I wouldn't like to think of any living there myself." Before Jude could pursue this, Debbie Lettice said "You need to let me go now. I have to get back to looking after children."

"A pity you didn't do that in Barnwall," Jude retorted, but only to a deserted phone. "Well, that settles it, Thom. We know exactly what we have to do."

He felt restrained for saying only "I don't know if I do."

"You heard what she said, and don't say not knowing what the house was makes any difference. If anything I think it makes things worse. It just means they won't know what's affecting them, Allan and Coral." As Thom tried to work out a response she said "We have to get them all out of that house, whatever it takes to move them."

SIXTEEN

"Allan, we both think the house we've found would be perfect for you and your family...." Jude looked up from the message she was typing on her phone. "I won't put you do if you don't," she told Thom.

"I'm sure it would be fine for them if they wanted to move again so soon."

"We have to convince them they should," Jude said, adding wrinkles to the cluster on her brows as if this might squeeze greater persuasiveness into the message. "It has more space for everyone than where you're living at the moment...."

"I suppose that could give Dean a room of his own for a schoolroom."

"Don't mention that if Allan calls. We want Dean back at school where he ought to be." Jude underlined this by reading aloud "There's a primary school with the highest rating in the next street to yours."

"Perhaps you shouldn't make it sound as if we presume it's going to be theirs."

"I want to make them feel it is. And there's a church with a Sunday school between your house and ours."

"I wouldn't have expected you to tell them that."

"It can't do any harm, can it? I told you before, I'll do whatever it takes to get them away from that place. Are you going to criticise everything I've put? Just say if you've any better ideas."

"I was only trying to decide how all that may sound to Allan and Coral."

"As if we care, I hope. As if we want the best for all of them, which we do." When Thom had to agree, though without finding words, she returned to the message. "The local police station is just a quarter of a mile away, not that there's much need of it round here. There's what they call a youth activity hub these days next to it for when Dean's older. If we can persuade them to enrol him now," she said as an aside to Thom, "that would be better still. Anything that brings him into contact with other children."

"I suspect they would need to be vetted first."

"We can do that in advance. I don't think his parents have any reason not to trust our judgment." This silenced him while she read him the rest of the message. "The sellers have lowered their price for a quick sale, and they're asking quite a lot less than you paid for the Barnwall house. It's a bargain you can't afford to miss."

"Now you're sounding like an advert."

He was afraid he'd antagonised her, but she gave a wry grin so lopsided it resembled a symptom of a stroke. "Fine, I'll take that line out," she said and did. "That should be enough now, shouldn't it? No, it's not at all."

Thom felt nervous of learning what she'd added until she showed him. *Meanwhile when do you want us again? We're assuming school's closed for the weekend.* She appended a link to the estate agent's listing and sent the message. "With any luck that should catch them at breakfast," she said.

She and Thom were at the kitchen table, on which her coffee had ceased to steam while she put the message together. A single lukewarm sip sent her to empty the mug down the tinny sink and chase the coffee with a resounding downpour. Having refilled the mug from the percolator, she cupped her hands around it on the table as if to drive away a chill. She might have been timing the inactivity of her phone with determined measured sips that made her mouth wince. Thom felt helplessly compelled to count them, and he'd numbered a dozen by the time the phone emitted its vintage ringtone, a reminiscence of the landline they'd bought for their first house. "Allan," it declared.

"Allan."

"We've got the message."

He sounded less enthusiastic than his mother or even the phone. "Have you had a chance to think about it?" she said.

"We've had a chance to talk."

"Shall we hear what you said?"

"We don't understand what you're trying to do."

For fear Jude might make this unnecessarily plain Thom said "Bring you closer to us."

"I don't think you can say we're all that distant. You see us every week."

"You know what your father means. We'd rather be with the three of you."

"My parents don't visit us all that often," Coral said. "Really not much more than you do."

"Then they should see you more as well. That's what our generation's for."

"If you think they should," Allan said, "I don't know why we've been sent this stuff about a house that's further from them than ours is."

Thom saw Jude pause to tone down her retort. "Not that much further, and a lot closer to us. Maybe it's time it was our turn."

"In case," Thom said, "we come to the point where we won't be able to drive to you any longer."

"Are you saying that's likely to be soon?" Allan said.

"I hope not." The disappointed look Jude gave him made Thom add "We can't say when."

"Then we can hope as you say it isn't soon. We'll have to see what we can do about the situation when it arises, if it does."

"It's already more of an effort," Jude said, "than Leigh and Kendrick have to make."

"You mustn't make it any more," Coral said, "if you find it's too much."

"Nobody said that, did they? You ought to know we don't mind making efforts for you. Now we've made some to find you a house."

"We wish you hadn't gone to any trouble," Allan said.

"It won't be any if you'll at least consider our idea." She was restraining herself so forcefully her fists on the table shook. "What did you think," she said, "of all the things I mentioned?"

"Any in particular?"

"You were looking for a Sunday school and you'll see we've found you one."

"Thank you for the thought, but we've decided such things are best taught at home."

"You surely can't think every subject is," Thom protested. "The school Dean would go to has the highest reputation."

"He's getting used to how we do it," Coral said. "I'm certain you wouldn't want to confuse him."

Thom sensed Jude's struggle to contain desperation. "You'd have the police nearly on your doorstep," he said as she might well have. "There'd hardly be crimes where you were."

"Elsie Doughty's only over the road if she's needed," Allan said.

"Are you going to reject everything we suggest?" Jude's restraint had given way, and Thom felt the protest might equally be aimed at him. "Don't tell us you couldn't use more space," she said. "Dean could have his own room for all his activities, and then he wouldn't bother you two while you're working."

"He already has his room upstairs," Allan said, "but we prefer to keep an eye on him."

Jude couldn't quite conceal her eagerness. "Is he there with you now?"

"He's where I just said. Do you think we'd be having this talk if he could hear?"

"We might," Coral said. "There's never any harm in his knowing what we've resolved."

"Doesn't he get to say how he feels?" Jude said. "He's affected too."

"We're very much aware he is," Allan assured her, "and we can deal with it."

Thom saw her stifle a response in advance of saying "I just wondered if we can see him now."

"What do you think you need to see?"

"I meant should we have our video call or wait till our usual time."

"It mightn't be convenient today. Will you be available tomorrow?"

"You know we're always available for you." As if it were a casual afterthought Jude said "What's the hindrance?"

"Allan just told you," Coral said. "It's not convenient today."

When the rebuff robbed Jude of any words she was prepared to utter Thom said "So the usual time tomorrow?"

"You'll need to be later," Allan said. "After mass."

"I was meaning to ask you last time you mentioned it," Jude said, "how long you've been going to church."

"Not long enough. Maybe that was one of our mistakes."

Thom sensed her effort to ask only "So what time are you telling us?"

"Of course you wouldn't know, either of you. We'll see about calling you once we're home. It should be some time in the afternoon."

"At least we can be glad you'll be out of the house for a change, wherever you're going. I hope Dean has a chance to play as well."

"When we give you your call," Allan said as the response he plainly felt her comment warranted, "please don't bring up what we've been discussing. No point in getting him worked up when there's no need."

"I wouldn't say we've had much of a discussion."

"Not the one we hoped we'd have," Thom felt he ought to add.

"We've hopes of our own," Allan told them. "We mean to see they're more than hopes."

"You aren't alone." Jude left this to be interpreted how it might be. "Now you haven't told us yet," she said, "when we'll be teaching again."

"We talked about that," Coral said.

For a moment Thom fancied this included him and Jude, a notion that made his memory feel dismayingly incomplete. He'd just grasped her meaning when a bell measured out four notes as if summoning the listeners to a distant church, and the reminiscence of the childhood ditty roused a phrase in his skull: "I do not know." Its source was the doorbell in Barnwall. "We have to say goodbye now. Speak more in due course," Allan said as fast as he ended the call.

Jude stared at the recumbent voiceless slab the phone had become. "Who do you think was at the door?"

"I've no more idea than you."

"I've one idea. I don't think they were just in a hurry to let in whoever it was," she said and raised her distressed gaze to his face. "I think they didn't want us to know who's come to their house."

SEVENTEEN

Jude glanced at Thom over the upright laptop screen as he quelled the spitting of the percolator. "What was the priest's name in Barnwall?"

"You aren't thinking of contacting him."

"I wasn't till you said."

"I hope you still aren't. How can it help?"

"I wonder whether he's another of the people who know more than they've been saying."

"I believe he did his best to help. Don't you think he would in his position?"

"You'd hope so, but it all depends on how much he knows. Just remind me of his name."

"Father Nicholas. Father just not Old Nick."

"Yes, I know. The kind of joke Allan would have laughed at when we knew him."

"We still do, Jude. He hasn't stopped being our son."

"I wish I could tell what he's being. I only hope he and Coral didn't hear Dean laugh."

Thom winced as a drop of the coffee he was pouring spattered his fingers on the handle of the mug. "You really think they wouldn't even like him to do that."

"Not at what Father Nick said, and we don't know how long they'd been lurking."

"We don't have to call it that, do we?" Thom objected as he dabbed his stinging finger with a kitchen towel. "They'd just come out to see how Dean was getting on."

"You're a lot more trusting than they seem to be."

This wasn't all she'd said that disconcerted Thom. "You asked me what the priest was called but then you said you knew."

"I need the rest of it. His last name."

"I don't believe he said."

"Then we'll have to hope there's only one of them in Barnwall. Nicholas, I mean. I don't suppose it matters how many priests there are."

As Thom binned the stained wad of paper she set about an onscreen search, producing a succession of clicks so incessant they put him in mind of one of the eye tests age had brought him. He was bearing the mugs and their trails of ephemeral fog to the table when she said "Nicholas Grimshaw. I ought to have known."

Wariness stiffened Thom's grip on the china handles. "Why should you?"

"Because he's the priest at their nearest church."

He set down the mugs as she brought up details from the map, not just the times of services at St John Bosco but the distance from Willow Grove to the church. "The masses can't be that long," she said. "The last one must have ended quite a while ago. They've had plenty of time to walk home."

"Maybe they've gone in the park."

"Let's hope they have. Let's hope they still at least do that with Dean." Jude had picked her phone up, but now she planted it on its back. "I'll give them as long as I can," she said.

She stared into the mist her mug was emitting before she took a sip followed at some distance by another. Each of them and their successors needed a visible effort, or the gaps she made herself leave between them did. Somewhere in the suburb the notes of a bundle of church bells tumbled clumsily over one another, and Thom couldn't help hearing a bid to capture the phrase of the doorbell in Barnwall. By the time the coffee in Jude's mug had shrunk an inch her splayed fingers were resting in front of the laptop as if they were about to leap onto the keyboard. They'd begun to drum in a rhythm suggestive of typing, though surely not of a delusion that she was, when the laptop uttered its fabrication of a ringtone as the boy hemmed in by his parents appeared on the monitor. Jude accepted the call at once, bringing herself and Thom onscreen, but the caller's icon stayed shrunken. "Who's there?" she said.

"Who do you expect it to be?"

"I thought it might be Dean now he's using that picture too."

"He doesn't need to make any calls," Allan said. "It'll always be one of us."

"Can we see all of you at least?"

"We've nothing to hide I'm aware of."

His face accompanied his answer, driving the image of his family off the screen. "Are they in the park?" Jude said.

"Who now?" In case he hadn't made her question sufficiently unwelcome Allan said "Who are you saying is out there this time?"

"Dean and his mother. We thought you might all have stopped off there after church when we didn't hear from you."

"It was the priest you met who kept us. We wish it weren't his church."

"Father Nicholas?" Thom said. "We liked him."

"We rather suspected you might have. I'm afraid he's not our kind."

"What kind is that?"

"I'm saying he didn't seem to realise when he wasn't wanted. He started asking our son about matters that were really none of his concern."

"Which were those?"

As Allan began to massage a prominent frown, Coral occupied half the screen to say "His beliefs."

"Aren't those rather what a priest is meant to be concerned about?"

"No, his own are, and we didn't care much for those either."

"He said there's just one god but people call him different things, and you can call him her as well because nobody really knows."

"Dean," Jude cried, "you've been there all the time. Come where we can see you."

His parents moved apart just enough to accommodate the boy's thin frame. They might almost have been restaging the image in the icon to exhibit the outcome of a childhood diet. "Now you see what we found objectionable," Allan said.

"You can't be talking about Dean," Jude protested.

Coral freed her lips from the clamp of her finger and thumb to say "You just heard the ideas the priest tried to give him."

"Make sure you put them right out of your head," Allan warned him.

Thom took this as a cue to ask "So what would you like us to teach?"

"And when?" Jude said. "As soon as you like."

Dean's parents glanced at each other over his head. "We've decided we prefer to handle religion ourselves," Allan said.

"We can offer all our other subjects too," Thom said. "Just say which."

"We haven't thought about it. We'll discuss it when we find the opportunity."

"We can talk about it now if you like," Jude said.

Allan jerked his head sideways at Dean, a gesture that resembled an inadvertent muscular spasm. "We don't."

"You enjoy our lessons though, don't you, Dean? We do."

"I do as well, gran. I hope mummy and daddy will let you do some more." As his parents turned their heads towards him, opening their mouths, he said "They had another one."

"They did." Jude sounded as puzzled as Thom hoped he had reason to feel. "What was it about?" she said.

"Mummy said it was like the other one they had. The lady made the house smell like that again."

"That's enough now, Dean," Coral said. "Go upstairs now so the grownups can talk."

"But my room's still smelly."

"Never mind letting everybody know," Allan said. "Please do as you're told and go there at once."

As the boy retreated his parents twisted on their chairs to watch him. "Close that door," Allan said, "and let us hear you shutting yours as well."

They gazed after him for at least a minute before returning their attention to the screen. Presumably whatever noises he'd made had fallen short of the laptop. "Have you had the crystal lady back?" Jude said at once.

"I think you know we have," Allan said.

"But yesterday you gave us the impression you thought your house was perfect and you'd never want to move again."

"There's nothing wrong with the house."

"And nothing in it that can't be put right," Coral said.

"I don't see the difference and I don't think you do either, Thom."

"I must confess I don't."

"You shouldn't call that a confession." Thom thought he was being absolved until Coral added "Confession's a serious matter."

"And you're never too young for it," Allan said, "whatever some church people would like us to believe."

"We still don't understand what you're saying about your house," Thom said.

"It was never the house," Allan said. "It was always someone in it."

"Allan," Jude cried. "Have we been talking at cross purposes all this time?"

"Now we're the ones who aren't sure what's being said."

"You gave us the idea you didn't think there was anything like that in the house."

"We tried not to believe it as long as we could, so that's something we have to confess. Trying to avoid the truth does nobody any good. In fact it can cause a great deal of harm."

"And we didn't want to upset you two," Coral said.

"You wouldn't have," Jude assured her. "We saw what was there when we were staying. We could tell it wasn't any threat to anyone."

Dean's parents stared in her direction. Coral mimed some kind of cogitation by pinching her mouth small, and so it was Allan who spoke while he kneaded a frown. "What do you think we're talking about?"

"Dean's friend you both seemed to think wasn't there."

"That was the start of it, true enough. We should have realised sooner what it showed us."

"Why, what do you think it did?"

"That he'd become involved with the occult somehow. We aren't suggesting anything like that was actually there, but the point is he wanted it to be."

"And what are you saying that was the start of?"

"Everything we're determined to put right."

Thom saw Jude was nervous of asking the inevitable question, and found he was reluctant to speak. He had to make quite an effort to say "What's that supposed to be?"

"Dean." Allan took Coral's hand, and they moved close together, blotting out the space their son had occupied. "I'm afraid he's all that's been wrong with our house," Allan said. "We can only hope Chloe's approach works this time, or we don't know what else we may have to do."

EIGHTEEN

Thom was striving to lie still despite the threats an ember of agony kept sending through his left thigh – he was hoping Jude had achieved sleep at last, since the rise and fall of her chest against his back had grown regular – when she spoke so close to his ear it felt as though a chilly breeze had invaded the bedroom. "I know what we have to do."

He tried not to find this as ominous as the darkness that surrounded them. "What would that be?" he almost didn't ask.

"Kissing," she said with an indistinctness that led straight into slumber, which he could tell by her breaths on his neck.

Since what he thought he'd heard made no sense he could grasp, what had she actually said? Surely not "kicking" or "kidding" or "kitting", but even less "killing", he fervently hoped. "Kitchen" conveyed nothing to him, unless her thoughts had recoiled from the problem that had kept them both awake in bed for hours – Dean and his parents. "You mustn't let it worry you. We'll have everything in hand," Allan had told them before terminating the call, apparently unaware of leaving them incapable of following his advice. He'd left Jude scarcely able to speak apart from repeatedly insisting they had to go to Barnwall. Thom had advanced some way towards persuading her that Chloe Sissons had convinced Dean's parents all was well, but he saw the possibility wouldn't content her for long, if at all. Now some notion seemed to have brought off the trick, at least enough to admit her to sleep. Thom's struggles to identify her last word cluttered his skull until at some point the dark settled into his mind, dousing all his thoughts.

Daylight and Jude's murmur wakened him. "Thom?"

"Yes." With some of the vigour hoisting his eyelids required he repeated "Yes."

"I let you catch up on your sleep because you're going to need it, but can you wake up now?"

When he peered at her face in search of the reason for her eagerness, panic seized him by the guts, because her features were a faded blur. Had his vision given way at last? He blinked so hard his eyes stung, which let him realise he was seeing her through the emanations of the mug of coffee she'd brought him. "Do you remember what I told you last night?" she said.

"I'm not sure if I heard you right."

"The kitchen, Thom. That's what we need."

"So that was what you said." He took a harsh sweet sip that seared his tongue but failed to rouse his brain. "In that case I don't understand," he said. "I assumed you were talking about the, you know, the Barnwall situation."

"I definitely am. I hope you don't think I'd have anything else on my mind just now."

"I'm still not with you, then."

"I hope you will be. I'd rather not be on my own with everything that's happening." When he shook his head in a guarded bid to reassure her Jude said "It can be our excuse."

His sore tongue winced from another sip. "Excuse for what?"

"To go and stay in Barnwall while we're having the kitchen made over."

"That sounds like an idea if you've decided we should have it done, but do we know how much it's likely to set us back?"

"I've been on the Richest Kitchens site while you were asleep. I'm not surprised they call themselves that. The site lets you work out what sort of price you're going to be looking at, and they're well out of our league."

"Then if we can't afford it," Thom said with increasing unease, "what are you saying we should do?"

"Don't you see it? You need to start thinking more like me." As though indulging a fault Jude said "We tell Allan and Coral we're having a new kitchen put in, but we aren't really at all."

"You think we'll be able to convince them."

"I can do a lot more than that if I have to for Dean, and I'm trusting you to. I'll call them right now."

"Can I just go to the bathroom first?"

"Of course you can if you need to. Don't be any longer than you have to be."

He was afraid her urgency would stop him up, and so it did. Straining proved unproductive, and attempting to relax required more effort still. At considerable last, shutting his eyes not too desperately tight once he'd made certain of his aim achieved the goal. The instant he stumbled back into the bedroom Jude jabbed the number that was waiting to be activated. Her impatience failed to reach Willow Grove, where the ringtone showed no inclination to relent. Thom was anticipating an electronic response by the time Allan spoke. "Mother, yes. Why are you calling now?"

"I won't keep you long if it isn't convenient." Thom heard her resolution not to let Allan's brusqueness deflect her. "You told us Thom gave you an idea," she said. "Now Coral's given us one."

"We're very much a team, but shouldn't you be ringing her?"

"I would have if we had her number."

"That's true, you don't need it. So what shall I tell her you said?"

"Just that I'm taking her advice about having our kitchen done." As Thom wondered how carefully Jude might phrase the rest of her plan, she demanded "What's that?"

While the screams were growing higher and louder, this simply emphasised their remoteness. "What's happening to him?" Jude pleaded.

"He's happening to himself. Don't say you've never heard a child having a tantrum."

"We heard you once when you were about his age, and you didn't sound like that."

"You think his behaviour sounds worse. I won't disagree with you, so—"

"I didn't say that and I didn't mean it." Jude's forcefulness faltered as she said "What's somebody done to him now?"

The closing of a door must have muffled Dean's screams. Of course nobody had gagged or otherwise muted him, but Thom felt relieved to hear Allan say "He's been put in his room."

With a desperate wiliness Thom hoped he was alone in noticing Jude said "Can you let him know we're here at least? I'm sure he'd be disappointed to miss us, and we would to miss him."

"We'll let him know you were."

"I think that's far too cruel, Allan."

"So how cruel are you saying we should be?"

"Not at all. Not even slightly."

"Sometimes you have to be cruel to be kind."

"I've never understood that saying, and I certainly don't believe it."

"Some of us do. Perhaps it's a good job."

Thom had begun to feel as if he could hear nothing but the screams. "What's upset him so much?"

"We said he could watch a programme we thought was going to be educational, but it turned out not to be."

"Why, what was it about?"

"Mathematics."

"I don't see how that could do him any harm."

"It wasn't the programme that was at fault, it was Dean. He wanted us to think he understood it so he could keep on watching it, but we tested him and he didn't understand at all."

"Maybe he would have. That's how learning works."

"We know how he has to learn."

"We could help," Jude was eager to propose. "Watch the programmes with him and then talk about them."

Thom saw she hoped this would release Dean, but Allan spoke over the screams. "We've decided we prefer to keep control of what he's taught and how."

"You don't mean you don't want us any more."

"I'm afraid that has to be part of it, yes."

For a breath or rather the lack of one Jude seemed rendered speechless. "Can we speak to him at least?" she found the means to ask.

"I thought I'd made it clear he has to stay in his room."

"If he absolutely must, but you could take your phone to him."

"He has to stay there on his own, unless you want to suggest a different way to punish him."

"We don't want to punish him at all."

"For what exactly?" Thom protested. "For not understanding a lesson? We'd never have punished a pupil for that."

"He's too good at not getting what he's told but no, not this time. For lying about it, which is a great deal worse. We won't have lying in this house."

In a last bid to sway him Jude complained "It feels as if you're punishing us as well."

While the stare this prompted was unreadable, it seemed to cut off Dean's screams. No, they had only been muffled further, though they were as violent still. Thom managed to conclude another door had shut once he heard Coral say "Who are you talking to?"

"Just my mother and father. She wants you to know she's taken your advice about the kitchen."

"You're going to be happy, Judith," Coral called.

"And she thinks Dean sounds as if something she doesn't like has got into him."

"I said nothing of the sort," Jude declared, "and you mustn't say I did. I'm saying nothing more in case I'm misrepresented further."

Thom was about to speak when she ended the call. "You've done yourself out of your plan," he said without knowing how this made him feel. "You were going to tell them we wanted to stay with them while the work was being done."

"We'll be staying there all right. I just don't want to warn them in advance. We need to see what's going on before they have a chance to hide it." She hurried to her wardrobe and dislodged the suitcase that was nesting on top. "I'll pack for us while you get ready," she said, "and then I don't care what anybody tries, we're going to see our grandson."

NINETEEN

At first the protracted slope of the extravagantly winding country road seemed too gradual to present Thom with any problem. As it grew steeper a lorry long as several houses reduced the car to a funereal speed. Thom was braking ahead of a bend while oily fumes seeped into the car and red lights flared raw in his eyes when he heard a vast gasp at his back. The twin of the lorry was looming behind him to trap him and Jude in a space very little larger than their car. As the blind bends multiplied, his right foot had to dodge from pedal to pedal despite the ache that kept seizing the cramped angle of his leg. When the lorry that had filled the mirror with its grille began to add the blare of a horn to the enormous panting of brakes, Jude twisted in her seat beside him, dragging at her safety belt. "We can't go any faster," she cried. "I only wish we could."

"I don't think he's honking at us. I think he means the other chap."

"But we're stuck in the middle. Can't you overtake?"

"That's not a good idea just now. We might never get there at all."

The possibility – the threat he hadn't intended to convey – silenced her. Presumably from her position she couldn't see how perilous the road was. Her enforced muteness didn't help much; his sense of her dismayed impatience was no less insistent than the pain that repeatedly surged through his leg. It took fewer bars of the pursuing lorry's grille to fill the mirror now. Fumes began to clog his nostrils while the horn brayed at his back and the blocked view ahead kept blazing crimson, and his leg shivered with the effort of overcoming the ache. He was having to stifle a groan by the time the road straightened and levelled out, allowing him to swerve the car onto the verge and let the lorry race past with a final complaint of its horn. "I'll just take the chance to give my leg a stretch," he said once he'd unclamped his aching teeth.

"If you need to, but try not to take too long."

As Thom hobbled around the car tufts of grass snagged his feet, jerking his legs and reviving the pain. Each circuit of the vehicle showed him a clump of buildings about a mile away, fronted by a roadside inn. He kept catching sight of Jude's concern, which he knew wasn't wholly or perhaps even mostly for him. Before the ache had entirely subsided he let her gaze urge him back into the driver's seat. He trod on the clutch as a preamble to starting the car, and the agony that had been lying in wait coursed through his leg, dislodging an exclamation of pain not much under a shout. "I don't think I can drive right now," he said through his teeth. "I think there may be a hotel up the road."

"Supposing there is, what are you saying?"

"If you can just get us there we can stop till I'm fit to drive."

"Come round, then, and let me take over."

Thom limped around the car again and eased himself into the passenger seat, gritting his teeth just short of grinding them. By the time he succeeded in extending his leg past the ache Jude had strapped herself in and started the engine. "Forget the hotel," she said as he hauled the safety belt across his torso and groped for the socket with the metal tag. "I'm taking us to Barnwall."

"We aren't even halfway, Jude. You don't like driving all that distance."

"I don't have to like it to do it if I have to," Jude said and sent the car onto the road.

She made it plain at once that she meant nothing to delay her. She slowed only when she came to some of the bends in the narrow unmarked two-way road bordered by hedges too tall to see over – just the sharpest bends, where she barely braked. Thom had to struggle not to mime tramping on the pedal, and her headlong sally at a perilously sightless curve in the road sent a twinge through his leg. She sped around the bend to meet a pair of cars racing abreast towards her, taking up the whole width of the road.

The car on the wrong side didn't fall back. As it gathered speed in a bid to overtake its rival it flashed its headlights, apparently in case Jude couldn't see it was rushing straight at her, too close to be able to swerve aside in time. A convulsion jerked Thom's leg, rousing an ache that felt like an omen of the injuries the crash would bring. Jude twisted the wheel so fast she was scarcely able to keep hold. The car veered off the road, nearly tilting into a ditch, too late to avoid the oncoming vehicle. Thom heard a vicious crack, and Jude's wing mirror slewed towards her window. The next moment the pair of cars vanished side by side around the bend.

Jude stared at her hands, which were trembling so hard the wheel shook. She stared at them until they grew steadier along with her breaths, and then she lowered her window to adjust the mirror. While the casing was splintered, the glass was intact. "They aren't going to take away my confidence. Nothing's going to," she declared and eased the car onto the road.

She didn't take long to regain her speed, but soon the road began to hinder it with roundabouts. Thom had forgotten how numerous the junctions grew on the last ten if not more miles to Barnwall, and he sensed her frustration as the impediments multiplied. More than once she drove onto a roundabout in defiance of oncoming traffic. In some ways reaching the suburban outskirts of Barnwall came as a relief.

He heard no children as Jude drove along the promenade. He tried not to find their absence ominous. In the harbour boats nodded their masts at one another as if they were sharing whatever secret the sibilant whisper of waves expressed. The pavement outside Crystal Distillations was deserted, but of course Chloe Sissons had no reason to hide. The unnamed van had moved from the corner of Childer Grove, revealing the plaque on the garden wall, and Thom wondered how he could ever have misread the street name. Perhaps he'd been too anxious to believe evil was remote from Allan and Coral's house.

Willow Grove was feigning innocence. Sunlight scoured the houses, lending all the bricks a guiltless gleam and displaying rooms like invitations to move in. The windows of the house beside the path to Childer Field seemed to open onto a furnace, where the blaze blotted out every front room. Jude parked at the far end of the road, barely in sight of the house and practically hidden by a van indistinguishable from the vehicle that had helped to confuse Thom elsewhere. "We'll leave the luggage in the car for now," she said. "I don't want to announce we're here."

She eased her door shut with hardly a sound and put a finger to her lips as Thom clambered out of the car. The street was full of a hush it felt uncivil to break, and he tried to find it no more than sedate, though he suspected Jude thought it ominous. He closed his door as gently as he could and risked testing his leg while she locked the car. Planting his weight on it set off a twinge that portended a limp, but at least he could walk. He relinquished the support of the roof of the car and was trying not to wince at the tentative steps he took when Jude said "Here's somebody I want a few words with."

Thom had to reach into his memory to name the man who'd turned the corner of Willow Grove: broad face his small mouth didn't need, though his wide eyes and thick nose did – Oliver Dodd, the social worker. "No need to park all the way down here," Thom's limp apparently prompted the man to advise Jude. "There's space by the house."

"The walk will do us good."

"I suppose that's true after your drive." He might have been weighing her veracity. "Another trip to see the family so soon," he said. "It's good to know you're all so fond of one another."

"Yes, I remember you told us you like to see families together."

"I do, and not just because of my job."

"Even in that house."

The social worker brought a finger to his lower lip as if he intended to measure his mouth. "Which one would that be?"

"The house they built so they could pretend nothing happened there."

"Nothing did, to be fair. It's a new house."

"You think it's fair to trick people into living there when it's the same place."

"I'll take the word back if it offends you, but I don't think I could really have stopped anybody moving in."

"You didn't stop anything, did you, Mr Dodd? You didn't stop what happened to that poor helpless child."

Oliver Dodd ran his finger back and forth below his lips as if to conjure up the best response. "Believe me, I wish I'd realised what was going on."

"Perhaps you should have been more vigilant. Well, now you have a second chance."

"Pardon me, to do what?"

"To keep an eye on a situation that needs watching. We don't think all is well with our grandson."

"Why, what has he been up to?"

"Not with him, with how he's being treated. It reminds me too much of the way that other awful business must have started. It needs someone to stop it before it gets any worse."

"I take it that's why you're here."

"Both of us, that's right, but we can use some help from somebody whose job it is."

"Leave it with me and I'll see what seems appropriate."

They had nearly reached the top of Willow Grove, Jude matching his pace whenever he increased it, while Thom limped to keep up. "May I have your number?" Jude barely asked.

She dodged around him to take the card he passed her. "And can you tell us who put up the new house?" she said.

"It was Considerable Constructions across the park. More considerable than considerate, some of us thought. We were breathing in the dust while they were knocking down the other house for weeks." He glanced beyond her, and his face grew rigidly professional as he raised his voice. "Good afternoon, both."

As he caught sight of the watchers, Thom did. They were standing in the doorway of the house with their arms around each other's waists as though to demonstrate they were a unit, incidentally cutting off the view along the hall. "What are you two doing here?" Allan said in surprise if nothing worse.

"I expect Mr Dodd can tell you," Jude said.

"I was just remarking on how nice it was that you're all back together."

"We wouldn't say otherwise," Coral told him. "It's a bit unexpected, that's all."

"I didn't get a chance to ask when we called you. We were hoping we could come and stay because of what we were discussing. If it's too inconvenient we can always to go to a hotel."

"We wouldn't like anyone thinking we've no room for my parents," Allan said. "You can have the room you had again."

"If you're sure Dean wouldn't mind."

"I can't see any reason why he should."

As Jude sent the social worker a look close to conspiratorial he said "I'll ask you to excuse me now. I have calls to make."

He hastened across the road, leaving Jude and Thom outside the garden gate. "We'll just fetch our luggage," Jude said.

"I'll give you a hand." Allan strode along the path while Coral remained in the hall, and then he peered about. "Why on earth are you parked all the way down there?"

"I didn't know if there would be room by the house."

"Don't keep behaving as if you aren't welcome, mother. Bring the car up, for heaven's sake. No need to create problems where there don't have to be any."

He gazed at his father over the gate as Jude headed for the car. "So was that all you were saying to Oliver?"

"Just family matters. Just about the kind of thing you heard."

Allan's scrutiny lingered until they heard the car approaching. As the handbrake rasped, Allan opened the gate. Thom hobbled after him, but Allan lifted both cases out of the boot as if to establish that nobody else was required, not to mention displaying his strength. "I'll take these up for you," he said.

Coral waited on the path for Jude as Thom limped upstairs after Allan. All the doors were open, revealing empty rooms even quieter than the road. Dean's room was so neat it felt as if the boy had been tidied away, along with the toys in the plastic baskets, and the quilt on his bed was as flat as a slab. As Allan planted the cases in front of the wardrobe, Jude hurried into the room. "Where's Dean?" she said at once.

Coral followed her in and sent Allan a faint wry smile. "Where do you think he might be?"

"Not at school." This must have been meant to express a hope, since Jude declared "At school."

"You were right the first time. You ought to know how we feel by now."

"Where, then? What have you done with him?"

"What do you think we should have done to him?" Allan said.

"I don't know. That's why I'm asking." As if Allan's words had caught up with her Jude said "To him, nothing at all."

"Then you've answered your own question."

"I don't see how I can have. What's supposed to be so funny? Why are you grinning like that?"

"Do calm down, mother. No need to act that way. Can't you see him?"

"How can I when he isn't here? What are you trying to say?" The desperation that had raised her voice turned shrill as she cried "Dean."

"Gran."

The response was so distant Thom couldn't locate its direction. Jude stared wildly about and then dashed to the window, which was just a few inches ajar. She heaved the sash as high as it would slide and leaned over the sill. "What's that meant to be?" she demanded.

"If you mean the sandbox," Allan said, "I made it for our son. We've had too much work to have time to take him to the beach."

When Thom joined her at the window he saw a wooden tray almost as wide as the back garden and filled with sand in front of the shed. Ranks of crumbling sandcastles stood against all four raised edges, implying an absent bucket and spade. "But he isn't there," Jude pleaded.

"Can you still not spot him?" Allan said with an approximation of a laugh.

"Heard but not seen," Coral said. "That's the wrong way round." Thom grew aware of movement twitching like a nervous tic on the edge of his vision. It was beyond the shed and the trees that bordered Childer Field. A figure was waving to him and Jude from the top of the slide in the playground, and as he narrowed his eyes to improve their watery focus he saw their grandson. Leigh and Kendrick were flanking the foot of the slide as a safety measure. "There he is, Jude," he said. "In the park."

"I can see that. I just didn't know where he was to begin with, that was all." She turned to confront Coral and Allan, so that Thom felt nervous of what she might say, but she said only "Now I see why you've given us his room."

"He won't give us any trouble. It'll do no harm to have him in with us," Allan assured if hardly reassured her as Thom heard Kendrick telling Dean "Now all the family's assembled. I expect your grandma's fine, whatever she sounded like."

TWENTY

As Dean set about carrying breakfast dishes and utensils to the sink Kendrick said "What news of your progress?"

"We're doing sins, grandpa."

"Not committing them, I hope."

"We hope that too," Coral said.

"You're saying you've been learning all about them, aren't you, Dean?" Jude said. "Which can you tell us about?"

"Eating too much."

"I don't think anyone could say you were guilty of that. Some of us might think you ought to be a bit more so."

"We don't want him guilty of anything," Allan said.

"You look like a healthy boy to me," Leigh said. "Not an ounce too much."

Thom saw Jude preparing to object and felt it wise to step in. "Which do you think is the worst one, Dean?"

The boy climbed on the kitchen stool to consign another armful to the sink before responding. "Not believing in God."

"So just make certain you do," Allan said, "because he's watching you every moment of your life."

"And not doing what mummy and daddy say, grandad."

"I don't think that's meant to be quite so deadly, is it?" Jude said.

"It could be," Allan said, rubbing his ridged forehead as if to compress his thoughts.

"I meant it isn't on the deadly list."

"Then perhaps it ought to be."

"Before we get too deep into a theological discussion," Kendrick said, "I should explain I wasn't asking how Dean was progressing."

Thom felt oddly wary of asking "What did you have in mind, then?"

"The work you're having done at home."

"They hadn't started when we left," Jude said.

As Thom hid his appreciation of her ruse Allan said "If you're away they send you updates."

"Nobody told us that."

"They say so on their site. I'm surprised you didn't see it. It's one of their selling points. If you move out while they do the work they'll send you daily videos."

"I don't suppose they've anything to send yet."

"I'd have thought they would by now. Why don't you give them a call?"

Thom saw Jude was starting to feel trapped if not harassed. "Maybe I will later," she told the tabletop instead of Allan.

"I didn't catch that."

She raised her voice to be heard over the thunderous downpour with which Dean was filling the sink. "Maybe later."

Kendrick stood up as Leigh did. "We're off for a drive and a walk," she said, "so we don't disturb anybody at their lessons."

As Thom tried not to be reminded of Chloe Sissons and how her activities had been described, the Bentons let themselves out of the house. Jude took a last mouthful of coffee as a preamble to asking "Have you two changed your minds about us?"

Coral grasped her mouth before releasing words. "In what way?"

"Your mother seemed to think just now you were involving us again."

"I don't know if she did," Allan said, "but I'm afraid we haven't changed. We won't be doing that."

"Then," Jude said not far from a rebuke, "we'll be getting out of your way as well."

"Would you like to join my parents?" Coral was already heading for the hall. "Let me see they don't drive off without you," she said.

"I'm sure they'd rather just be on their own together. We'll take the chance to walk around your town."

"That's very thoughtful of you, mother."

"We'll see everyone for dinner, then," Coral said.

"Yes, everyone." Jude had only just reached the hall when she turned back, and Thom thought she'd changed her mind or found a further argument. "Be good for your mummy and daddy, Dean," she said, and he swung around to wave a hand transformed into a swollen pallid decomposing mass – a glove of bubbles. "I know you will," she told him.

She didn't speak again until she and Thom were past the garden gate. "I do realise we could have had a word with Leigh and Kendrick while we'd got them on their own."

"What kind of word?"

"The kind we need to have with people. I want to talk to some of those while we have the chance."

"Should I know who?"

The look she gave him was at the very least reproachful. "I think you should, yes."

Willow Grove felt as if the house they'd left was enjoining secrecy on its neighbours. A few minutes' purposeful walk or in Thom's case a determined limp through the politely muted suburb brought them in sight of a church. Jude was heading for it when she glanced along a side street. "There's somewhere I should have thought of," she said. "I'm getting as forgetful as you, Thom."

The sounds of children – cries and equally playful shouts – had diverted her attention, and she made for Childerfield Primary at once. Clumps of the eldest youngsters stood in the schoolyard while numerous juniors chased in a variety of ways around them. A woman shorter than several of her charges appeared to be overseeing all of them by herself. "Excuse me," Jude called through the railings, "would it be possible to see Jane Thorndyke?"

The woman took a step towards the railings. "Who's looking for her?"

"Mrs Clarendon."

"Oh, it's you." The woman trotted swiftly closer, peering at Jude's face. "You're seeing who you wanted," she said. "You let me think you were somebody's mother."

"I am. I'm Allan's, and this is his father."

"But you were never Dean's parents."

She was at the railings now. Her voice stayed louder than the phone call had led Thom to expect it would be. Perhaps she was compensating for her stature if not turning up the volume to denote authority, which fell short of daunting Jude. "No, we're his grandparents," she said, "and we thought you were as concerned about him as we are."

"I told you I was concerned for him."

"And you said you'd call me if you had anything to tell us."

"I said that. There hasn't been."

"Don't you still come to work past their house?"

"I've made a point of doing so."

"Have you seen him at all?"

The teacher lowered her voice at last. "Not him or anybody, sadly."

"Or heard them?"

"Not that either, none of them. It's been as quiet as I told you."

"Don't you find that at all worrying?"

"I can't say I did. He was always the politest child in my class."

"Not so quiet it was unnatural, surely."

"I wouldn't have called it quite that. I did wonder if they'd gone away, but then I heard some activity out the back."

"What sort of activity?"

"Somebody sawing and nailing something. It sounded heavy, whatever it was." A bell shrilled inside the school but failed to quell the schoolyard clamour. "I have to leave you now," Jane Thorndyke said.

"Thank you for the information, and we'd be very grateful if you'd keep us posted." As the teacher set about gathering children into queues Jude said "I'd like to know what Allan built, if it was Allan."

"Surely it would have been the sandbox."

"She told us it was heavy, but it didn't look that way to me. I'll find out what it was when we go back," Jude said and turned towards the church.

She didn't slow down even for Thom until they reached the churchyard, which was planted with a scattering of headstones sufficiently pristine for an undertaker's window. Thin pointed arches framing abstract mosaics of stained glass relieved the long rectangular red-brick church, which was surmounted by a sketchy neon cross. The door beneath the cross was shut, remaining immobile despite Jude's double-handed bids to twist the doorknob. "I suppose we have to expect that these days," Thom said.

As she abandoned her assault on the doorknob they heard a series of faint thuds like the blows of a muffled hammer in the church. Jude flattened an ear against the door and then knocked hard on a panel. "Is that Father Nicholas?" she called.

"One moment." In not many of them he unlocked the door and stepped back. His round ruddy jocund face was propped on a heap of the hymnals he'd been dropping on ledges in front of the pews. "I came in the side way and forgot to open up," he said. "I try to be here as much as I can. I only wish we could leave churches open all the time. I want everybody to feel welcome."

"We know our family was," Thom said.

"Was and is, as many of you as there are."

"We understand you had a disagreement with our son and his wife," Jude said.

"I'm sorry if that happened." The priest hoisted the stack of hymnals so as to level not just his gaze but his face at her. "I think I know you both, do I?"

"We met in the park last time we were visiting. You were having trouble with your dictation."

"Sorry not to have recognised you sooner. Of course, the family in Willow Grove."

"If that's what you choose to call it. I remember you said you knew its history. I didn't realise what you meant then."

She sounded more accusing than Thom felt was called for. "Can you tell us what the disagreement was about?" he said.

The priest stood the hymnals on the nearest ledge, exposing the pallid celluloid collar whose restrictiveness contradicted his demeanour.

"I did think I'd begun to forge a link with them before," he said, "but they didn't seem to find me Christian enough."

"As I recall you believe people should find their own way to religion."

"Within reason, certainly." Father Nicholas glanced towards the altar as though anxious not to be overheard. "I hope God will forgive me for saying so, but there are people who should never set foot inside a church, not unless they change their way of thinking."

"I don't know how it makes me feel to hear you say that," Jude confessed. "So what are you saying we should do?"

The priest's cheerfulness had begun to recede into his face, and now the last of it did. "I can't think of anything at all."

"There's such a thing as being too tolerant, especially when it puts a child at risk."

"I absolutely agree, but I'd ask you to appreciate I wasn't involved."

"How can you say that? You must have seen how they were."

"Regrettably not. I wasn't here then."

"Who do you think we're talking about? I mean our family, mine and Thom's."

"Do forgive me. I thought we had Joan and Daniel Day in mind. I'd hardly say your family were of that order."

"Not yet they aren't, and we mean to see they never are, but I think living in that place has changed them."

"They did seem different last time I spoke to them, but I don't know if that's the explanation. Your son rather gave me the impression their work was causing them some stress."

"It isn't just that. You must have believed something was wrong with the house or you wouldn't have sent them to Chloe Sissons."

"I only recommended her because I was asked about an exorcism. In fact, you suggested it." The priest let this weigh on Jude before he said "You'll understand why I was opposed to such a course, but what Ms Sissons does is different. Gentler, above all. As I may have said, it's a common practice in some cultures."

"Whatever it was, it hasn't worked. I think that place is haunted by what it was before it was demolished."

"I'm afraid that's rather outside my area of expertise." As Jude started to protest Father Nicholas said "I take it you're concerned about your grandson."

"Do you even need to ask?"

"Have you considered approaching his school?"

"They've taken him away from there as well. We were hoping you could see your way to helping, particularly now I've made the situation clear."

"I'm sure you'll appreciate I wish I could, but since they aren't parishioners of mine and determined not to be, there isn't really much I can do in the way of intervention."

"How little is not much?"

"Very little." When her gaze showed no sign of yielding the priest said "Less than that, I fear."

"So you can't offer us any hope at all. I thought that was supposed to come with your calling."

"There's always hope. It's a sin to think otherwise." The priest gave this time to exhibit its importance. "Do I recall one of their neighbours is a social worker?" he said. "Might they be someone to consult?"

"We have," Thom said.

"Then I trust it was productive or will be." When nobody found an answer to this, the priest hefted the pile of hymnals, jamming them under his chin as if to hinder any further discussion. "There is one way I can help," he said.

"Tell us by all means."

"I'll pray for everyone."

"Thank you," Jude said, and perhaps Thom was alone in realising how much of an effort this took. "Yes, thank you," he said with as little conviction. As he limped after her between a pair of ashen upright slabs each distinguished only by a name and a brace of dates he said "Is that everybody now?"

Jude glanced back from the churchyard gate just long enough to give him a reproving blink. "Not even nearly," she told him and led the way to the house.

Thom thought she was planning to confront Allan and Coral until she made for the path to the park. She halted halfway down the path, tilting her head towards the house, but it was as silent as Jane Thorndyke had described – as silent as the stones outside the church and even less communicative. "I wonder what kind of lesson Dean can be having," she muttered.

"Maybe everyone's on their computers."

"Let's hope that's all that's going on. I'd pray if I thought it would make any difference."

She loitered unhappily until Thom saw determination overtake her, and then she strode into Childer Field. As the playground and the cries of children fell behind she hesitated, and he had no doubt she was listening for one cry in particular. "Come on," she urged as though Thom was the hindrance, and he watched her force herself to stop looking back.

Beyond the park the sunlight gleamed on the nameplate of Childer Grove as though mocking Thom's persistent misperception. He didn't know where he was bound until Jude made for Crystal Distillations. The window merely hinted how crowded the shop was not just with crystals but tarot packs and boxes of incense perfuming the air and jewellery shaped into obscure symbols and packages of herbs, no doubt including sage, though it was keeping its smell to itself. Chloe Sissons stood up to greet the newcomers from behind a counter displaying shelves of crystals and topped with a stand of books on healing. Today's kaftan was leafily green, as if she meant to cling to the end of summer. "Hello?" she said with real or at any rate persuasive enthusiasm.

"Hello," Jude said more neutrally, and so did Thom.

"Are you looking for anything special? We've plenty of special items here. I like to think the whole shop is."

"I don't doubt it," Jude said.

Chloe Sissons examined her face and perhaps her tone as well. "Will you let me offer a suggestion?"

"I'd be interested to know what you suggest to your customers."

"For you I'm going to say quartz. For both of you. I find that's the best for calm. Amethyst is good too, and I carry morganite and lepidolite, but I always recommend quartz. If you'd like a pair I can do you a deal."

"I certainly feel as if I could use some calm," Jude said and let a pause imply the reason. "Do you really not recognise us or are you trying not to?"

"Aren't you from somewhere up by the park?"

"You see, you do know us, and you know where we met. You've been back since."

"Yes, I remember."

Thom thought Jude might pounce on this, but she said "So what can you tell us about that house?"

"Not a thing except I was asked to give it the works."

"Twice, to be exact. Don't you know its history?"

"I don't. They didn't say and I never think I need to have that kind of information, not that I do that kind of job very often at all."

"Then what did you sense about the place?"

"The same thing. Nothing, I'm afraid I mean. You asked me that before."

Jude's visible frustration prompted Thom to say "But you seemed to be sensitive to us just now."

"I am to people, not to places. I don't mind admitting I learned how to purify a house from one of the books I sell."

"If you're so sensitive," Thom said, "you must surely have felt something about our son and his wife. Don't worry, you can tell us everything. Whatever you say, it won't get back to them."

"I'd have said they could use some of my crystals too. More so than the last time I saw them."

"Any reason that occurs to you?"

"Stress, but I couldn't tell you why."

Jude's frustration was etching lines into her forehead. "How about our grandson?"

"I did think they could let him act more like a boy his age."

"We think so too," Thom said. "Why did they say they'd asked you back?"

"They told me there was still evil in the house."

"Who said that? Was it Coral?" Thom hoped aloud.

"No, her husband."

As Thom found he didn't want to question Chloe Sissons any further Jude said "And what did he want you to do about it?"

"To purge the house again."

"The whole house."

"Mainly they wanted just one room."

The hint of relief Jude's voice had admitted didn't linger. "Which room?"

"Their son's. Your grandson's."

Seeing Jude's reluctance to continue, Thom felt compelled to say "Did you ask why?"

"I thought to protect him from whatever they believed was wrong with the house."

"But you didn't think anything was."

"I did get the feeling something wasn't right. To tell you the truth, I was glad to leave." With a pause so brief it conveyed her wish to change the subject she said "Did you want to look round the shop?"

"Maybe another time," Jude said.

"Then I hope I was some help."

"We hope you were as well." By the time she reached the door Jude seemed to find this unnecessarily ambiguous. "Thank you for being honest with us," she said.

As soon as she and Thom were on the pavement she murmured "Well, that told us nothing we didn't know."

"I don't know if I did."

"Then you should have. I don't suppose you know where we're going now either."

"You'd better say."

"I want a word with the builders who were responsible for the house."

"I couldn't even tell you where they are."

"They won't hide from us," Jude vowed and took out her phone to activate the map.

It sent them up the hill to Longboat Road, a stubby street that paralleled the promenade. Considerable Constructions and Demolitions was at the far end, if it could be called far. "It's a shame they didn't do it that way round," Jude said of the firm's name, mostly if not wholly to herself.

One of a number of overalled men was propping roof tiles with a concatenation of clatters against a wall of the builder's yard. Several of his colleagues, whom dust had turned prematurely grey-haired, were loading a truck with outsize bags of flour – sacks of concrete. Someone out of sight was dealing measured blows with a hammer, an activity Thom found disturbing in a way he couldn't place. A brick shed housed an office, where a receptionist took some time to raise her eyes from typing calculations on a laptop. "How can we help?" she said.

Thom couldn't have told her, though she was regarding him as if the firm's services were a male preserve. "Can we speak to the boss?" Jude said.

"Mr Len's out on jobs just now. Can I be of assistance?"

"We want to talk about some work he did."

"Considerable guarantees all its work. If you can let me have the details—"

"There's no problem with the building work. We just want to ask him about a house he put up."

"If you care to wait he should be back here in an hour or so."

"We haven't really got that long. Can't we catch him at a job?"

"I was only thinking you mightn't want to walk that far." It was apparent the receptionist had observed Thom's limp. She consulted the laptop so as to announce "He should be at Viking Mansions up by the park in a few minutes. That's the closest you're going to find him."

"You won't mind if I forge ahead," Jude told Thom in the guise of asking, "if you can't keep up."

He was anxious that he should. By the time she reached a house diagrammed with scaffolding he was just a block behind. A sports car boastfully exposing a plump pair of leather seats was parked half on the pavement outside the house. A broad man rendered even squarer by the shoulders of his grey suit finished addressing workmen scattered on the levels of the scaffold and tramped fast to the car. "Mr Len," Jude called and more urgently "Mr Len?"

He met this with a look that didn't quite attain amusement. "That's what some folk call me."

"It's the name we were given when we went to your office."

"Aye, that's Martha's way." This might have been indulgent or resigned. "So what's the hurry you've chased me down for?"

"We wanted to ask you about a property you were involved with. The house in what used to be Childer Close."

He swung the car door wide before replying. "The council hired us to knock it down."

"And then we understand you bought the site and built a new house."

"No sense in leaving land like that with nowt on it when you've got folk desperate for housing."

"Land like that." Jude might have been isolating the phrase for investigation. "Did anything happen while you were working there?" she said. "Anything you'd say was unusual."

"Too damn much did. Souvenir collectors that tried to pinch bricks while we were demolishing till we chased them off. There's some website for their sort of, I won't say the word I'm thinking, that tells them where to go to steal the stuff they do Christ knows what with."

"I wouldn't like to think. What else?"

The builder climbed into his seat to be greeted by a leathery exhalation, and dealt the door a decisive slam. "What else of which?"

"You said too much happened."

"Too much of what I just told you. Didn't mean nowt else."

"What about when you were building the new house?"

"What's going to happen then? They wouldn't want to grab any of that."

"Anything else out of the ordinary, I'm wondering."

"Nowt worth wasting anybody's breath on," the builder said and revved the engine as if to blot out any response. "Got to be off now. Another job wants a look."

As the car roared out of sight Thom let go of the gatepost he'd been clutching for support while an ache lingered over fading from his leg. Jude performed a shrug eloquent of frustration and was turning away from the house, visibly unsure where to head next, when an oddly muffled voice halted her. "Len never talks about it much."

Their informant was a workman whose face from the eyes downwards was hidden by a black gauze mask. "About what?" Jude said.

"About the demolition. He was always peeved we ended up one lad down."

"How did that happen?"

"Harry wouldn't work on the job even when the boss said he'd fire him if he didn't, so he got given the push."

Thom was starting to suspect he might prefer not to learn any more. "Do you know why he refused?" Jude said.

"Len thought he was smoking too much dope on the job."

Jude shook a frown onto her forehead. "Why would that be a reason to refuse to work?"

"Not the dope, what he said he saw." The mask winced inwards with a breath, as though the fabric was striving to shape a mouth. "There was nothing when we went to look," the man said.

"What did he say there was?"

"First off he thought it was a worm, the way he told it." The shiver of another inhalation passed through the mask. "That's because it was squirming about in the rubble," the man said, "but he swore it was a little finger. He said it only looked like a worm because somebody had pulled the nail off."

TWENTY-ONE

As Coral placed a plate of poached cod and infant potatoes and slivers of carrot in front of him Kendrick said "So what did everyone find to do here while we were off on our jaunt?"

"Everyone didn't," Jude said.

"She and my father went out for the day, mother's saying. They've been seeing what there is of Barnwall."

"You sound as if you don't think there's much," Thom objected.

"There doesn't need to be when we have this house."

"And we've all been working hard at home," Coral seemed to want a number of the listeners to appreciate.

"We found a nature trail, Dean," Leigh said. "There were lots of squirrels in the trees. I expect you could go and see them sometime."

"Expect so, nan."

Thom thought he sounded less convinced than dutifully agreeable. As Coral set the last platefuls before herself and Dean the boy brought his right hand out from beneath the table. "No sauce," she said.

"I don't believe he was being cheeky," Leigh protested.

"I'm telling him he mustn't touch the sauce. We don't want any kind of restless night when he's going to be in our room."

"I think you've made it really quite mild."

"I imagine his mother knows what's best for his diet, dear," Kendrick said.

Thom dipped the points of his fork into the cheese sauce he'd poured from the jug and found it not merely mild but bland. He thought Jude was about to comment on it until she asked the question he could see she was nervous of voicing. "What have you done to your hand, Dean?"

The boy clenched his forefinger as if to hide it afresh, and winced. The top joint was wrapped in plaster. "Someone split his nail," Coral said.

"Who did?"

"Who on earth do you think? You're looking at him."

"It was the way you put it. How did you manage to do that to yourself, Dean? There's such a thing as working too hard."

"He tripped while he was running up the stairs," Allan said in answer to the gaze his mother trained on him. "We hope at least he's learned not to run inside the house."

"Do be careful what you're doing, Dean," Leigh said.

"I do try, nan."

"Why was he running at all?" Jude said.

"I should think he was being a boy," Kendrick said. "Didn't Allan shoot about a lot at his age?"

"He had plenty of life in him when he was a child."

Thom couldn't miss the implication about Allan's present state, and doubted anybody at the kitchen table other than their grandson would. He thought Allan meant to placate her or at any rate dismiss the subject of himself by asking "What have you heard today?"

He'd roused Jude's wariness. "About what?"

"The work you're having done at home."

"Oh, I see, yes, of course, I forgot." All this apparently gave her time to compose more of an answer. "Nothing yet," she said.

"They haven't been in touch at all? That's really not up to their standard."

"We haven't asked them to be."

"Look, if you don't feel comfortable doing it for any reason, let me contact them for you."

"I've already told you I'll see to it in my own time, Allan. There's no need to make me look incapable."

"I don't believe I was. If anyone—" Allan said before truncating the comment with a forkful of fish.

The silence he'd imposed upon himself grew infectious, emphasising the squeaks of Dean's utensils on his plate. The clumsiness his injury imposed made Allan massage his corrugated forehead while Coral kept clutching her mouth. Jude might have been trying to distract them by saying "Whose turn is it to read to Dean tonight?"

"It's ours now," Coral said.

"You're claiming this one for yourselves," Kendrick said.

"We'll be doing all the reads in future."

"That's a bit disappointing," Leigh protested. "We like reading to him, and I'm sure Judith and Thomas do."

"We'd prefer to keep control of what he hears," Allan said.

"Can we all listen at least?" Jude said.

"You'll be welcome if you think it will do you any good." As his gaze strayed back to Dean and his efforts to quieten his knife on the plate Allan said "It ought to."

Thom didn't expect Dean to be sent upstairs as soon as he'd finished washing up the dinner items. "You've earned your bathtime," Coral told him.

"Does he have to earn it now?"

"She was joking, mother."

"I'm sure your mummy meant you've been a helpful boy," Leigh said, not just for Dean to hear.

"Who's going to supervise the bath?" Jude said.

"You can." Immediately and less indulgently Allan added "All of you."

"We'll just see to the bath first," Coral said.

This entailed not merely filling it and testing the temperature but covering the water with an extravagance of foam to conceal Dean's nakedness. "You can come in now, everyone," Allan announced.

Dean seemed amused to see the room growing crowded with grandparents. Once his parents left them alone he admitted to the wince he must have hidden at the kitchen sink. "You should have told mummy and daddy it hurt," Jude said.

"It doesn't very much. Some boys get hurt worse."

Thom thought she might interrogate this, but she said "Was it why you were making all that noise when we called your parents this morning?"

"I'd been bad, gran."

Though this was plainly meant as a denial, Thom wasn't sure what kind. Dean retrieved the toy submarine he'd been allotted for the bath, only to flinch from winding it up. Thom would have turned the key for him if Kendrick hadn't claimed the honour. "Full speed ahead, captain," he declared each time he planted the boat in the foam, where Dean used his feet and his uninjured hand to guide its largely invisible course. He grew so engrossed in the task that Leigh said "Don't get cold in there, will you?"

His response sounded oddly wistful. "It doesn't go cold any more like it did, nan."

"Just the same, we think it's time you were out," Allan said.

Thom hadn't realised Dean's parents were loitering so close to the bathroom. As Allan grabbed a towel from the rail, Coral brought a pair of Dean's pyjamas bunched in her fist. "We'll take over now," she said.

Jude moved at once, but only to sit on the topmost stair. Thom tried to find comfort some stairs below while Leigh and Kendrick stayed on the landing. None too soon Allan emerged from the bathroom, guiding if not propelling Dean with a hand on the back of the boy's head. On her way to the parental bedroom Coral let her gaze trail over the spectators. "Quite an audience tonight," she said as though she'd forgotten anyone was there.

Thom thought she and Allan had begun to read to Dean at once, if so quietly it challenged the listeners outside the room to hear, and then he realised the murmur consisted of prayers that included Dean's restrained voice. Several minutes' worth of these ended with the creak of a temporary bed. Dean could barely have slipped into it when his father set about reading aloud.

Thom identified the material in seconds, though it sounded like a version simplified for children. "The young man's outfit was so white it nearly blinded them.... He isn't here, he's risen from the dead...." This seemed benign enough, together with the aftermath in which Christ walked beside the disciples without revealing his identity until he dined with them. "Tomorrow you can hear how Jesus went to heaven," Coral promised.

"Just remember he could come back from the dead," Allan said, "because he was never anything but good."

"And you remember what they did to him because you didn't behave like he wants you to."

"I remember, mummy. You and daddy read it all to me."

"Now call good night to everyone."

Jude had gripped the banister to haul herself to her feet, but subsided as Dean raised his voice. "Good night, gran and grandad. Good night, nan and grandpa."

"No need to hurt everybody's ears," Allan said as the chorus responded. "And don't forget we're here."

"I won't ever, daddy. Good night and mummy too."

Presumably the ensuing pause denoted a ritual kiss and its twin. As the grandparents trooped downstairs Jude waited until Allan and Coral emerged from their room. Thom saw she meant to confront them once Dean was beyond hearing, but it was Leigh who spoke as the family gathered in the front room. "Do we gather Dean's had the crucifixion for his bedtime story?"

"We've been giving him his last days," Allan said, having shut the door to the hall.

"Whose?" Jude blurted as much like a gasp as a word.

"You can't really be that uninformed about religion, mother. The days before the crucifixion."

"Don't you think all that could be a bit overwhelming at Dean's age?" Leigh said.

"It's what happened," Coral said. "It's the truth."

"I assume you wouldn't have gone into too much detail."

"No." Coral sent her mother a single lingering blink. "We didn't go into too much."

Thom thought the answer silenced Leigh more than it satisfied her. "I still don't think it was the best choice for bedtime," Jude said.

"It gives him plenty to reflect on while he goes to sleep," Allan said. "And it should take his mind off his little injury if needs be."

"I'd think they're more likely to keep him awake, both of them."

"Maybe one will remind him of the other," Coral said.

Kendrick tilted his head towards the ceiling. "He sounds asleep to me. I expect he'll let us know if he's in any distress."

"Let's hope so," Jude said forcefully enough to be aiming to speak for everyone in the room.

As some form of response Leigh said "We've been looking up places we could take him."

"What sort of places would those be?" Coral said.

Her mother read out names and descriptions from her phone: the Woodland Wander arboreal labyrinth, the Overkill Overhead Adventure constructed in another section of the forest near Barnwall, Wings With Zing that sounded like a spicy dish to Thom but proved to be a bird sanctuary.... Dean's parents objected that his temporary guardians might lose him in the maze and could hardly be expected to protect him from the perils of the rope course. "How about the sanctuary, then?" Jude said.

"You sound as if you think he needs one," Allan said.

"He has one," Coral said. "Our house."

"I certainly think he could do with a treat now and then."

"We can take him if he deserves it," Allan said. "No need for anyone else to go to the trouble."

"But we like to," Kendrick said, "and I believe I'm speaking for everyone here. We're more than happy to relieve some of the pressure on you both."

"There is none," Coral said. "We've organised the household so there isn't."

Thom felt it was past time he contributed. "Not even on Dean?"

"We can't see any reason why there should be," Coral said and squeezed her mouth as if to trap anything she might have added.

Thom found too much of an answer to voice but thought Jude might instead. She seemed equally to be waiting for someone else to speak up, and perhaps despairing of them. As though to ensure the discussion was done Coral switched on the television and brought up the Worth Mirth channel. All the episodes of comedies it offered proved to deal with families in chaos, a spectacle several audiences that sounded suspiciously alike found a good deal more hilarious than anyone in the room did. When the credits of the third half-hour began to flee at speed up the screen, Allan broke the silence. "By all means watch as long as you like, but I think we're ready for bed."

"Do you mind if Thom and I have the bathroom first?" Jude said at once. "We can go together."

Thom suspected she'd had enough not just of the alleged comedies but of the infrequent determined expressions of amusement everybody in the room seemed to feel compelled to utter. As he and Jude scaled the stairs he heard a jolly signature tune fall silent to make way for a murmur of conversation. Jude halted halfway up but presumably managed to distinguish no more words than he could. She loitered on the landing, but the top floor was utterly hushed. Once Thom bolted the bathroom door she told him "I wanted to make sure we're up here when they are."

The mirror showed Thom his attempt not to look too concerned. "Why, what are you thinking of doing?"

"Listening, and I hope I'll find there wasn't any need."

This left him nervously alert once his bed finished creaking with his search for the least uncomfortable position. When he heard footsteps padding upstairs he grew tenser still, not least because he sensed Jude had. Two sets of them turned stealthy as they entered the room next door, and he couldn't help holding his breath, clenching his teeth until his chest tightened around a pain. Nobody spoke, and he heard no other noise from the parental bedroom. Before long muted footfalls headed for the bathroom, and soon they made way for their partners. A similar muffled routine signified that Leigh and Kendrick had come upstairs, and then stillness settled on the house. At some point the hush became sleep.

A high sound roused Thom – the cry of a bird, he thought, or the squeal of a swing in the park. He was trying not to decide which so as to avoid wakening further when he heard a fumbling at the door.

Had the shrill noise disturbed Jude's sleep too? He hoped she was only going to the bathroom. He struggled to free his hands from a tangle of the quilt and then groped to widen his eyes with a finger and thumb while he strove to focus. Despite the clumsy dogged sounds at the door, the room in front of it appeared to be deserted. Was Jude too sleepy to let herself in? He was about to stumble to her aid when the door wavered open, revealing a silhouette in the dimness.

It wasn't Jude. It was far too small. It lurched towards him at once, exhibiting no more of a face. He felt his chest clamp his breath until the silhouette produced a voice. "Grandma? Grandad? I'm scared."

Before Thom could respond, Jude was instantly awake. "What's the matter, Dean?"

"I'm scared of them in there."

"Why, what have they done?"

"They aren't my mummy and daddy."

As Jude threw off her quilt and made to go to him, a whisper as sharp as bared teeth followed him out of the dark. "Dean. Dean, come back here at once."

The last word hissed like a snake. "Who's speaking?" Jude demanded.

"Who do you think it's going to be, mother?" A silhouette twice Dean's size darted into the room and loomed over him. "You were having a dream," it told him. "Now do as you're told and stop disturbing people."

"What dream?" Jude was determined to hear.

"It doesn't matter now. He's bothered you enough." The larger silhouette grasped the shoulder of the smaller and turned its captive towards the door. "I'm sorry he behaved like this," it said. "It won't happen again. Now please try and get back to sleep or we'll feel worse about him still."

"Allan. Allan," Jude protested as if trying to fix his identity. "We don't mind being bothered. It's one reason we're here," but by now she was talking to the door he'd shut. She shoved herself off the bed and tiptoed rapidly to the wall the rooms shared, gesturing Thom to follow her and crossing her lips with a finger. As he floundered to join her they heard the door of the parental bedroom creep shut, and she pressed her ear against the wall. Thom did the same in time to hear Allan say just audibly "Don't you ever dare say anything like that to anyone again."

Quite as low Coral said "Even if you were dreaming, that's no excuse."

"I wasn't, mummy." Dean's voice stayed unrestrained. "I was awake."

"Then that's even worse, and don't let anybody hear you say it. You'll be sorry if you do."

"Just you remember what happened to the other little boy who used to live here," Allan said, "the one you tried to bring back."

"And think how much your finger hurt."

Jude let out a cry of dismay before she could cover her mouth, and the next room grew instantly silent. She made for the door at speed, and Thom was limping to head off the confrontation when she halted, clenching her fists. "No," she declared, "not yet. We'll wait till everyone can hear."

TWENTY-TWO

As Jude took hold of Dean's doorhandle Thom said "What do you mean to say?" Her question felt close to a demand if not an accusation. "What do you think we should?"

"Do you want to find out first if Leigh and Kendrick heard?"

Sounds of the Bentons heading for the stairs had given him the notion, a final delay of whatever confrontation Jude was planning. "That's an idea now you mention it," she conceded and left the room at speed while Thom limped to keep up. "Leigh," she whispered urgently. "Kendrick."

The Bentons were almost downstairs. Perhaps they didn't hear her, since neither of them looked back. Before Jude could call to them again, they disappeared towards the kitchen. "I don't think I'd have done it quite like that," Thom murmured.

"You haven't done very much at all." She swung to face him, and he thought she might have toppled down the stairs if she hadn't grabbed the banister. "Please do your best," she said, "to back me up for once."

"I think I always have," Thom protested, but she seemed not to have time to hear. She went downstairs so swiftly he was afraid she might trip, and every hasty step he took to follow her reminded him how much his legs could ache.

The Bentons were pulling out chairs from the kitchen table to sit down. Dean's parents had boxed him in on a bench while he pored over a book, where the dual columns of print on each page made it plain to Thom it was the Bible. "Here's the sleepyheads," Allan announced and stood up. "Usual coffees for everyone, yes?"

"Too many things round here seem to be usual, Allan."

His studied exuberance faltered. "We don't know what you think you heard, mother, but—"

"Thom heard too, didn't you, Thom?"

"I certainly heard things I'd rather not have."

Jude held out her hands to Leigh and Kendrick. "Did you two hear what was going on?"

"It seems not," Kendrick confessed as Leigh shook her head. "It seems as if we never do."

"I wonder how you and Thomas managed, Judith," Coral said, having appeared to pinch the thought out of her mouth. "Nobody was making much noise in our room that I remember."

"Just a moment, everyone." Allan abandoned ferociously rubbing his brows to hook a finger at their son. "Take your reading upstairs, Dean," he said, "while the grownups finish talking."

"Before you do if people really think you have to," Jude said, "just tell your nan and grandpa what happened in the night."

"He had a nightmare," Allan said.

"Can he be allowed to speak for himself?" When Allan dealt the air a backhand slap, presumably gesturing Dean to respond, Jude said "Go on, tell them."

"Daddy said I had a bad dream."

"That's what he said, but do you think you did?"

"Maybe I did because I was bad. That's why mummy says I have them."

"That's complete nonsense, so don't you believe it. Dreams are just dreams, and anyone can have bad ones. What else did daddy say to you?"

"He said I won't have them if I'm good."

"We all think you are, don't we?" When Thom and the Bentons murmured agreement without using words Jude said "I meant what else did he say last night?"

"If there's to be any discussion of that," Coral said, "do as your father told you. You've already disobeyed him once."

"Blame me for that," Jude said, "and do whatever you'd do to him to me." As Dean marked his place in the Bible with its ribbon and clambered off the bench, she added "Just one more question, Dean. How exactly did you hurt your finger?"

"It doesn't hurt much now, gran."

"That isn't what I'm asking. How was it done?"

"Daddy said. On the stairs."

"Don't just repeat everything your parents say. Tell us in your own words."

"He doesn't need them," Coral said, "unless you're saying someone's lying."

When Jude audibly parted her lips and then shut them with less of a sound Coral said "Off with you now, Dean, and shut the doors behind you. We want to hear where you end up."

His footsteps dwindled beyond the kitchen door, to be terminated by a faint thud from his bedroom. Allan left the percolator untouched and returned to the table, on which he planted his folded arms to lean over them like a judge. "Now just what are you claiming you heard?"

"You tell them, Thom. Don't leave it all to me."

"We heard you frightening Dean. That's hardly the best way to stop him disturbing people, if that bothered you so much."

"You did worse than that." Thom sensed some of her dismay was aimed at his reticence. "We heard you threatening to treat him like the Days treated the boy they had," she said, "if you haven't already started."

As Leigh and Kendrick made to respond their daughter said "Either your hearing let you down or your mind did."

"You won't deny you talked to him about the Days, will you?"

"We may have mentioned them."

"So you're admitting you knew about them."

"I don't know why you'd call that an admission," Allan said, "when you seem to know about them yourself. If anybody needed to own up—"

"We didn't mention it for Dean's sake. Just when exactly did you find out about them?"

"After he kept insisting there was someone else in the house. We looked into the history and turned that up."

"Then surely you must be able to see how the place has been affecting you both."

"In what way, mother?"

"Calling me that and your father father for a start. You never used to." When Allan gave this a barely patient look she said "How you've been behaving towards Dean. You never acted like that till you moved here."

"We only realised what he's like when we did. Where we lived before we could have blamed it on bad company, but now we've isolated him we can see it's only him."

"There's nothing wrong with him except what you're making happen," Jude cried. "I don't know what you imagine all this religious stuff you're loading him with is achieving, but we're sure it's doing him no good at all."

"We pray it is," Coral said. "We only took it up because of him."

"Well, someone besides us could see what's happening to you."

Kendrick cleared his throat and seemed inclined to let this stand as a response. "If you mean us, Judith—"

"I hope we can but no, I wasn't meaning you just then. I'm thinking of the couple who sold Allan and Coral this house."

"Why should they agree with you?" Coral said.

"Because they say it changed them as well. The way you've started to feel about Dean, the house made them feel like that about the children they work with. That's not really how they are at all, and they stopped once they moved away."

A pause massed like a noiseless storm before Allan said "You've been talking to them."

"We've spoken to quite a few people," Thom said.

His bid to support Jude only squeezed her lips as thin as her frown. Presumably she'd planned to reveal the information at her own pace. "About us," Coral said.

"About your situation."

"So who have you been discussing our business with?" Allan demanded.

"We talked to the builders who put up the house. We talked about the one they had to demolish. One of them thought that hadn't got rid of everything that was wrong."

"That doesn't sound very professional. Are we going to hear what he said?"

Thom was hoping to avoid explicitness in case it proved unpersuasive, but Jude intervened with some force. "Someone found a finger. Just a finger, and somebody had pulled its nail off."

"How would they know anyone had done that?" Coral objected so vehemently she might have felt accused. "Did they call the police?"

"It seems as if it wasn't physically there, but things like that don't need to be to have an influence."

"I'd say somebody was being far too imaginative."

"Thom will tell you I imagined nothing anyone we spoke to said."

Allan dealt his brows a vicious rub. "Who are we going to hear about now?"

"Jane Thorndyke at the school for one."

Thom found a point to make. "She agreed with us there are things Dean can't learn at home."

"I'm sure she did her best to justify her job," Allan said. "And I'm not surprised she agreed with you. You've both been trying to justify yours."

"How can you say that?" Jude protested. "We tried to help you with Dean's education, since you're so suspicious of the school."

"And maybe you were trying to see all you could."

Jude glanced at the Bentons in the hope Allan's wariness disquieted them, but not even their faces responded. "Let's stay with Jane Thorndyke," Thom said. "She thinks your house is too quiet for a house with a child in it."

Coral released the handful of her mouth to say "She's been spying too, has she?"

"She often walks to work past here, and she's still concerned about Dean."

"Then it's time quite a few people stopped interfering. She's got no rights in the matter now he's left the school."

"And you can't be too quiet when you're learning," Allan said. "Thank heaven we took Dean away from her kind of class."

"You shouldn't let that trouble you so much, Judith," Kendrick said. "We appreciate it was your profession, both of yours, but perhaps some children aren't best taught at school. It must have been approved by the authorities or it would never be allowed."

"Jane Thorndyke's not the only one who thinks like us," Jude said. "There's Father Nicholas."

"Good God, mother, have you been bothering him as well?"

"He was already bothered about Dean. I'm sure he feels you're being too extreme with him."

"I don't doubt we are by that priest's standards, if you can even call them that. If he's representative of how churches have ended up we're glad we're keeping Dean well clear of them."

"He cares for people, and that matters."

Jude said this to the Bentons, but Allan retorted "I'm amazed you aren't saying it's all that does. Faith matters more to some of us, especially when we have to find it for ourselves and our child."

"I will admit," Kendrick said, "for a priest he did seem a little casual about it."

"Remember he believed there was something in this house that needed dealing with," Jude said. "He just didn't want to be responsible for an exorcism. It would have been too close to the kind of thing the Days did."

"Some of us might wonder what drove them to behave that way," Coral said.

Jude stared at her and then at Coral's parents. "Did you hear that? Can you still ignore what's going on here?"

"You didn't really mean anything by it, did you, Coral?" Leigh said, though not entirely comfortably. "It was just a manner of speaking."

"And I thought we were talking about the priest," Allan said. "We'd say he didn't want to take responsibility for anything. Very much the wrong type for the job."

"He recommended Chloe Sissons, didn't he?" Jude said.

Coral met this with a laugh more like a denial of one. "Is she yet another of your informants?"

"We went to see her, yes. I must say you both seemed anxious not to let us know she was here last time you brought her in."

"Why would you imagine we'd care about that?"

"Because you made her concentrate on Dean's room."

"Did she see anything wrong with that?" Allan said. "Tell the truth."

"With his room? Nothing at all, and we haven't either."

Allan uttered a breath that left his words redundant. "With being asked."

"She didn't say." As he gave this a stare no less expressive than the breath Jude said "She told us she couldn't sense anything about the house, but then she never does. That doesn't mean there's no influence."

"Judith," Leigh said with a gentleness Thom for one found ominous, "have you forgotten how she got involved in the first place?"

"I rather think I just said. Father Nicholas suggested her."

"But surely you remember bringing someone to the house was your idea. If you're looking for some sort of influence that's been affecting the household, and please forgive me for saying this, perhaps it's you yourself."

Jude found no answer, or at least none she chose to voice. "So," Allan said, "if you've finished talking about us—"

"I haven't." Jude's gaze lingered on Leigh and included Kendrick. "There was something I think you'll have to admit you both saw."

Neither of them seemed eager to respond. As if he was the loser in a silent game Kendrick said "What would that be, Judith?"

"Or I should have said you didn't see. None of us saw Dean in the bath."

Leigh's gentleness had infected Kendrick. "You'll excuse me, but we all did."

"He was always covered up one way or another. We never saw him with nothing on."

Less mildly than warily Kendrick said "Why would you want to do that?"

The listeners might have thought she'd decided not to answer. "To see he was all right," she eventually said.

"I don't think any of us need to see him like that to know."

Thom felt he was trying to deal not just with his own unease by saying "Is that all now, Jude?"

"You should know it isn't." In the same accusing tone she said "What has somebody been knocking up?"

"I don't think even Thomas knows what you mean by that," Kendrick said.

"Then he should." She rested a sad gaze on Thom's baffled face. "Jane Thorndyke heard someone hammering out at the back."

"We've all seen what they were making," Leigh said. "A sandbox for Dean."

"Perhaps it wasn't that," Coral said.

While Thom couldn't read the look she sent her husband, it prompted Allan to stand up. "By all means come and see," he said. "I think you should."

As everyone trooped out of the house Thom glanced up at Dean's room, but the boy wasn't to be seen. Tools in the shed emitted an eager clatter, apparently roused by the force with which Allan threw the door wide. He stood back, extending his hands to the shed like a conjurer exhibiting a trick. Thom saw Jude recoil and hurried to discover what she'd seen. A heavy unadorned cross more than four feet tall, evidently the item Allan was displaying with pride, stood propped against a workbench. "All my own work," Allan said.

"But whose idea was it?" Jude said, perhaps in some form of hope.

"Ours."

"Yours and Coral's, you must be saying."

"Our son thought it was appropriate as well."

As this appeared to leave Jude reluctant to speak, Thom said "What are you planning to do with it?"

"It isn't finished yet. There'll be something to put on it first."

"Do we have to ask what?" Jude demanded.

"I should think even you must know that, mother."

"The Days had one like it." She was appealing to Leigh and Kendrick now. "I don't want to think what they used it for," she said.

"Plenty of Christians still have them, Judith," Leigh said.

"Thanks for the private view, Allan. If that's all at last," Kendrick said and paused in search of some assurance, "I think it's time we were getting ready for the road."

"You're leaving," Jude said not far short of disbelief. "You think you should."

"We can't see any reason not to," Leigh said.

"You don't believe we've given you enough of them."

"Not to be concerned in the way you seem to want us to be."

"But we're concerned about you, Judith," Kendrick said, "and the effect you may be having that we're sure you'd never mean to have."

Thom felt compelled to speak as soon as he could – instantly, in fact. All he could think of to say that mightn't exacerbate the situation was "At least Dean will have his room back."

Allan stared past him at the house while he locked the shed. "Perhaps."

As everyone made for the house Thom saw Dean dodge out of sight from his bedroom window. He didn't want to think of the boy as a prisoner, but he wished he'd had time to see Dean's expression. Had it been wistful or worse? Surely that was only because he felt excluded from the family gathering, unless he was yearning for the park. Thom was about to propose taking him there – he hoped this would help Jude too – when Allan said "How long are you two thinking of staying?"

"As long as you can put up with us," Jude said.

"I mean how much longer do you think your work will take."

"We haven't finished yet."

He held the back door open for her and immediately followed her into the kitchen as though to ensure she went no further. "The work on your house," he said.

"We haven't heard from anyone."

He ensured the door to the hall was shut tight and then turned to scrutinise her face. "Have they heard from you?"

"Since you seem to feel entitled to know all about it, no."

Her voice had risen as if she and it were determined not to be trapped. "I don't know what on earth the problem can be," Allan said, "but please let me solve it for you right now."

Jude managed to stay quiet while he took out his phone, but seeing him search his contacts list proved to be too much. "Don't bother trying. There's no point," she said with increasing defiance. "We found we couldn't afford the work."

Coral stared at her and then at Thom. "Do you mean to tell us it was never started?"

"Sadly," Thom said, "as Jude says—"

"You lied to us. You lied in front of our son."

"I don't think you need to bring Dean into it. He doesn't know we were a bit lax with the truth."

Allan's stare equalled Coral's for growing dislike. "He will."

"We just wanted to see everyone," Jude protested. "I'm sorry if you think we needed any more of a reason to visit you than that."

"For heaven's sake, mother, don't say any more. Everything you're saying makes it worse."

"Then what would you like us to do?" Thom demanded.

"Please just leave."

Jude gasped as if he'd punched her in the stomach. "You can't really be telling us to do that, Allan."

"I'm very much afraid we must. We've put up with a good deal lately, but we can't allow lying in this house."

"If you're so concerned with Dean you must see this is for his sake." With a surge of renewed anger Coral said "And you had the gall to make out we were lying about how he was hurt."

"Can you see what they're doing?" Jude appealed to the Bentons. "They're using all this as an excuse to get rid of us."

"Hardly to get rid," Kendrick objected. "I'm sure you'll be kept in touch."

"I expect things will be patched up in due course," Leigh said.

"I asked you not to say any more, mother. You really aren't helping your case."

"I didn't know we had one."

"We'd rather not talk any further," Coral said.

Despite the warning, Thom had to ask "When do you want us to go?"

"As soon as possible." With an indifference that rendered the word final Allan added "Please."

As Jude trudged and Thom limped upstairs Allan followed them, calling "Dean, go in our room." When the boy ventured onto the landing he gave his grandparents a puzzled blink. His father gestured him with a wave like a frustrated slap to do as he was told, and he left the open Bible weighing down the Lego box on top of the stacked baskets of toys with an account of the possessed swine rushing to destruction. Allan loitered outside the parental bedroom while Thom collected items for Jude to pack. She seemed to have taken the ban on conversation to heart, unless she'd been stunned into muteness, but as she dragged her suitcase out of the room she called "Goodbye for now, Dean."

"We hope we'll see you soon," Thom told whoever ought to hear.

Allan's voice was louder. "Stay where you are, Dean."

The boy called a bewildered goodbye over the rumble of the cases. Allan seized them and bore them downstairs almost at a run. Coral and her parents were waiting in the hall. "Travel safely," Kendrick said.

"And do look after Judith," Leigh said.

Jude let her distracted gaze stray over them and Coral before she lurched at Allan to deliver some form of kiss, but he stepped out of reach. "I don't think that's appropriate at present," he said.

Thom tried to take comfort from the last phrase and wondered if Jude had. She blundered out of the house as if their son had robbed her of sight and grabbed the gate for support before flinging it wide and stumbling to the car. "I hope you're seeing what you've done to your mother," Thom muttered.

"I'm afraid we have to be more concerned about what she might do to our son."

Allan carried the luggage to the car at a speed that suggested a determination to be rid of his parents. Jude climbed into the passenger seat without looking at him. "Thank you," Thom said, though barely, and found nothing more he wanted to say, if he'd even wanted that much. He eased himself into the car without rousing too many aches and gave Jude's limp unresponsive hand a squeeze that apparently conveyed too little consolation. He was starting the engine when Dean ran out of the house. "Grandma, grandad," he cried. "Don't go."

His father strode to shut the gate before the boy could reach it. "Don't start running off, son," he said loud enough for anybody in the house or indeed the street to hear. "We don't want you getting hurt, do we? We don't know what might happen to you if you weren't with us," and Thom saw Dean's face contract in the mirror as the car moved off – surely saw it shrink just with distance, not shrivel as though it and its owner were trying to hide.

TWENTY-THREE

They had just passed the end of the park when a blank white van pulled out of Childer Grove, obscuring the name of the road. The driver either hadn't seen the car or found it unworthy of notice. Thom stamped so hard on the brake the engine stalled, and the car juddered to a standstill, blocking the way into Childer Grove. Sunlight seemed to etch the letters on the street sign deeper as if to remind him of the mistake he'd made, a misidentification that felt like a desperate denial now. He shifted his feet to the clutch and accelerator, rousing twinges in his legs. As he twisted the ignition key Jude said "Blind fool."

"I hope I haven't been quite that useless."

"Not you, the van man. I expect you're being all the use you can be."

It sounded very little like an accolade, and he felt ashamed of having seemed to seek one, not least since he suspected any might be undeserved. At least he could drive, even if it took them away from her concerns without leaving those so much as slightly behind. He eased the pedals down, only for the action to pierce both his legs with agonising cramp. He was barely able to drive clear of Childer Grove before he had to halt the car by clutching at the handbrake. As he inched his feet off the pedals in search of a pose less productive of anguish Jude said "Have you decided to go back?"

His suffering reduced him to a syllable. "No."

"Don't raise my hopes like that, then. That's just cruel."

"Oh."

Apparently the approximation of a word failed to convey his state. "I'd go back this minute," Jude said, "if I thought they'd let us in."

With an effort Thom succeeded in voicing a sentence. "Better let things die down."

"Please don't talk about dying just now, Thom."

A shorter answer required no less exertion. "Why not?"

"If you don't know without being told there's no use my saying. If I prayed I'd pray I'm wrong." Her stare relented somewhat as she said "I'm sorry, are you still recovering from what he did?"

Syllables were deserting Thom again. "Who?"

"That driver. I know I could have meant Allan. I don't think I'll be recovering from that in a hurry."

"No." This had to do duty as more than one answer. "Cramp," Thom said through his aching teeth.

"Oh dear. How bad is it?"

"Bad." Edging his feet towards the pedals felt like a threat of more pain. "Can't drive," he barely said.

"I'll have to, then." She gave him some seconds to move before she said "Let me come over there."

He wasn't anxious to discover how much pain climbing forth might entail. As he straightened up on the roadway he suppressed all of a cry that he could. He leaned his hands on the roof as he hobbled to the passenger seat, but the support lessened his agony hardly at all. By the time he managed to lower himself onto the seat and risk extending his legs Jude had started the engine. While he fumbled the tag of the safety belt into its slot she lowered her head as if she'd succumbed to prayer. The car began to coast downhill, but they weren't even in sight of the promenade when Jude found a space beside the kerb and hauled on the handbrake. "I'm not going to be able to do this," she said. "Everything's left me too tense."

Thom hoped she could fill in the rest of the question his pain reduced him to abbreviating. "What, then?"

"As you say, we can't go back to the house. Are you going to be able to drive today?"

"Don't think so."

"Then we'll just have to find a hotel."

The prospect appeared to enliven her, Thom presumed because she wouldn't have to drive far. Less than a minute's descent of the hill brought them to the Wavelets Guest House, a three-storey building that had been extended to incorporate a twin on either side, although it looked to Thom as if its neighbours had reached out to hem it in. Jude parked on the concrete that had deadened three front gardens. "Wait while I see if they've room for us."

A pair of gnomes stood sentry beside triple steps that led up to a large central porch, one side of which had been removed to accommodate a ramp edged with plaster pixies angling for fish or else for water. As Thom eased his worse than aching legs away from the front of the car in a bid to judge how painful climbing out might be, Jude reappeared from the porch. "We're welcome here," she said. "They don't mind having us at all."

He heard she was thinking of people who did. He couldn't find an answer while he was busy dragging the agonies that were his legs out of the car. "I'll bring the cases," Jude told him. "Just bring yourself."

She wheeled one up the ramp as he hobbled to follow, clutching at the rail alongside which the plaster anglers were ranked. By the time he gained the porch she'd fetched the second case and was waiting for a chance to steer it past him. A maternal woman at least twice as broad as Jude hurried across the lobby to meet them. The badge pinned to the lapel of her dark suit identified her as RHODA MANAGER. "Will the gentleman want any help with a wheelchair?" she said.

Thom collapsed onto the closest of several armchairs overlooked by an extensive oak reception counter. "Don't need any of those yet," he gasped, and made an effort to anticipate "I'll be fine."

The manager seized Jude's luggage by the handle and propelled it to the counter. "How long are you planning to be with us?"

"We've a few years yet, we hope," Jude said.

"I'm certain that has to be so," Rhoda said with an equally polite laugh, though Thom was unsure whether Jude had meant or even seen a joke. "How long would you like your room for?"

"Just overnight, do we think, Thom?"

"I expect one of us will get us home tomorrow if we both don't."

Once Jude filled in a registration form the manager gave her a key on a numbered wooden paddle twice its size. "I'm keeping you on the ground floor," she told Thom and sped Jude's case along a protracted corridor into the left-hand house while he limped in pursuit of the women and the cases, frequently floundering against the walls and at one point into a room where a chambermaid was stripping an extra bed.

The room the manager loitered in the corridor to indicate contained a generously capacious bed. "You lie down," Jude urged, and Thom set about doing so in painful slow motion. As soon as she'd unpacked their toiletries she joined him. "I'm going to see if I can get a little sleep till it's time for dinner," she said.

She slipped an arm around Thom's waist, and he felt her breathing grow more regular against his back, but every time he thought she'd found sleep a spasm seized her body, jerking her awake. Eventually she said "What are we going to do?"

"I think we've done everything we can for the moment."

"Maybe, but it's nowhere near enough."

"I don't know what else we'd be able to do." When the long breath she took resulted in no words he risked saying "Do you think perhaps you went a bit far at the house?"

"I don't at all. How in particular?"

"The business with Dean in the bath for a start. You must have seen Leigh and Kendrick were taken aback."

"And so they should have been, but not because of me. I'm still convinced there was something his parents didn't want any of us seeing. Just think how they behaved about it. They made such a fuss about me not telling all the truth, but they have their own ways of not doing that."

Thom could only hope his silence soothed her, although he was unable to judge. He dozed and thought she'd finished twitching awake until she roused him in the dusk that had sneaked into the room. "Whenever you're ready let's go and have dinner, and then maybe I can get to sleep."

Thom swung his legs off the bed at increasingly less speed and succeeded in restraining himself to a wince that comprised most of him. "I'm not going to be able," he said as distinctly as the pain permitted, "to walk very far."

"Then let's see if we can dine in the hotel."

She supported him all the arduous way to the lobby, gripping his arm harder whenever he staggered towards either wall of the corridor. The breakfast room beyond the central staircase had been transformed into its evening self, which enticed diners with a menu on a stand. An eager waiter ushered Jude more than Thom to a table beneath a chandelier dangling crystal slivers like omens of winter. "We'll have at least a bottle," Jude declared. "Whoever will be driving needs to sleep."

"Do you think we should let Allan know we're here?"

"I don't believe he'd want to know or Coral would."

Thom supposed he understood the reason for her vehemence, which sounded determined to convince him. "I was only wondering if we could offer them a meal to patch things up."

"I'd say most of that is up to them after the way they treated me."

He'd hoped she would at least consider the proposal. He didn't want to ask what she had in mind instead in case she couldn't answer. The return of the waiter ended their wordless awkwardness. They were halfway through a bottle of merlot by the time their meals arrived, and the alcohol seemed to have left Jude content with silence. Thom's steak Americano proved to be tender although only obscurely transatlantic, while Jude's sea bass Thai style was imbued with an oriental tang. When at last she lined up her knife and fork beside the glistening skeleton that appeared to have an eye on her she said "I wish we could have treated Dean to this kind of dinner."

"I'm sure we'll be allowed in due course. We just need to give them time. After all, we're still his grandparents."

Jude gave him a sadly affectionate look while she emptied the second bottle of merlot into his glass. "You do like to believe the best, don't you, Thom."

"Of people, do you mean? I'd like to."

Her gaze lingered on his face. "Then I hope you will of me."

"I can't imagine any reason why I wouldn't."

"I just hope you won't end up imagining too much about me."

Thom felt he'd lost his grasp on the conversation, perhaps because of all the alcohol. Jude could have too. At least the wine appeared to have assuaged or at any rate dulled his pains to an extent, so that he managed to limp largely unaided back to the room. "When you're done in the bathroom I'll have a wallow," he said. "Maybe that'll send away the aches."

He lay in the water until his second helping of it began to grow lukewarm. It reminded him how cold Dean had once said his bath had grown and why, a thought that sent more of a chill through him than the water did. He padded unsteadily into the bedroom to find Jude asleep, her slack lips trembling with her breaths that sent faint ripples across the pillowcase. When he wriggled in tentative stages towards her under the quilt she didn't waken. As his arm ventured around her waist she mumbled "Good," though he could have imagined a reversion to sleep had truncated the rest of a word. It took him no time he was aware of to join her in slumber.

Daylight found him through his eyelids. At least no pains had wakened him. He set about straightening his legs inch by timid inch. Even at their fullest extent they stopped short of reaching any ache. He could sprawl them so wide because he was alone in bed. "Jude," he said, "I'll be able to drive after all."

This prompted only silence from the bathroom. Of course she couldn't be expected to welcome the development too enthusiastically when it meant they would be travelling away from their grandson, but Thom hoped the journey would at least not make her nerves worse. "Did you hear me?" he called.

There was no sound beyond the open bathroom door, not so much as a hint of movement. A jab of undetermined panic jerked him up against the headboard, to see that their suitcases were still in the room. They gaped at him from a stand against the far wall beneath the blank slate slab of a television screen, and his case lolled out a shirtsleeve like an idiotic tongue. "Are you all right, Jude?" he shouted.

He heard a response from the bathroom – a faint moist noise that suggesting the parting of lips preparatory to an answer, but nothing more. Was she unable to speak for some reason? When the sound came again he recognised the dripping of a tap. He kicked off the quilt and bruised his feet with the floor. As he stood up his legs reminded him they still had aches to offer. He limped rapidly across the room and was drawing breath to remonstrate with Jude for withholding any answer, however relieved he would be to find her unharmed, when he saw her robed arm lying on the bathroom floor, twisted at an angle that must surely be excruciating if she was conscious. He grabbed the doorframe for support as he stumbled through it at a run, and halted there. The sleeve was as empty as the rest of the bathrobe that had fallen off a hook on the door, and the bathroom was deserted.

He fumbled with the lock and chain and poked his head into the corridor, hiding the rest of his naked self behind the door. The empty passage led at length to emptiness. He lurched against the door to slam it and padded fast although unevenly to grab his phone from the table on his side of the bed. Jude's table was bare except for a glass practically bereft of water and printed at the rim with a trace of lips reminiscent of a kiss – no phone beside the glass, no wristwatch. He brought her number onto his screen and prodded it so vigorously his nail sent a twinge through his finger. The phone stayed mute for most of half a minute before informing him it was unable to complete the call. Surely it could still locate Jude – they'd set up that mutual facility – but when he directed it to find her it seemed reluctant to respond. "Jude Clarendon was at the Wavelets Guest House," the relentlessly bright voice told him at last, "about an hour ago."

"Where is she now?" Thom pleaded, but the phone ignored him. For a moment – no, far too much longer – its inertia took hold of him, and then he dropped it on the bed and grabbed the bedside phone. The zero he had to dial felt like an undefined but ominous negation, one he might prefer not to find words for. "Hello?" he demanded as soon as he heard a responsive click. "Hello?"

"Mr Clarendon? This is Rhoda at the desk."

"Yes, hello." It felt like delaying a question or several. "Have you been there long?"

"When I'm needed. We've had some sickness among the staff."

"I meant would you have seen my wife."

"I did."

"When?" He was equally anxious to learn "What was she doing?"

"Just leaving the hotel." Thom was about to repeat his initial question when the manager said "About an hour ago."

"Did she say where she was going?"

"I didn't ask her, Mr Clarendon. I'm sure she would have said if she'd wanted me to know." As Thom strove to produce a simulation of gratitude the manager said "She did tell me what to say if I saw you."

"What?"

He was barely able to restrain a repetition of the word as Rhoda paused, apparently silenced by his brusqueness, before saying "Just that you shouldn't worry."

"About what?" Thom had to learn.

"Wherever she's gone, I should think."

"Thank you," Thom managed to pronounce on the way to embedding the receiver in its stand. He was staring at the cluttered icons on his phone in the hope that some aspect of the screen might inspire him when a thought sent him stumbling at speed to the window. His and Jude's car was still parked outside the hotel; he could see the left-hand corner of the rear. He would have turned away if the brake light hadn't flared as vividly red as the paintwork. He clutched at the latch of the window to raise the sash and shout to Jude to wait for him. He was making to crane out when he saw the brake light dull, but only because a cloud had obscured the sun again. He leaned over the windowsill, bruising his stomach, and then gripped the sill so hard his hands ached. The car wasn't his and Jude's, which was nowhere to be seen.

He was staring at it as though the fierceness of his gaze could effect a transformation when his phone shrilled on the bed. He shoved himself away from the window and nearly fell before he could reach the phone. "Allan," it announced as he snatched it up. Surely it was bringing him some reassurance. "Allan," he blurted. "Thanks. Is—"

"Are you having some kind of a joke?"

"I wouldn't say so. What do you mean?"

"What are you thanking me for?"

"For calling. Is—"

"Who else would we call? Don't you think we'd think of you first?"

"I'd hope so." Thom was growing desperate to clear the irrelevant discussion out of the way. "Is—"

"You'd hope that, would you? That's even more of a joke. Don't say another word." As Thom opened his mouth to disobey Allan said "Except you'd better tell us this right now. Do you know what's happened to our son?"

TWENTY-FOUR

For a moment that felt longer and then grew prolonged, Thom was afraid to speak. He wasn't even certain of the question: was he being ordered to confirm what Allan knew or to provide him with the information? No answer he could find seemed less than perilous. "What are you saying has happened to him?"

"You're asking everyone to believe you don't know."

"I'm asking, yes, because I don't. I give you my word."

"You've given us reason to wonder how much that's worth."

"I don't think that's fair, Allan."

"You aren't the one who should be talking about fairness, the way you've both behaved."

While loyalty prompted Thom to defend Jude, he couldn't postpone saying "You still haven't told me what's supposed to have happened to Dean."

"Supposed." This was Coral in the background, loud enough to be addressing an audience. "It's a lot more than supposed," she cried.

"He's been taken from us," Allan said.

"Good Christ, how—"

"No need for that kind of language, father. It isn't going to help."

"I'm just shocked, that's all." In fact Thom felt a great deal worse, too belatedly swayed by Jude's concerns. "How could that have happened," he demanded, "with all the care you wanted everyone to see you were taking of him?"

"It shows we weren't vigilant enough," Coral said with a bitterness Thom could practically taste, "and we let him be too trusting."

As Thom wondered what else he dared ask Allan said "Why aren't we hearing mother? Isn't she at home?"

Besides confusing Thom, this robbed him of a hope he hadn't realised he was harbouring. "She isn't with you, then."

"Would I be asking if that were the case? Can you promise us she isn't there?"

"I don't know what kind of promise that would be. I can only tell you I've no idea if she is."

"Do you honestly expect us to believe that? Has something gone wrong with your head as well?"

"Not that I'm aware of," Thom said, though his mind felt besieged by perplexity that for the present delayed his grief. "Why are we arguing about all this when you, when you've lost Dean?"

"Because we hope it may help us find him."

"Just lost, not— I thought you meant—" Thom said and cut short his comment with a grunt that lopped off an unamused laugh at himself.

"We mean he's been taken from the house."

"I wish you'd made that clearer sooner. All right, I'm guilty too."

Coral's voice was louder than before. "He's admitting it now, did you hear?"

"Guilty of not being clear enough. I'm saying I'm not at home."

"Why is that?" Allan said.

"Because when we started off yesterday we found neither of us could drive."

"So where are you?"

"Still here. Still in Barnwall."

"No need to make people think we wouldn't have put you up," Coral said.

As Thom attempted to make sense of her change of mind Allan said "What stopped you driving?"

"I had a cramp and your mother said her nerves were bad after everything that happened yesterday."

"I hope you aren't holding us responsible for her behaviour," Coral said.

"I wonder if they were so bad."

"Why would she have said it otherwise?" Thom demanded.

"For an excuse to stay in town so she could steal our son."

More from dismay than unbelief Thom protested "Who says she did?"

"Oliver across the road saw the car before. He's here with us now."

Like a warning Coral said "And Elsie Doughty is."

As Thom found nothing he wanted to say – perhaps even think – Allan said "Just where are you exactly?"

"The Wavelets hotel."

"And you really had no idea what mother meant to do."

"She said nothing about it to me. When I woke up this morning she'd gone."

"But you surely must have seen how she was acting before that. We did."

"You ought to have stopped her," Coral said.

"We were to blame as well. We should have told Dean he mustn't go with her."

"Though we'd never have thought she was capable of doing what she's done."

"We'll see nothing like that can ever happen again. Wait there," Allan told Thom, "and we'll pick you up."

In a bid to regain at least an illusion of control Thom said "I'll meet you in the lobby when I'm ready. I haven't been up long."

"Please make sure it's as soon as possible," Coral said. "We may need your help."

"You need me to be involved all right," Thom retorted, although to a deserted phone. He dropped it on the bed and trudged to the bathroom, where he returned the contorted robe to its hook. His thoughts felt as substantial as the glass panel of the shower – certainly solid enough in their way to intrude between him and the vigorous downpour, but too disorderly to be arranged into any kind of use. He was groping close to blindly for the controls, having grasped that the ferocious filaments of water were too hot, when he heard a solitary high note above the muffled thunder in the bath. His phone had taken a message.

He fumbled at the slippery metal knob, reducing the shower close to chill, and shivered while he hastened to spray himself clean of shower gel before hoisting one leg and then its equally uncooperative partner over the side of the bath. He towelled himself as he tramped into the bedroom, printing the carpet with his progress, and only just thought to rub his hand dry as a preamble to grabbing the phone. The terse message was from Jude. *Don't worry*, it said. *He's with me.*

Thom was struggling to decide how he felt about the confirmation – dismayed or reassured or an unmanageable amalgam of both – when he heard a car halt with a rasp of its handbrake outside the hotel. If Jude had returned, what must he do? Heading for the window felt like striving to outrun any resolution. He heard a car door slam and then another: Jude and Dean? When a third door slammed it left him more remote from knowing how he felt than ever. A fourth door made itself heard, and he was just in time to see Elsie Doughty and Oliver Dodd following Allan and Coral to the porch.

He was tempted to linger over dressing, but what could postponing any confrontation achieve? As he performed the ungainly slow-motion jig that donning his trousers entailed the room phone rang, and his shackled legs sent him sprawling across the bed in his haste to seize the receiver. "Your family is here for you, Mr Clarendon," Rhoda said.

"They aren't my family. Not all of them." Thom thrust the receiver into its plastic niche before muttering any of this. He struggled around on the rumpled quilt that felt too emblematic of Jude's absence, and hauled his trousers up over his feet before groping for his shoes and stuffing his feet into them so carelessly he trod the backs down, a peccadillo Jude would have reproved. The room had begun to ache with his sense of her departure, and he sent himself into the corridor.

Beyond it the policewoman and the social worker perched on the edge of armchairs while Allan paced about the lobby in the fashion films required expectant fathers to act and Coral gripped the banister at the foot of the stairs as she glared upwards. Thom was less than halfway along the corridor when Elsie sat further forward. "I believe this may be him now."

She and Oliver stood efficiently up as Coral swung around to stare at him while Allan took several steps towards him. From the counter Rhoda sent him a smile that looked more automatic than welcoming, and he wondered what she might have heard while everyone waited for him. "Will somebody come to my room," he called. "All of you if you like."

"Why is any of that necessary?" Coral objected.

"I'll need help with the luggage, and there's something you may want to see."

Oliver was the first to move towards him. "We should make sure we're a team," the social worker said.

As Thom headed for his room he sensed all of them crowding at his back, compelling him onwards if not ensuring he couldn't flee the hotel. Opening the door reminded him he'd had no time to pack. His case was still dangling a sleeve to signify his negligence, but Elsie strode to stand over Jude's case. "It looks as though your wife may intend to come back."

"I think she just didn't want to waken me."

"So she didn't trust you either," Coral said.

"I don't know why you wouldn't, Allan. I don't know what you think I've done to you."

"Coral's saying mother doesn't any more than she trusts us. I'm afraid that's how she's gone, Oliver."

While Thom wasn't entirely convinced Coral had meant to defend him, the social worker gave a saddened nod. "Was that what you brought us to see, Thomas?" Elsie said.

"No, it's this." Thom picked up the phone he'd abandoned on the bed, only to wonder whether Jude might have sent another message. None had arrived, and he showed Allan and Coral her assurance, which instantly turned into a confession. "It's from my wife," he told the policewoman and the social worker.

"Have you tried to locate her phone?" Elsie said.

"I did before. I mean, I tried, but she must have turned it off." As the policewoman held out a hand for his phone Thom declared "That's perfectly all right, thank you. I'll do it myself."

The hand hovered to encourage him or extend its permission if not conveying impatience along with eagerness to take over the task. Thom asked the phone where Jude was and felt unsurprised to learn she'd shut hers down again. She'd apparently sent the message from an unnamed location close to the motorway that led to Manchester. As everyone clustered around the phone Elsie said "Does that suggest anything to you, Thomas?"

"I'd say it looks as if she was making for home."

"I should think that would be a likely possibility."

Thom was overtaken by a sense of having betrayed Jude, however inevitably necessary it was. "Why did you need me to do that? Won't your people be on the lookout for the car?"

"We're hoping all this can be settled without having to involve the force. The outcome may be up to Dean's parents."

"That's why I've come along," Oliver said, "to help the situation if I can."

"If you can pack now," Coral urged Thom, "we need to be on our way."

It took her very little time to despair of his pace. She dashed into the bathroom to return with Jude's bag of lotions and the like. Once she'd dumped that in Jude's suitcase she hurried to pull out drawer after empty drawer as though searching for evidence. The sight of a Bible in a bedside drawer detained her for a moment, so that Thom wondered if it prompted a silent prayer. The instant he zipped his case shut Allan grabbed the handle while Oliver took hold of Jude's, and Coral threw the door wide. "Can we go now, please?"

"I know how worried you must be," Thom risked saying, "but I'm absolutely certain Dean is in no danger. Aren't you, Allan? You know your mother well enough."

"I wish I believed that."

Thom could only cling to the conviction that he did. He limped after the suitcases with the women close at his back. As everyone reached the lobby Allan said "Have you paid for your stay?"

"I'm just about to."

"No, allow us. We ought to take some of the responsibility. Too many people haven't been." Producing a wallet fattened by plastic cards, Allan said "And we apologise for thinking you were implicated in what's happened."

"Whoever's paying," Coral said, "can they make it quick?"

The manager gave up pretending not to overhear and was ready with the bill by the time Allan went to the counter. As the touch of his card drew an appreciative beep from the reader he said "Could you give me a ring if my mother comes back to the hotel? I'll leave you my number."

"Is anything the matter I ought to know about?"

"Some confusion," Allan said for her to interpret how she might.

Coral barely waited for him to provide the number. She'd secured herself in the seat beside the driver's by the time he and Oliver wheeled the cases to the car. Thom eased his legs past the back seat, only to be nudged into the middle by the policewoman and the social worker climbing in on either side. "Make yourself as comfortable as you can," Allan said, speeding the car onto the road.

Before long Thom felt hemmed in by mannerisms intruding on any bids he made to relax. Oliver kept tracing his lower lip as though searching for words if not sealing them in, while Elsie fell to fingering her eyebrows with a single uninterrupted movement that encompassed the width of her skull. Thom remembered how amused he and Jude had been by the prevalence of tics among the residents of Willow Grove, though he doubted the mannerisms Allan and Coral had developed would have entertained her: Coral frequently reaching to squeeze her mouth into a puckered grimace while Allan took the opportunity to rub his ridged brows whenever a deserted stretch of road let him. Thom could only close his eyes in the hope of growing unaware of the nervous activity surrounding him. He didn't succeed at any point during the hour it took to reach the motorway, where unconsciousness managed to catch up with him, occupying his mind until a voice recalled him. "Your home," it said, or "You're home."

AN ECHO OF CHILDREN

He opened his eyes to find Allan staring back at him. As his vision gradually fastened on the blur beyond his son's unfocused face he grasped it was his and Jude's house. The sight felt like a promise of comfort, and then he remembered why everybody in the car was there. At once the house stood out from its neighbours, isolated by the guilt it was trying to hide. Coral had already left the car and was gazing urgently at him. "Let us in," she said, gesturing as well.

She watched him clamber out of the car after the policewoman and wobble on the pavement while he recaptured some control of his legs. As he limped towards the house everything reminded him of Jude: the flowers she'd planted in old superseded chimneypots on either side of the garden path, the lion's head sporting a massive brass ring through its nose on the front door of their half of a conjoined pair of bulky white houses, the lisping name plaque Juth Home on the garden gate. Everyone massed on the path at his back as he reached to press the bellpush, but he couldn't tell which of them muttered "Don't let her know we're here." He supposed refraining was advisable, whatever it prevented, though he found himself abruptly unable to think. He slipped the key into the lock and eased the door open. They made no sound, and neither – even when he held his breath all the way to the edge of a helpless gasp – did the house.

TWENTY-FIVE

The whisper felt as if someone had spat in Thom's ear. "What are you waiting for?" Its fierceness seared away its gender. He couldn't have said whose it was until he turned to find Coral wiping her lips. "Listening," he hissed.

"For what?" Still lower, which only lent her voice more force, she urged "Just go in."

"I thought we weren't meant to be heard."

"I didn't tell you that. It wasn't me."

He had a sudden disconcerting notion that he'd imagined the directive or addressed it to himself. The silence of the house was at his back now, which only rendered it more ominous. "Call to her if you like," Allan murmured over Coral's shoulder. "It might be best to let her know she's not alone."

Thom swung around and had to grab the doorframe to save himself from toppling into the hall. "Jude," he shouted. "Jude, everybody's here."

The house swallowed his voice, leaving no trace. It felt as if the hall and the equally deserted stairs, not to mention every room, were challenging him to make more noise. "All right, she knows now," Coral said and pushed past him. "Let's find them and get this dealt with."

Allan sidled past him with an apologetic grimace, and Thom limped after them. By the time he reached the kitchen they'd searched it and the other rooms downstairs. The house appeared to be exhibiting how hastily he and Jude had departed: a pair of mugs stood mouths down in the sink, while in the front room a cardigan hung over the back of

Jude's chair, dangling its handless arms. The dining-room might have been awaiting her and Thom and whichever guest they might care to invite – in her case, Dean. "They must be upstairs," Thom said and supposed he hoped.

"Then someone's being far too quiet about it," Allan said and raised his voice. "Dean? Dean, we've come for you. Can you answer? Answer at once."

As everyone gazed up at the hush his shout had gained if not prompted, Elsie took hold of the banister. "May I, Thomas?"

A final feeble hope of keeping some control over the situation made Thom say "I'll go first if you don't mind."

He surely had no cause to fear what he might discover. As he propelled himself up the stairs by grabbing handfuls of the banister he sensed impatience massing at his back, but could limp no faster. The toilet and the bathroom were worth no more than a glance each. While the toilet smelled faintly of a cleaning spray, the bathroom had been robbed of any trace of scent. His and Jude's bed suggested a determined bid to flatten away every vestige of their presence. There was still the guest room, but Allan's and Coral's faces left him in no doubt what they'd found. He felt doggedly stupid for needing to peer past them so as to confirm "Nobody's here."

"I'm sorry," Elsie said, "but it looks as if I'm going to have to put out a call."

"You did your best," Allan told her. "Nobody can blame us."

The family and Oliver trooped downstairs after her as she took out her phone. Thom was plodding at the rear of the party one unhappy step at a time when his breast pocket emitted a ping. Snatching out his mobile felt like lightening the heart it had rested against, especially once he saw the onscreen name. "Jude's sent another message," he announced.

Don't worry. For a moment he thought the phone had simply reiterated her previous text, and then he read the rest. *Not home. Stopped off.* As soon as he displayed it Coral urged "Call her. Call her now."

The stares they brought to bear on him looked determined not to give way to a single blink. As the indeterminately distant phone rang Coral pinched her lips white with a fist while Allan knuckled his brows red. Thom took his gaze away rather than establish whether the policewoman and the social worker had recourse to tics as well. The mobile treated him to a generous silence before informing him that the phone he was calling could not be reached. "She's switched it off again," he said.

"Locate it," Elsie directed. "Find where she messaged from. She can't have had time to go far."

Thom might have thought the phone was on Jude's side, since it situated her five minutes ago. "She's in York," he said. "She's in the Shambles, or she was."

Elsie consulted the map on her phone. "There don't seem to be any hotels in that area."

"She's tricked us," Coral cried. "We're no nearer finding them."

"Unless she could have gone to your parents," Allan said.

"I don't believe she'd dare. She must realise they'd tell us." Another clutch at her mouth let Coral decide "I should tell them to be on the lookout in case they come across her and Dean."

In a desperate attempt to regain some semblance of the domesticity he'd lost Thom said "Shall we all sit down at least while we think what else to do?"

Coral jabbed her phone on the way to the front room. She marched to Jude's chair with a kind of defiance if not a challenge and sat on the edge as though to avoid any contact with the garment Jude had shed. She pressed the phone against her cheek, a gesture that suggested she was striving to squeeze out a response, and then gazed at it as Kendrick spoke. "Coral. Always a pleasure to hear from our daughter."

"It won't be this time."

"Don't say you've disowned us."

She plainly had no time for his sally at a joke. "I'm saying it won't be a pleasure."

"Dear me. What's to prevent it?"

Thom saw reluctance to admit her lack of vigilance come close to gagging her. "Have you seen Judith?" she said.

"Which Judith would that be?"

"Which do you think? Allan's mother, of course."

"We do have a friend of that name, you know. Just Judith, not the rest of it. We wouldn't automatically think you meant that interfering woman. But no, we haven't seen her since you sent her on her way for fibbing. Why do you ask?"

"She's done a lot worse than fib. She's abducted our son."

"Good lord almighty." This was directed away from the phone. "Coral says Judith Clarendon has kidnapped Dean."

"Coral." The cry had ambitions to convey disbelief and outrage and support rendered helpless by distance. "You'll have called the police," Leigh hoped aloud.

"They're here with us right now, mother."

Thom felt he should have intervened sooner in Jude's defence. "We don't believe Dean will come to any harm."

As Allan and Coral stared at his presumption, perhaps just in assuming he could speak for them, Kendrick said "If you'd dealt with her sooner this wouldn't have happened."

"We trust you'll find the courage to deal with her now," Leigh said.

When Thom thought of nothing further he could trust himself to say Coral said "We've discovered they're in York. I can't imagine she would come to you unless she's made up a massive lie about the situation, but if you're out and about at all, could you keep on the alert?"

"Like a pair of hawks," Kendrick said.

"And more power to you for staying so calm about it," Leigh said. "You're certainly our daughter and we're proud of you."

As Thom saw Coral stiffen to retain the control they wanted her to have, Kendrick said "Keep us posted on any developments when you can."

"May they be all we could wish for," Leigh said, "and very soon."

Coral and her phone had run out of words when Elsie said "I think together we might all make that happen."

"How?" Allan said as if she wished he could be briefer.

"I've identified the hotels closest to the area we know Judith was recently in. If we each call some of them perhaps we can track her down. Just make it clear we don't want her to be alerted. I'd suggest saying we're planning a surprise."

She read names off the map and assigned them to her companions, reserving several for herself. As everyone set about phoning, Thom thought the room sounded like a call centre if not a criminal simulation. The Skeldergate Hotel proved unhelpful, and the Hotel Romanus had no guests of the kind Thom described either. The Archway Hotel hindered him with an extensive list of options before letting him anywhere near a receptionist. "Archway on Skeldergate," she said.

He fended off confusion by realising Skeldergate was the name of both a road and a hotel. "Can you tell me," he said for a dogged third time, "if an elderly lady and a little boy have checked in?"

"What name, sir?"

"It could be Jude or Judith Clarendon."

"Let me see for you." An outburst reminiscent of a hailstorm denoted typing on a keyboard. "You said Judith Clarendon," the receptionist reminded him.

"Or Jude."

"I'm afraid we don't have any guest with either name."

"But do you have anyone like the description?"

"Can you tell me the boy's name?"

"It's Dean."

At once four stares converged on Thom. He was about to make his companions aware he hadn't found the fugitives when the receptionist said "Then they're here."

"They're there, they're there right now?"

As his babbling intensified the stares the receptionist said "No, I mean they're staying with us." A succession of plastic clicks led her to add "We have the lady down as Judith Beverley."

"That's her middle name. I expect there was some misunderstanding. So they aren't there at the moment."

"No," the receptionist said while all the stares subsided, "the lady's left the key with us."

"How long is she planning to stay, do you know?"

"She's paid for one night."

"Would you mind not telling her I rang?" Thom had to force himself to say "We want to give them both a surprise."

"Is it an occasion? Is there anything you'd like the hotel to do for it?"

With an effort Thom managed to say and say only "Just what I asked."

Everyone else stood up as he ended the call. "Well done," Elsie said. "Thank you, Thomas."

"For what? For lying?"

"For doing what had to be done. I'm sure we all appreciate it must be painful for you."

"I only did what all of you were doing." This gave him no comfort, and he turned on Dean's parents. "You don't seem to mind lying any more. If you hadn't made Jude feel unwelcome for not telling you the truth, maybe we wouldn't have this situation now."

"Please don't try to blame us for her behaviour," Coral said. "She's responsible for it, and you're making us think you are."

"We'll do whatever's necessary to get our son back where he ought to be," Allan said. "It's a great deal less of a sin than what's been done to him."

Thom felt he was retorting on Jude's behalf. "By whom?"

Allan gave him a saddened look. "My mother and nobody else."

"As Elsie says, thank you for seeing what's right," Coral said and halted in the doorway, having strode to it. "Now can we go and find them while we know where they're going to be?"

Thom tried to keep himself a window seat in the car, not so much for any view as in a bid to feel less trapped, but the social worker came at him from one side while the policewoman commandeered the other. Well before they reached the motorway Allan and the passengers reverted to their mannerisms, until Thom felt close to fancying the actions were a form of communication if not a way to signify some element everybody had in common. Closing his eyes still didn't help, and he sensed the silent tics massing around him like a discussion so bereft of language it might as well be mindless. He could only stare between the seats at the unrolling road and struggle to ignore how everybody in the car seemed to feel repeatedly compelled to check some aspect of their face.

Soon the motorway began to climb for miles towards a Yorkshire peak. A procession of elephantine panting lorries occupied the inside lane while smaller trucks laboured up the incline beside them. Allan veered into the third lane without losing speed and then, as a series of brake lights flared ahead of him, the fourth. On the far side of the central barrier massive lorries hurtled downhill as three lanes of vehicles competed to outrun them and one another. The cars in the lane closest to the barrier were racing so fast that Thom almost overlooked the red car driven by an intent woman with a small boy in the back.

He slapped a hand over his mouth before he could blurt a word, and felt as if he'd been infected with a tic. He was tempted to keep what he'd glimpsed to himself, but Oliver twisted on the seat beside him, dealing him a vigorous presumably inadvertent nudge as he peered through the rear window. "I didn't imagine that, did I? Wasn't it Judith and Dean?"

"Where?" Coral demanded, turning as much of herself as she could.

"I thought I saw them in a car we just passed on the other side. Did anybody else?"

For a moment Thom clung to his secretive silence, but what could that achieve? "I wasn't sure," he said.

"See if you can call her." Coral thrust an urgent arm towards him, clutching at the air just short of him. "Call her now."

"I don't think that's advisable if she's driving on the motorway."

"He's right," Elsie said, although as if this was uncommon. "Try locating her instead, Thomas."

He felt sure Jude would have blocked this, and his phone confirmed it. "She's switched it off."

"Call the hotel, then. Let us all hear."

"Make it quick," Allan said like his wife's gesture translated into words. "We're coming to an exit soon."

The last number Thom had phoned brought him a voice he recognised. "Archway on Skeldergate."

"I was speaking to you earlier about Mrs Clarendon. You have her staying there as Mrs Beverley. I wonder if you could tell me—"

As Allan took one hand off the wheel despite his speed to grind his knuckles against his forehead the receptionist said "I'm really sorry, sir."

Thom found it called for some effort to ask "For what?"

"I didn't realise the lady and the little boy were here while we were talking. As soon as you'd gone she came over to give me quite a telling-off."

"Why didn't you let me know she'd heard?"

"We hadn't stored your number or I would have. I do apologise."

"Have you any idea what she did after she spoke to you?"

"Checked out, I'm afraid. She just threw her key on the counter and went. She'd paid in advance, so of course we couldn't stop her. I can only apologise again."

"You keep asking for absolution," Coral cried, though Thom didn't think the receptionist had. "He can't give you that."

"I'm sure you did all you could. It wasn't your fault," Thom felt provoked to ensure the receptionist understood. "Thank you for your help."

Coral turned her eloquently dissatisfied back on him as Allan outdistanced the last of the effortful lorries and swerved into the inside lane to be ready for the exit. He didn't quell much of his speed while he drove around a roundabout beyond the exit ramp to return to the motorway. His urgency brought Thom closer to panic before he grasped why. Suppose Jude had seen them? Might that make her reckless? She was already racing faster than he'd ever seen her drive.

As Allan sped along the motorway, a process that felt like a bid to rescind the previous journey, Thom grew tense and parched whenever he saw traffic slowing down ahead. Now the tailback was virtually at a standstill, and even when it gathered a tentative halting speed it felt sluggish enough for a funeral procession. The cause was an accident, and one of the cars boxed in by police vehicles and an ambulance was red. Allan's was alongside before Thom was able to identify it for certain. Half the number plate was bent beyond legibility, but the letters he managed to read had none in common with the registration he'd been afraid to see, and the speed Allan regained felt so much like a release it was shameful.

No further accidents delayed them. Just lethargic queues did. Thom stayed alert for a red car and saw many, but not Jude's, until its absence made him nervous of not seeing it at home. Where was it in their street? He hadn't thought to look for it last time, but now he was desperate to locate it. There was a red vehicle at the end of the street – yes, a red car in their drive – yes, their car. As Allan parked across the entrance to the drive, blocking the way out, Thom saw Jude in the front room. She planted her hands on the window and dodged back at once. "Let me go first," he said.

Elsie left the car as Dean's parents did, and Oliver wasn't slow to emerge either. Everyone waited with varying fractions of patience for Thom to clamber forth. As he limped up the garden path he heard a decisive clank he hoped he'd misidentified. He slipped his key into the lock and turned it, but the front door didn't yield. He had indeed heard the door being bolted. He levered the letter flap open, bruising his fingers on the metal edge, and stooped to the slot, spreading an ache through his spine. "Jude," he called. "It's me."

Her answer came from well along the hall. "I don't care, Thom."

"Don't be silly. Let me in."

"I won't be doing that for anyone." Her voice retreated as if she was determined to distance herself from him. "Me and Dean, we can't trust anybody out there," she said. "I won't be letting any of you into this house."

TWENTY-SIX

Before Thom could think what if anything else he might say he was seized by the shoulders and propelled none too gently aside. "Let me do this, father," Allan told him.

He fell to his knees on the doorstep, giving Thom the grotesque notion that he meant to lead them all in prayer. Allan's fists thumped the front door for support if not to announce his determination. He ducked to peer through the slot and held the metal flap open with his knuckles. "Dean, are you there?" he shouted. "Dean, answer me at once."

"I'm here, daddy."

Thom thought the answer sounded timidly uncertain how it might be received. "Where?" Allan demanded. "Let me see you. Let him, mother."

"Here, daddy."

"Why were you hiding in the kitchen? Did your grandmother tell you to hide from us?"

"Granny said I could have a drink."

"That's tremendously thoughtful of her, I'm sure. Now will you ask her to let us in."

"Please may you let my mummy and daddy in, please and thank you."

"I'm afraid I can't do that, Dean."

Elsie stooped to murmur in Allan's ear. "Keep her talking," she told him and dodged around the side of the house.

"Ask your grandmother why she can't, Dean."

"Granny, daddy says I have to ask—"

"Because it's for your good. You feel safe in my house, don't you?"

"Yes, gran."

"Then that's why. I'm keeping you safe because I'm the only one who's trying."

"Ask her safe from what."

"Granny, daddy—"

"Safe from things I can't tell you about and wouldn't want to. Things people wouldn't want me saying either."

Thom heard how she was aiming this at the listeners outside the house. As he watched Allan search for words, Elsie returned to murmur "I can't find any way in short of breaking in. The back door is bolted too."

The information appeared to prompt Allan if not goad him. "Dean, never mind your grandmother. You come and let us in."

"He can't do that," Jude said.

Coral lurched at the door so fiercely she came close to toppling Allan. "God help you if you even touch him, Judith."

"I don't need to do that, though I'm sure he wouldn't mind."

"You think you can overrule us, do you? You'd better know you can't where our son's concerned. Dean, your parents are talking to you. Do exactly as we say."

"Go along then, Dean. Show them what they're asking for."

It dismayed Thom not to know how threatening this ought to sound. He heard small footsteps run along the hall and halt at the front door. Dramatic gasps expressed exertion, and then Dean complained "I can't reach."

Jude's voice was almost as close as his. "Now you see why I said he can't do what you're asking."

"Fetch a chair to stand on, Dean," Allan shouted as if the boy was still at the far end of the hall.

"I'm sorry, Dean, you mustn't move anything of mine."

"Do as you're told, Dean," his father yelled and thumped the door again. "Do as you're told by us."

"He knows he must do as I say in this house. At least I'm glad you taught him obedience."

"All right, if you aren't going to be reasonable we won't be." Allan dealt the door a parting thump to help shove himself to his feet. "We'll just have to break a window."

"Do that and I'll have the police on you."

"They're here, and you'll support us, won't you, Elsie?"

"That's unfortunately the case, Judith. Now please just open this door. The outcome will be exactly the same in the end."

"Perhaps there's something you should hear first, Ms Doughty, is it?"

"That's my name and I'm listening."

"Then make certain you hear this. Dean, what do you truly want to happen now?"

"Please may you let my mummy and daddy come in, please and thank you?"

"That's what you really want," Jude said more like a disappointed refutation. "You're sure you'll still feel safe."

"Yes, gran."

"Yes what?"

"Yes, granny," Dean said, apparently in case this was expected.

"I'm asking if you're saying yes to both the things I said."

"Yes, gran."

Had Thom heard Dean's answers start to falter? Perhaps the repetitions had robbed the boy of vigour, but he seemed to have infected Jude. "And you, Thom," she said.

"What about me?"

"What do you think should happen now?"

"I think we'd better do what everybody wants."

"So you're with them too." She sounded not just disillusioned but betrayed. "If that's what you want," she said, "it's what you can have."

Thom did his best not to take this as a threat, however ominous he found its vagueness. In a moment he heard the bolt slammed back, but it took him longer to grasp this was the only concession Jude meant to offer. He turned the key that was still in the lock, and felt compelled to announce "Coming in" as if he'd ceased to be an owner of the house.

Jude had retreated halfway to the kitchen and was standing by the stairs, so that he might have fancied she'd given herself a choice of ways to flee. Her arms were draped over Dean's chest in a loose hug that looked close to growing more possessive. They framed his face, which seemed hardly to have room for all the bewilderment it contained. Allan pushed past Thom so resolutely it was plain he would have been rougher if he'd felt the need. "Come here now, Dean," he said.

Thom thought he saw Jude's arms tighten near the boy's neck as she ducked towards him. "What do you want to do, Dean?"

"Go to my mummy and daddy."

"You don't want to stay with me. You wouldn't lie to your old grandmother for any reason. Nobody's making you do that, are they, because remember you've been told it's a sin."

As Allan took a heavy step towards them Dean said "No, gran."

"It's no to everything I said, is it? Go on then," Jude urged, flinging her arms wide in a mime of helplessness if not repudiation. "Go."

Dean took a pace away from her, and Thom saw him try not to flinch at the sight of his father bearing down on him. "No need for that behaviour, Dean," Allan said and grasped the boy's shoulder. "We know whose fault it must have been."

Jude sank onto the stairs as though exhaustion or failure had caught up with her. "Well, you've all got what you came for, and now you can leave my house."

Thom was hoping the instruction didn't include him when Elsie said "I'm afraid it won't be quite so simple, Judith."

Whatever she intended, her words sent Thom to stand by Jude, not quite touching her while he couldn't tell if she preferred him not to. "Didn't you hear what I said?" she demanded.

Surely she was addressing the rest of the party as they followed Thom into the house – surely she didn't mean him. In what might have been an attempt to recapture some element of normality she said "Hasn't anybody even brought my suitcase?"

"It's in our car, mother."

"Then might someone have the decency to bring it in for me?"

"We'll see to it when we've dealt with what we need to," Allan said and steered Dean into the front room.

Jude leapt up from the stairs as if she meant to confront an intruder and marched after them to claim her armchair. Dean's parents sat with Elsie Doughty on the couch and held the boy in front of them. Thom offered Oliver Dodd the second armchair, a gesture that felt grotesquely if not desperately domestic, but the social worker moved to stand beside the policewoman. "So what's not supposed to be simple?" Jude challenged all of them save Dean.

"The question," Elsie said, "is whether Dean's parents choose to prosecute."

Jude's mouth jerked wide, and Thom thought he should head off her response, at least for the moment. "Should Dean be hearing this?"

"Oh yes," Allan said. "We think he definitely should."

"Then I'll say whatever has to be said. How can you even dream of prosecuting your mother?"

He was hoping to regain her trust as well as prompting Allan to reject the policewoman's suggestion. While Jude withheld any comment Allan said "To make absolutely certain nothing of the sort can ever happen again."

"She wouldn't have done it if you hadn't barred us from your home for something you've admitted wasn't that serious."

"We never barred you, Thomas," Coral said.

"And you oughtn't to have done it to her either. Grandparents should have rights too."

"Perhaps they should," Elsie said, "but the law doesn't give them automatic right of access to their grandchildren."

"And they certainly don't have any right to steal them," Allan said.

"Who are you saying stole anyone, Allan?" Jude was provoked to retort. "I didn't steal you, did I, Dean? You wanted to come with me."

Thom wasn't sure whether Coral gripped the boy's arm harder as she said "Why would he want to leave us?"

"He only wanted an adventure. That's what I told him he'd have."

As Thom deduced this was meant to protect Dean, Allan said "We wouldn't call putting him in danger an adventure."

"What are you trying to make people think? He was never in danger from me, and he's never likely to be."

"You don't think sending texts while you're driving on the motorway is dangerous."

"I didn't and you know I didn't, Thom. What have you been telling everyone?"

Whatever trust he'd managed to recover had deserted her. "I never said you had," he protested.

"I sent the message before we got to the motorway." With a defiant stare at Elsie she said "I'd stopped on the side of the road."

"I'm sure you had," Thom said, "and everybody else should be."

"Sadly that's not the case," the policewoman said. "I think we have to see it as one aspect of a larger pattern of behaviour."

"Which is what we have to put a stop to," Allan said. "At the very least we'll be taking out an injunction."

Jude's question resembled a plea. "Against what?"

"Against you, Judith," Coral said. "You won't be seeing our son again till we're satisfied the situation has been resolved."

"If it ever should be," Allan said.

Oliver ran a finger underneath his mouth as if feeling for the words he spoke. "There was the alternative we discussed."

Since Jude seemed distressed beyond answering, Thom said "What might that be?"

"Appropriate treatment."

"For what?" As if the question had caught up with her Jude said "For whom?"

"For you, mother. For your mental health."

"You want to bin me, you mean."

If this was meant as any kind of joke, its humour failed to cross the room. "We've concluded there are grounds for sectioning if necessary," Elsie said.

Thom's intervention tasted of the bile that had invaded his throat. "You'd do that to your mother, Allan."

"We think it may well be the best course before she can do any more harm, and I mean to herself as well."

"She can't be very happy as she is right now," Coral said.

More bitterly still Thom said "I don't doubt for a moment that's true."

"Then you ought to welcome the solution we're offering. You both should."

Thom's throat felt clogged with words, none of which he succeeded in dislodging. He willed Jude to answer while he struggled to, but it was Allan who spoke. "There's someone here we haven't heard from yet. What would your choice be, Dean?"

"What one, daddy?"

"No need to make it sound as if I'm telling you what to say." As Allan turned the boy to face Jude, Coral helped propel him, so that Thom could have fancied a solitary mind was at work. "Do you want your grandmother to go to prison," Allan said, "because of you?"

"She mustn't." The boy's features strove to shrink together in dismay. "Don't let her, daddy," he begged.

"Would you rather she went into hospital?"

"Yes, to get well."

"There you are then, mother. Even Dean thinks you should."

Before Thom could swallow his disgust at the proceedings so as to intervene, Jude found a response. "Thank you, Dean," she said. "Thank you for showing me what I have to do."

TWENTY-SEVEN

As Thom halted at the entrance to Calm Gardens the concrete gatepost greeted him by clearing its throat. "Her husband for Judith Clarendon," he told the metal grille.

"We see you, Mr Clarendon. Drive straight in."

The high spiked gates confirmed the invitation by swinging apart with a faint terse squeal. A man with grey hair as dishevelled as his large loose face made for them at once, only to be retrieved by a nurse in a pale blue long-legged uniform. The wanderer looked content to be ushered back towards the wide recycled red-brick mansion, indeed pleased to have gained her attention. Dozens of his fellow patients were roaming the extensive lawns on both sides of the drive or sitting singly if not in occasional pairs on benches, but none of them was Jude. Solitary trees rusted by autumn stood about the grounds, all of them too thin for anybody to hide behind. Of course Jude had no reason to hide from anyone, surely least of all Thom, and he restrained himself to advancing up the drive as sedately as a mourner at a funeral.

Gravel fragments ground under the wheels as he parked near the capacious pillared porch. Paint not quite the shade of the nurses' uniforms sought to renovate the extravagantly spacious lobby, and a white reception desk assisted the trick, but Thom still felt overwhelmed, close to intrusive. The receptionist behind the desk extended him a smile he'd grown to know. "Mr Clarendon," she said. "Did you see your wife?"

"Not yet. Where is she?"

"Out in the air. You know we like our guests to enjoy that when they can."

"Out of the grounds, do you mean?"

"We hope she may be ready for that soon. Shall I see if I can find doctor if you'd like a word?"

"I'd rather find my wife. I looked for her as I came up but I couldn't see her."

"I think she may have dressed up for you. I expect that's why you didn't recognise her. I'm sure she's out there somewhere. I would have seen her if she'd come back in."

Thom thanked her and limped down the steps from the porch, keeping hold of the chilly handrail. Beneath his feet the gravel felt treacherously unstable, and proclaimed his progress with a shrill clatter. Beyond it the left-hand lawn offered softness that he fancied might have been designed to soothe anyone who trod on the precisely trimmed turf, but he couldn't yield to the sensation while he had yet to find Jude. Why hadn't he asked what she was wearing? He might have called her name if visitors weren't requested to keep their voices down to avoid disturbing any of the patients. He could only plod unsteadily towards the gates, peering about for anything familiar. He'd begun to feel the yielding lawn was meant to slow him down by the time he realised Jude was the woman sitting by herself on a bench.

It faced a view of distant mountains, beyond which more remotely still lay Barnwall. Jude was wearing her new coat for the first time, one of the items she'd bought for her stay in the hospital. Rather than enlarging her, the long bright blue padded garment made her appear dwindled, a child dressed up for a special occasion. Surely just the wind across the discreetly restless grass was responsible for disordering her hair so much. She didn't look away from the mountains until Thom moved in front of her, and then her eyes took some moments to focus. "Oh, Thom," she said as if she hadn't had a chance to comprehend his presence. "How long have you been here? I didn't see you coming."

"Not long." He stooped to kiss her forehead, which wrinkled at his approach and then at his touch. "I was looking for you," he said. "I missed you at first because of the outfit."

"Oh dear, do I look that awful?"

"Of course you don't. I wasn't saying that." With some determination he added "You look absolutely fine."

"So long as I do for you. Perhaps I will be soon." A search for a thought pinched her brows as if they were striving to hold it in. "Never mind about me," she eventually said. "Sit with me and tell me how you've been doing."

"Oh, pretty well." This was meant to sound carelessly satisfied, but in case it conveyed insufficient reassurance Thom added "Really perfectly well."

Surely Jude was shuffling away from him along the bench only to help herself scrutinise him. "Don't say it like that or you'll have me thinking you don't want me to come home."

"There's nothing in the world I'd like more. You have to know how much I miss you. I just didn't want you worrying."

"So you're saying I should."

"No, I'm telling you you needn't."

"You know I wouldn't have agreed to come here if I'd thought you wouldn't be able to cope on your own."

"Well, I can. Of course I can." He was distracted by wondering whether she'd forgotten how she had become an inmate at the hospital. "Set your mind at rest," he tried urging.

"I do try. That's meant to be why I'm here."

"I just hadn't fully appreciated everything you do for us at home. I promise I'll be doing a lot more of my share once you're back."

"That's very sweet of you."

She might have been addressing a child who was anxious to impress, and Thom was afraid he'd failed to reach her, because she seemed to be growing intermittently remote from him. "That's enough about me," he declared. "How are you progressing?"

"The doctor says I'm coming on. You met her, didn't you?" As Thom refrained from pointing out he'd done so several times Jude said "I think she's quite nice. The place is too, and the other people."

"Quaite naice, you mean."

Once she would have laughed, however briefly and dutifully, but now she frowned at him. "Whose voice was that supposed to be? It didn't sound like you."

"It wasn't meant to. It was just my feeble attempt at a joke."

"Oh, a joke. Thank you, then," Jude said and summoned up an appropriately debilitated giggle. "Only don't do it too often, will you, or you'll have me wondering who's got into you."

This seemed to strand the conversation until she cried "Look at the little bird coming to see us."

Thom glanced where she was gazing and felt his guts clench. As the small brown shape fluttered down to land between them Jude said "Don't start panicking about me. I can see it's just a leaf."

"Was that your joke for me?"

"Yes, that's it, a joke. You're right, a joke."

Fewer words might have convinced him. Jude fell silent as if the task had exhausted them or her, and then she said "They tricked us, didn't they? Unless I tricked myself."

"How did anyone do that?"

"I said I'd come here because I thought it would be easier to leave than prison. I didn't know they'd fix it so I'd be kept in."

"It's only for a while, Jude. I'm sure it won't have to be for very much longer."

"It feels long. It feels like my life." As Thom sought to manufacture further optimism she said "I was wrong to say the neighbours were plotting with Allan and Coral, wasn't I?"

"I don't think it can have helped."

"No, I should have kept it to myself and then I mightn't be locked up now." Perhaps she took his dismayed silence for agreement, since she said "You saw how that Doughty woman didn't want the other police to know she was helping track Dean down. I used to like that name of hers, but it means she's determined not to see what's wrong. Doubty with a b, that's a better name for her."

Thom still felt bereft of any answer when Jude said "I've only told you that. I won't be telling anybody else. And at least I was clever otherwise."

He couldn't very well not say "When was that?"

"When I collected Dean from that house. I didn't know how I'd have to do it till I got there, but I saw him by himself in the front room and made him see he had to shush because we were going to have a special secret all of our own, and then I managed to show him he had to open the front door without letting anybody hear. They had some religious programme blaring out on the kitchen radio, so they didn't hear him open it or me shut it either. Then I told him I was taking him on an adventure and I wouldn't tell him which because it was going to be a surprise, and he had to come with me right now, so he did. I wasn't lying, anyway, and they can't say I was. It seemed like an adventure to him." Her sense of triumph faltered as she said "I don't suppose it would be so easy now. They'll be on the lookout, and lord knows what they've told him about me."

"Jude, you have to put all this out of your head if you ever want to come home."

"Don't worry." As he risked hoping not to need to she said "I've already told you I won't be mentioning it to anyone but you. I just wanted you to know how it can be done. They'll still let you go to that house while you've made them think you aren't on my side."

More desperately than altogether accurately Thom vowed "You know I am."

"Then it's all I need to. Just hold my hand so I'll know you're here."

He tried not to grip it too vigorously, since it felt depleted of both strength and substance. The intermittence of her pulse distressed him until he realised it was the flutter of the fallen leaf beneath their hands. Soon the breeze that had roused the leaf swept it off the bench, and Jude watched wistfully as it sailed to merge with the autumnal mosaic on the lawn. When she raised her eyes to the mountainous horizon Thom could tell she had Barnwall in mind. "There was something I was trying to remember while I was waiting for you," she said. "Something about breathing."

"I can't think what that would be."

"Then let me try to."

The energy this used up seemed to let her hand grow limp. After a considerable pause she said "I think—"

"Ah, you have. Go on, then."

"I think I'd better go in now."

Thom wasn't sure whether this felt like a disappointment or relief that she hadn't said worse. "Would you like me to come in with you?"

"I've tired you out enough. You go and drive while you're still fit." As he helped her off the bench, though he wasn't sure which of them was doing most to support the other, she said "Do you think they'll ever bring Dean to see me?"

"I can ask. I'll more than ask."

"Don't antagonise them on my behalf. We need you to be able to do what I would."

Thom thought it unwise to respond. They held hands all their halting way to the porch, where Jude dealt him a kiss and an equally imprecise hug. He was turning away, not least to hide his face, when she said "Keep looking, Thom. I don't believe we know everything there is to know."

"I'll do my best." He saw his deliberate vagueness was inadequate but could only add "You know I always will."

Although he had his back to her Jude said "Is something the matter with your eye?"

"It must have been the wind," he said and delayed dabbing at it further. "Gone now."

"Be careful driving if your eyes are playing up again. Let me have a look."

He made himself swing around and send her a smile he held until it earned a tentative imitation. "See, there's nothing to worry about," he said. "I'm ready for the road."

"Don't let me keep you, then." As he started to protest he hadn't meant to sound impatient Jude said "Just make sure you look after yourself. We don't want both of us in hospital."

"I'm sure it won't be either of us soon."

His bid for comfort felt like one more linguistic stumble, and he fled to the car without another clumsy word. When he looked back the porch was deserted. Before he was even clear of the grounds he had to stop the car, because his vision was dangerously blurred, not just by age. He hoped Jude couldn't see he'd halted, or she might imagine he was coming back to her. As soon as he'd finished mopping his eyes with a handkerchief he sent the car out of the alerted gates, and managed not to have to stop again for the half an hour it took him to drive home.

The house felt as if the family had sought to erase every trace of her presence, which was why he'd left her cardigan draped over her chair, eager to be inhabited once more. Changing the bedclothes could wait to celebrate her return; he was only postponing the task. Most of the meals he'd bought in these lonely weeks were designed for the microwave: to be honest, pretty well the lot of them, but he needn't inflict so much honesty on Jude. While he realised she was anxious to believe he was taking sufficient care of himself, he'd refrained from letting her know how much. He'd settled into clinging to the banisters whenever he used the stairs, for fear of falling if not worse with nobody to come to his aid. The habit felt as though age had overtaken him all at once, and resembled an omen of being left alone for good. He'd tried sleeping in his armchair, having done so inadvertently several times, but always wakened with an unpleasant sense that his cranium and eyes and in particular his mouth had grown stuffed with dust. In any case he spent enough time in the chair, striving to retreat into books or television broadcasts, all of which stayed unreachably aloof. Just now bed was his solitary refuge, and less often sleep.

The sounds he made once he let himself into the house felt dulled, much like him: the mutter of water pouring into the percolator, the clunk of the pot on its stand, the note of the clapperless bell of a mug he removed from its wooden hook to plant it on the kitchen counter. He needed a fierce coffee to ward off any exhausted doze that would help rob him of sleep when he retreated to bed. While the percolator multiplied its muted bubbles he sent Allan a message. *Visited your mother again today. If you have any news I can pass on I know she would be pleased to hear.* Although he was tempted to leave it at that, he felt bitterly provoked to add *It might help her recover.*

He was sipping coffee that assaulted him with blackness by the time the answer came. *Please tell mother everything is as it should be here. We hope she will be also soon.* At least their son wasn't saying these unaffectionate words to her face – for the present he and his family had been advised not to visit in case this disturbed more than helped her – and Thom could add some humanity when he relayed them. They dismayed him as much as her not asking after the family had. He assumed she was nervous of learning of any developments in Willow Grove, unless she felt she knew the situation there all too well.

Yet she wanted him to disinter more of the history of the place. Presumably this was what she'd meant when she'd exhorted him to keep looking – he hoped so, at any rate. Would it be best to pretend he had and found nothing of significance? Perhaps better to search and establish there was nothing to be found. He typed Joan Daniel Day Barnwall in the scrawny rectangle and dragged the results up the screen. Surely he should feel reassured that they were all references he'd previously seen, except that he mustn't have scrolled to the foot of the listing last time, since he'd never heard of the book it cited, *Killing for the Almighty* by Jonathan Dashwood. It apparently contained a chapter on the Days and was available as an ebook.

Could that be worth ten pounds? It must be if it could help Jude in any way at all. Thom retrieved the laptop from the front room, where it lay like a blackened sandwich bereft of any filling on the dresser, and raised its screen on the kitchen table to download the book. The crude image that did duty as a cover – a crucifix whose arms were tipped with instruments of torture – might have been designed by a child or a computer. The next page proclaimed that everything the book contained was true and described the author's copyright at considerable length before threatening pirates with a fearsome curse, perhaps as a joke. Since no contents page was provided, Thom skimmed through the book.

The first chapter – *Babble from the Bible* – offered an unimpressed summary of Biblical instances of exorcism. *The Claptrap Trap* listed such statistics as the author could find of faith abuse and made the appalled point that the police believed the practice was far more widespread than reported, whether the perpetrators were Christian or Hindu or Muslim. Too often the abuse went unremarked until it caused the victim's death. *The Blair Bitch Project* cited exorcisms that might have been suggested by the famous film – "a movie the gullible took away the wrong ideas from". *Lout of Africa* dealt with beliefs that had emigrated to Britain – "an import we can live without and too many children couldn't live with". *Black Hands, Black Heart* pursued the theme with examples until Thom began to suspect some racial bias might lie at the core of the book. How could any of this help Jude? He supposed he should at least search for the Barnwall couple, and their surname brought up a chapter: *Days of Torture, Nights of Hell*.

It was indeed about the Childer Close murder, revealing more details than Thom had previously learned – too many of them. Once he saw the list of items the police had collected from the house as evidence – pliers, a hammer and nails, an electric kettle, a large pair of scissors – he stopped reading well before the end, but caught sight of a remark made by Daniel Day: "Whatever helps to drive a devil out has to be God's plan." He couldn't tell Jude any of this, and wished he'd never let it into his mind. As he sent the chapter crawling up the screen the account grew more explicit, and he did his utmost to avoid even glimpsing what it said. He was hoping to race to the end of the chapter without being further distressed when a paragraph snagged his attention: a description of the Days. While he saw no reason to discover more about them, at least it ought to be relatively innocuous. He read several sentences before his hands began to shake.

Jonathan Dashwood had attended the trial and noted in detail the Days' behaviour under questioning. They'd exhibited a variety of mannerisms "either to distract the jury from their answers or to try to look more human". When Daniel Day wasn't drumming his crossed arms with his forefingers as though to hurry up the lawyers he resorted to running a fingertip under his lips "like he was trying to zip his answers in". Simply a coincidence, Thom strove to think, but Dashwood hadn't finished with the man, who had kept chafing his brows "like he wanted to rub out his memory". As for his wife, she didn't just finger the width of her eyebrows "like she was checking what was in her skull" but would rub her mouth as if to scour it or to wipe away any responses that might incriminate her. Dashwood thought all these quirks were a pretence, since the Days persisted in believing they'd acted for the best in their treatment of their victim. He was least impressed by Joan Day's favourite affectation: pinching her lips as if she wished she could seal her words in.

Thom shut his eyes and covered his face with his hands, all of which merely immured him with his thoughts. "You were right. You were more right than you knew," he said as if Jude could hear, but only his moist enclosed exhalations responded. "It isn't just Allan and Coral, it's the neighbours too. They breathed in that house. When they thought it was being destroyed, they breathed it in."

TWENTY-EIGHT

"**Your mother** would really like to see you, Allan."
"You've changed your mind about us, then."
"I'm afraid I have, yes."
"Why be afraid? I don't understand."

In haste, which he hoped was less apparent than persuasive, Thom said "I don't understand why you thought I'd changed it."

"Because you gave us the impression we weren't welcome. We're sorry if you and mother felt that way, but we only did what had to be done."

"Yes, we all have to do that sometimes." Once again Thom felt in danger of betraying too much, and tried to outrun it by adding "I don't believe your mother ever wanted you to stay away."

"It's just you that thought we were wrong, then."

"Let's leave all that behind, shall we?" Everything Allan said made it harder for Thom to speak. "As I say," he persisted, "I hope she can look forward to seeing you very soon."

"Then I expect she can if the hospital's agreeable."

"It will be as much as I am."

"How will they fix it? Should I contact them?"

"There won't be anything to fix." Thom felt his mouth refrain from grinning mirthlessly at the inadvertent lie. "Just show up," he said.

Allan rubbed his abruptly ridged forehead, a sight that made Thom clench his fists, though not before hiding them from the laptop. "Hold on," Allan said. "Have we been talking about visiting?"

"That's very much the idea, yes."

"I thought you meant seeing her the way I'm seeing you right now."

"I'd much prefer you to be there. That's to say Jude would."

"Then I'll have to do my best."

"I know how you feel." To leave this hurriedly behind Thom said "Can you soon? Can you tomorrow?"

"It's a possibility. I should be finishing the job I'm on today."

"And Coral? Will she be able to make time?"

"Hello, Thomas." She greeted him further by appearing on the screen and then mimed pensiveness, squashing her lips between finger and thumb. As his aching fists contained his distress she released her mouth to say "It's not about time."

"I really think it is. Jude hasn't seen you for weeks."

Coral offered this a terse laugh in case it had invited any. "I'm saying I'd have the time all right, but somebody has to stay here with Dean."

"I meant she'd like to see all of you, Dean in particular." It took more of an effort to ask "Why do you want to keep him there?"

"You truly believe the hospital would be suitable for him."

Thom strove not to fancy she could have incarcerating her son in mind. "I'd say it lives up to its name."

"We hoped it would. Names can be treacherous."

"A lot of things can be."

"Yes, people too."

Thom didn't want to know what thoughts he might have roused. "So can I count on you?"

When she and Allan started to enact deliberation, only digging his nails into his palms let Thom keep his gaze on the screen – on the sight of the resurrected mannerisms. He watched the faces turn to each other but saw no communication pass between them before Allan said "We'll see how it works out."

"Can I take it you'll be going tomorrow?"

Had he betrayed too much nervous eagerness? "That's what I had to mean," Allan said.

His impatience sounded like a threat to end the call, a prospect that made Thom blurt "I haven't spoken to Dean yet."

"What would you want to say to him?"

"How about hello for a start?"

"You can say that tomorrow, surely. You'll be there, won't you?"

"Where else would I be?" In case this suggested an answer Thom rapidly added "Of course."

"Then no doubt you can have a word with him then."

"Is there any reason I can't now?"

"He's praying," Coral said.

Jude wouldn't have let this pass unquestioned, and it felt as though she was urging Thom to ask "What for? I mean, for what?"

"For his soul, we hope."

"And never to be tempted to leave us again," Allan said.

"Let's hope seeing where his grandmother has ended up will show him some of the consequences," Coral said. "We wouldn't be taking him otherwise."

"Do you hear that, Dean?" his father said. "You're going to see what your little escapade led to."

Thom was just able to catch a murmur of contrition, which prompted him to shout "Hello there, Dean. It's your grandad."

"Since you've been interrupted now," Coral said without endorsing the situation, "you may as well come and show your face. We don't need anybody thinking we don't want it to be seen."

Did the boy have to struggle off his knees, or was he loath to be looked at? Thom's breaths had grown shorter and more numerous by the time Dean ventured into view beyond his parents. As they moved apart to confront their son Thom saw a good deal besides his face. The breath Thom took to speak felt like an expression of dismay. "What have you done to your hands?"

"Nobody's done anything to them, have they, Dean?"

"No, daddy."

"So you've no reason to keep doing that to make your grandfather think anyone has."

"No, mummy."

"Then stop it. It's devilish behaviour, if you ask me. Stop it this moment, right now."

The spectacle of Dean flexing all his digits in a quest for some sensation made Thom's fists ache not just with tension but in sympathy. As the boy quelled them by pressing them against his chest, a gesture reminiscent of a religious image or else the occupant of a coffin, Thom protested "Then what's wrong with them?"

"Nothing whatsoever. We told you what it was." When Thom stared at her Coral said "Praying."

"Nothing wrong with a little fervour," Allan said.

Thom had to believe them if he wasn't to feel utterly helpless. Dean took the pause as his cue or else a desperate chance to ask "When are you coming to stay with us, grandad?"

"I couldn't tell you just now." At least this gave Thom the excuse to add "I expect your mummy's parents will have."

"Not since you were here," Allan said, "so you've no reason to be envious. You know that's a deadly sin, Dean."

"I was only thinking Dean would appreciate seeing them as well."

"We'll look into setting up a link," Coral said.

Thom might have insisted on his meaning, but it seemed more crucial to establish "When will you be there tomorrow? Seeing Jude, that is."

"When do you need us to be?"

"It's your mother who does." Why had Thom said that? He could only hope it didn't sound suspicious. "Of course I do as well," he tried declaring. "Can you be there by noon?"

"We should be able to. We'll see you there, then."

"I've already said you will."

Why couldn't he just have said yes or some comparably unemphatic phrase? He didn't need to sound so anxious to convince. As he reached to end the call before his face could betray him any further he heard a heartfelt murmur – the beginning of a prayer. "Please don't let," Dean entreated, and then blackness engulfed his voice.

Thom's hand trembled on the lump of plastic, a style of item he'd always found more reminiscent of an outsize insect than a mouse. He felt desperate to call back for Dean's sake, but for Dean's sake he must resist the impulse. He only wished he weren't forced to postpone any intervention until tomorrow. "You have to," he muttered and sent the limbless oval carapace skittering away from him.

"You have to." That didn't mean just the delay, but summed up his solitary course of action. He repeated the phrase, quite possibly aloud, whenever all the thoughts he was alone with began to clamour. He could imagine Jude saying it to him, and sometimes when he lurched awake he fancied she had. At times this let him sink back into jerky sleep, away from the prospect of tomorrow that had already turned into today, despite the dark. The jabs that were his reawakened awareness of his plan of action felt more viciously insistent than any cramp.

They sent him out of bed once dawn began to crawl over the suburban roofs. The shower he took must have been hot, since it hid the face he could do without confronting in the mirror. He felt as if he had no time to sense the heat or to taste the cereal, however doggedly sugared, that was all the breakfast he could justify. A mug of ferocious coffee nudged him towards consciousness. As soon as he persuaded himself he was capable of driving he locked the house and left it a wistful backwards glance before hastening to the car.

Fifteen minutes brought him to the motorway, and in another fifteen he could see the exit that would take him to Calm Gardens. He sped past it in the middle lane and kept his gaze ahead. How soon might he pass the car he had to watch for on the opposite side of the road? The need to ward off intermittent assaults of low sunlight with the windscreen visor didn't help. When he reached the long climb to the highest stretch of motorway, two sluggish cavalcades of lorries forced him into the third lane, and he veered into the fourth to overtake a faster procession of traffic. He'd sped just a couple of hundred yards when the mirror framed a van racing up behind him. He tramped on the accelerator, ignoring a sharp twinge in his calf. As he strove to outrun several cars in order to retreat out of the path of the van he caught sight of a vehicle speeding towards him on the other side of the barrier – Allan's car.

Allan was driving, intent on the road, while Coral had twisted in her seat to address Dean behind them. Nevertheless Thom covered as much of his face as felt even slightly safe and peered through his fingers while he struggled to control the wheel with just his left hand. The oncoming van flashed its lights and blared its horn at him. Had any of this drawn Dean's attention? Thom thought the boy's head turned towards him as the family sped past, but he had no time to make anything like certain. He barely managed to gain enough space to flee into the third lane before the van passed him, still sounding its horn.

He took refuge in the inmost lane as fast as he could, just as the road levelled out ahead. His loud unsteady heart set about slowing while the motorway began to slope downhill at length. The sun he had to fend off with the visor felt like a lamp in an interrogation room. For miles he was afraid Allan was about to phone or send a message demanding whether they'd seen him, but no question had caught up with him by the time he arrived in Barnwall.

He was abreast of Childer Grove when he pulled over to think. How close to Willow Grove could he risk leaving the car? Surely nowhere anyone who would recognise it might see it, but he didn't want to carry the contents of the boot any further than he had to. He drove alongside Childer Field to the entrance nearest to Willow Grove that was still out of sight of the houses there. He scraped a tyre against the kerb as he parked, and then he levered himself out of the car onto flagstones cracked and canted by some vehicle heavier than his. Once his legs settled on the aches they had to offer he limped around the car.

He mustn't have screwed the cap of the plastic can as tight as it required, despite bruising his fingers in the process. Some of its contents had trickled into the boot and greeted him with their sharp oily smell. He stood the container on the crooked pavement and eased the boot shut while he glanced about to see nobody was watching, and then he gripped the handle of the can and made as fast as he could for the park.

Only one of the pair of gates was ajar. Its twin's rusty bolt was immovably embedded in the concrete path. Thom had to sidle through the meagre gap, balancing the can in front of him and grazing one awkwardly outstretched elbow on a rail of the bolted gate. At least Childer Field appeared to be deserted apart from a few distant walkers – trotters if not inadvertent runners, rather, hauled along by eager dogs – and an argumentative pair of children taking turns to propel an empty supermarket trolley through the park. Thom struggled free of the gates and tramped at an increasing limp along the path.

Willow Grove wasn't as close as he'd hoped. Once he left behind a miniature range of hillocks that had blocked his view he saw the family house beyond the unpopulated playground more than a quarter of a mile ahead. Surely that wouldn't be too much of a trek, even given how burdensome the plastic can was growing. He'd begun to regret having bought a ten-litre container; half that might have sufficed. Since the can had just a single handle, he could only grasp it with one hand, which felt painfully cramped by now, not far from agonised. The weight had started to exaggerate his limp – he must look like a comedian portraying an injury – but when he switched the can to his left hand it turned him yet more clumsily lopsided. Clutching the handle in his right hand while he supported the can with the other didn't douse the insistent flares of cramp, and hugging the container with his free arm didn't help. He could only resort to dumping the can on every bench he came to, and every time the effort of retrieving it was more of a strain. The red of the sunlit plastic seemed far too bright, an alert to anyone who saw it, and the faint moist rectangle the can left on each bench was altogether too suggestive of evidence. At least there were only six more benches between Thom and the alley leading into Willow Grove – six more tremulous bids to heft the can. He grabbed the handle and stumbled towards the next bench while heat that felt like being swathed in nettles surged through him. He was halfway to the bench when his phone rang in his pocket. "Allan," it said.

Thom could have fancied he'd been caught in the act he had yet to perpetrate. He dropped the can beside him on the path and fumbled with his practically unworkable fingers for the phone. "Allan," he said as automatically as it had.

"Yes, it's me. We're all here."

Thom found this far too ambiguous. "Where?" he said and peered towards the house.

"Where you wanted us."

This sounded ominously knowledgeable. "The hospital, you mean," Thom said and hoped.

"The place that's supposed to calm people, yes. Where are you?"

"Unfortunately I've been delayed."

"Are you on the road? Don't let me distract you if you shouldn't talk."

"I can still do that. I'm resting at the moment."

"You're saying you're at home."

Could Allan hear the contentious shouts of the boys with the supermarket trolley? Surely they could be outside where Allan thought his father was. "I wish I were with your mother," Thom felt provoked to say.

"We aren't either," Coral said.

Thom's hand had grown steadier, but it recommenced trembling so much he had to clasp it with the other to support the phone. "I thought Allan told me you were at the hospital."

"That's precisely what I did," Allan said. "When are you likely to be here?"

"Not for quite a while, I'm afraid."

"Then just what are you trying to do?"

Once again Thom felt discovered – certainly in danger of it. "To let Jude see you," he said, truthfully enough.

"Well, we haven't, Thomas," Coral said.

"What's preventing you?"

"No need to make it sound as if it's any of our doing," Allan protested. "Her doctor says you didn't let her know you'd invited us to visit, and she thinks it's premature. She says seeing all of us just yet might cause a relapse or at least undo some of the progress mother has made."

"I didn't realise." This was painfully the case. "I should have thought to ask."

"Yes, we think you should have before bringing us all this way, particularly Dean."

"He wasn't too well in the car, were you, Dean?"

"I'm better now, mummy."

"No thanks to someone when it wasn't even worth you feeling sick."

"Just you tell grandad how you really feel now we're here."

"I was looking forward to seeing grandma, grandad. I'm sad the lady won't let us."

Thom yielded to the hope he was suddenly able to experience. "I expect we'll all be seeing one another soon, and perhaps mummy and daddy will appreciate why I've done what I did."

"No doubt we'll have to try," Allan said. "Now if nobody has anything else to say we'd better be starting back."

"Maybe take your time so Dean won't be so ill."

"We already meant to, thank you," Coral said.

He couldn't condemn her resentment, especially given its reason – her concern for Dean. For the first time in far too long she and Allan had let their son speak for himself, and Thom was sure he'd been right to entice them away from the house in Willow Grove, just as the Lettices had reverted to their old selves once they'd moved elsewhere. If Allan and Coral hadn't regained their personalities while they were searching for Dean and confronting Jude, that must have been because the presence of their equally infected neighbours had prevented them. Thom felt desperate to believe he'd done enough, but he knew he'd scarcely begun. "Travel safely," he said and ended the call.

He pocketed the phone and flexed all the muscles he felt able to risk testing before the next stage of his trek with the plastic can, and couldn't help envisaging the grotesque possibility that someone might happen along and offer to help with his burden. As he bent with a groan to seize the handle he heard a squeak of wheels behind him. One of the pair of teenagers, if indeed they were even so aged, was rushing the supermarket trolley along the path. "Fuck off out of the way, you old cunt," he offered by way of a greeting.

"No," Thom said and stood his ground beside the can, blocking the path. "No, I don't believe I will."

The youngster propelled the trolley at him with all the force he could summon. As Thom braced himself to catch it the wheels twisted, sending it past him onto the grass, where it juddered to a standstill. He grabbed the handle and hauled the trolley towards him. "Give it back, fucker," the second whippersnapper said.

"I won't be doing that, son," Thom promised and hoisted the can with a concerted surge of strength to brandish it at them. "Would you like me to give you a splash of petrol? I've a lighter here as well."

"He's fucking mad, him. Leave the cunt," the initial urchin said.

They'd barely started to swagger away when Thom had to drop the can. At least it landed in the trolley. He was afraid the thin metallic clash might make the miscreants glance back and see how enfeebled he'd grown, but they sauntered out of sight around a hillock. As soon as he felt strong enough he set about urging the trolley towards Willow Grove, only to worry how conspicuous he must look. He fumbled to unzip his coat and drape it over the can, and then he laboured with the trolley to the exit from the park.

As far as he could see Willow Grove was deserted, even mostly by cars, and yet he felt watched. He pushed the trolley through the passageway between the houses and manoeuvred it into the front garden. There was no sound except his uneven footsteps and the insistent squeaks of the wheels, but the silence around him wasn't enough. He had to be certain nobody would intervene until he completed his task — until its effects were beyond prevention. "Hello?" he yelled with all the voice he had.

No answer came, not so much as an echo. It felt as if Willow Grove had denied his presence. He tried again, shouting the syllables so far apart they might have been an inadvertent pair of words, but the street remained as innocently unresponsive as the house in front of him. He was making to steer the trolley around the house when a voice called "They've all gone out. See, their car's gone."

Thom swung around, clutching at the handle of the trolley for support. Eric Bowler was across the road, leaning his folded arms on the garden gate while he drummed on his biceps. The sight sent a shudder through Thom, jerking out an answer before he could think. "They won't be here much longer."

"We've not heard that. How come?"

"This isn't a good place for children."

"It's fine if they're good themselves." The owner of the amusement arcade raised a hand to shade his eyes while the left one persisted in its rhythm. "What were you trying to bring them?"

"Just a leaving present."

Bowler lowered his hand to unlatch the gate. "You can give me it and I'll pass it on when they get back."

"Don't worry. It's all right. You needn't bother." None of this deterred Bowler from starting to cross the road. "I can let myself in," Thom tried asserting.

The man's advance might have been miming skepticism. "They've let you have a key, have they?"

"Why wouldn't my son let me have one?"

Perhaps it was the lack of an answer – at least of any he could own up to knowing – that halted Bowler in the middle of the road. "If you want to be neighbourly," Thom felt compelled to say, "there is something you could do."

"Let's be hearing it, then."

"If anyone's proposing to live here with children, tell them it's no place for them."

"What would any of us do that for?"

"I believe you know the history. I don't think I need to say any more."

"I don't think you should either, and we won't be bothering anyone."

"It's a great deal more than a pity none of you did at the time." Thom was further provoked to add "It won't be happening again if I can help it."

"How do you reckon you're going to do that?"

Did Thom sense a threat? He suppressed an answer and found another. "I'll be putting all the truth online."

"Some of us mightn't want you giving our road a bad name."

"It already had one. Changing it won't change the place." There was no mistaking the threat now, especially since the man was advancing on him. Thom could only protest "Aren't you concerned about your local villains any more?"

"Who says I'm not?"

"I saw a couple of them with a trolley just like this." Progressive inspiration let Thom add "They were heading for the promenade. I expect they'll be on a thieving expedition. I heard one say they'd be going to your arcade while you weren't there."

"The new lad I've got won't be any bloody use. I'll sort the buggers out," Bowler vowed and ran to slam his front door, then sprinted to his car.

Thom watched until the vehicle swerved out of Willow Grove, trailing a trickle of greyish fumes, and then he struggled to steer the trolley around the house. As soon as he managed to labour to the back door he reached up to grope for the key he'd seen Allan hide somewhere above the lintel. His fingers encountered a stretch of brick, but nothing else. Had Allan or Coral removed the key so that nobody could let Dean out of the house? He stepped back to peer at the wall above the door in the hope he'd misunderstood where the key was kept. A narrow rectangular section immediately over the lintel was a little paler than the surrounding brick. As he fumbled at it with both hands it came loose, and the key it concealed slid off the lintel to clatter on the doorstep.

Thom unlocked the door and was about to replace the strip of plastic masquerading as brick when he saw how pointless this would be. He wrangled the trolley into the kitchen and locked the door. He had to shove a chair against the table before he could manoeuvre the trolley into the hall – the chair Dean had occupied last time Jude and Thom were there. "Untidy child," Thom muttered, struggling to trundle the trolley along the hall. At the foot of the stairs he sweated over twisting it to face the kitchen, and then he dragged his coat aside to take hold of the plastic can.

He'd forgotten or at any rate tried to forget how much of a burden it was. As he stumbled upstairs at an unsteady plod, hugging the container so fiercely it bruised his chest, he kept blundering against the wall. At least this saved him from toppling backwards under the weight of the can. Well before he reached the top he fell to resting the can on each successive stair in front of him, and every effort his shaky hands had to make to retrieve it was more of a task. At last he was able to dump it on the landing, and clung to the banister for quite a few strenuous breaths as a prelude to hauling himself onto the upper floor.

The house felt as stealthy as he'd tried to be – as if it was concealing some aspect of itself from him. He limped into Dean's room, only to wonder why he had. Of course, he intended to salvage Dean's toys; there was no reason why the boy should lose them when he would be unavoidably upset enough. The plastic baskets in which they were stored could be detached from the stack. Thom lifted off the topmost and was staggering with it across the room when a Lego piece that had strayed out of its carton slipped through the mesh and fell on the carpet. As he trod on it, the miniature brick almost sent him sprawling. "You damned untidy creature," he snarled. "I've doing all this for you, if you only realised. Maybe I shouldn't have gone to so much trouble, in fact any. Maybe you deserve what you've been getting."

He dumped the basket on the bed and took hold of his mouth while he considered the possibility, and then his words and feelings and the gesture he'd acquired caught up with him. For a moment he felt so terrified he might have fled the house, but clenched his fists instead. "You won't get to me," he vowed, "not when I know what you've been doing."

He crouched with a grunt of pain to retrieve the Lego fragment and restored it to its box, and then he tramped downstairs to plant the basket in the trolley. Two more trips dealt with the rest of Dean's toys, and it distressed Thom to realise how few. He collected all three laptops from the workroom and stacked them in the trolley, which he guided effortlessly along the hall and through the kitchen, inadvertently colliding with Dean's chair. "You aren't untidy, you poor child," he said loud enough to be heard throughout the house. "You deserve a lot more freedom."

He left the trolley by the back door and stumped upstairs at a determined pace that felt like a hope of leaving thoughts behind. He unscrewed the plastic cap of the container and flung it across the landing, proclaiming carelessness, and then he set off through the rooms, laying a pungent liquid trail. By the time he returned to the stairs the can had grown less burdensome, even given his increasingly depleted strength. He continued the trail all the way down the stairs and in and out of the rooms and the hall. When he reached the kitchen there was just enough left in the can to spill some fuel under the table and extend a final dribble not quite as far as the back door. He unlocked it and ran the trolley past the picnic table and Dean's sandbox and the shed, not relaxing his exertions until it was at the back gate. As he limped to the house he took out his lighter. Leaning through the doorway, he triggered a flame and dropped the lighter on the end of the trail across the linoleum. The flame went out as the lighter fell.

Thom lurched into the kitchen and stooped to grab the lighter. As he straightened up, encountering a jab of agony on the way, he turned the flame up to maximum and activated it again. He gripped the nearest chair for support while he leaned down to touch the flame to the last inches of the trail. It ignited with a timid whump like the withheld explosion of a disappointing firework. The flames it sprouted seemed feeble too, at least until they raced up a leg of the table and blazed in Thom's face. He recoiled so violently he backed into the door, slamming it behind him and dislodging the key, which skittered across the linoleum.

It came to rest in the midst of the flames that were setting fire to the table. When he floundered to seize it they seared his fingertips before he could touch the key. He jerked backwards and painfully upright, barely managing not to grab the blazing table for support. What could he use to snag the key? Which drawer contained the solution? He hauled one out from beneath the counter by the sink while heat massed at his back and his nostrils filled with an oily stench. The drawer was stuffed with a stack of wadded towels. He pulled out its neighbour, which emerged so readily it crashed to the floor, scattering cutlery over the linoleum. His senile clumsiness embarrassed him – he would have to clear up the clutter before Allan and Coral could see – until the situation he was growing desperate to deny came back to him. He bent despite a vicious stab of agony to catch hold of a fork as the top of the table began to split apart, blackening while a rush of flames crowded into the hall. Still in his aching crouch, he scraped at the blazing linoleum with the fork and dragged the key towards him. He was so desperate to let himself out of the house that he almost didn't think to protect his hand with a towel before attempting to retrieve the key. As he thrust the key into the lock he was suddenly terrified that its heat would distort the mechanism, and when he turned it he encountered some obstruction. He could smash a window and clamber out of the house – surely his body was still capable of this, however injurious the task might prove to be – or might he use the front door, if the hall wasn't too lethal by now? He felt the key twist, but only because the heat had warped the stem, jamming it in the socket. He made a final bid to twist it and heard a muffled grating sound – the head of the key snapping off in the lock. No, it had held, and as the hindrance gave way the key turned in the mechanism.

Thom threw the door wide, which appeared to rouse the flames. He felt them leap higher behind him and swung around to reassure himself they hadn't crept up on him. They were just an arm's length away, prancing as if frustrated by the distance. Ungainly spikes of fire crowned the table, while the doorway to the hall was an arch of flame. The spectacle – the belated sense of what he'd done – seemed to rob him of the ability to retreat as the flames on the linoleum made bids to snatch at him. Or was the house pinning him there, stealing his capacity to think? Panic at the possibility released him, and he limped out of the house as fast as all his aches would let him.

He stumbled to unbolt the gate and wrestled the trolley through. There was nobody to see him in the alley, and the park looked deserted too. He was urging the trolley past the playground when an old couple intermittently supported by sticks strolled around the nearest grassy hillock. They halted with a dual click of their canes and lifted them to point beyond him, uttering exclamations of dismay. Thom did his best to maintain his dogged progress until he realised his unconcern might seem suspicious and glanced back.

He saw Dean's bedroom window splinter while it filled with fire, and then the pane shattered, releasing flames that blackened the wall as they streamed towards the roof. Tatters of ash outlined by glowing red flocked out of the window, along with an outburst of black smoke that oozed across the garden as if it meant to follow Thom or at any rate indicate him. He turned away to find the old couple competing for the fastest call to the fire brigade. It was too late to prevent them by feigning a call, but he doubted their appeals would bring any immediate help, since there was no longer a fire station in Barnwall.

When at last he reached the exit from Childer Field he clambered up the hillock by the gate. The house was a block of fire, and flames had sprung out of the roof. He slithered down the hillock and trundled the trolley to his car. Once the boot was loaded he abandoned the trolley like the criminal he was. As he drove out of Barnwall he heard distant sirens, speeding towards Willow Grove too late.

The sight of the first country road prompted him to wonder if he might encounter Allan and the family returning, as they would imagine, home. What would he need to say to them? As he drove he rehearsed his side of the dialogue. "You can have our house till you find another one. If your insurance doesn't cover the price we'll help you out. I saved all your computers and Dean's toys. I hope in time you'll come to see why I had to do what I did for you. Just try and remember how different you felt once you were away from that house. Remember how you went back to treating Dean."

He reached the end of the road without having met them. Presumably he passed them at some point on the motorway, but he didn't see them, and assumed none of them had noticed him. Or could they be waiting for him at Calm Gardens? When he parked outside the hospital there was no sign of Allan's car. He couldn't see Jude anywhere either, which gave him more time to prepare what to say to her. He sent Allan some of the thoughts he'd composed on the way, and then he made for the reception desk as soon as all his aches would let him walk. "Please may I see a doctor, please and thank you?" he said. "I've come to join my wife."

ACKNOWLEDGEMENTS

Jenny was there as ever – my first reader and constant support. I'm also especially grateful to John Kaiine, who on learning that I'd almost run out of the exercise books I use for first drafts sent me several the great Tanith Lee hadn't got around to using. Perhaps I can view my use of them as a kind of posthumous collaboration. I'd be honoured. Gemma at Silvine (the manufacturers) was splendidly helpful too, and sent me the last few that remained in the warehouse, the line having been discontinued.

Once again Imogen Howson scrutinised the final version to its great benefit. My editor Don D'Auria continues to be splendid, as are Nick Wells and the rest of the Flame Tree team – Gillian Whitaker, Josie Karani, Sarah Miniaci, Olivia Jackson, Leah Ratcliffe, Mike Spender, Federica Ciaravella, Chris Herbert….

It was another well-travelled book. Its various states went to the fine Matina Aparthotel in Pefkos on Rhodes, the Festival of Fantastic Films in Manchester and Fantasycon in Birmingham. It's a compulsion, this writing lark.

ABOUT THE AUTHOR

Ramsey Campbell has been given more awards than any other writer in the field, including the **Grand Master Award of the World Horror Convention**, the Lifetime Achievement Award of the Horror Writers Association, the **Living Legend Award of the International Horror Guild**, and the **World Fantasy Lifetime Achievement Award**.

Among his many novels are *The Hungry Moon, The Influence, The Wise Friend, Thirteen Days by Sunset Beach, Think Yourself Lucky, Somebody's Voice, Fellstones, The Lonely Lands, The Nameless* and *The Incubations*. His trilogy *The Three Births of Daoloth* further develops the cosmic horrors he invented in his first published book, *The Inhabitant of the Lake*. The Spanish film *La influencia* was based on his novel *The Influence*. The television series *Los Sin Nombre* is based on his novel *The Nameless*.

FLAME TREE FICTION

A wide range of new and classic fiction, from myth to modern stories, with tales from the distant past to the far future. Flame Tree Fiction includes the trade fiction imprint, **Flame Tree Press**, featuring tales from both award-winning authors and original voices, along with short story anthologies, mythology and folklore collections and classic works in the **Beyond & Within, Collector's Editions, Collectable Classics, Gothic Fantasy** and **Epic Tales** series.

OTHER TITLES

SPECIAL RAMSEY CAMPBELL EDITIONS

The Incubations: A New Novel by Ramsey Campbell
The Invocations: H.P. Lovecraft Short Stories
The Damnations: M.R. James Short Stories

GOTHIC FANTASY COLLECTIONS

Lovecraft Short Stories • Lovecraft Mythos New & Classic Collection
M.R. James Ghost Stories • Algernon Blackwood Horror Stories

OTHER TITLES BY RAMSEY CAMPBELL

Ancient Images • Fellstones • Somebody's Voice • The Hungry Moon
The Influence • The Lonely Lands • The Nameless • The Wise Friend
Think Yourself Lucky • Thirteen Days by Sunset Beach

The Three Births of Daoloth trilogy
The Searching Dead • Born to the Dark • The Way of the Worm

Available at all good bookstores, and online
at **flametreepublishing.com**